Praise for Lisa Amowitz's debut novel, Breaking Glass:

"Jeremy's story is gritty and suspenseful, and at times downright spooky, but his intelligence, tenacity and quick, sarcastic sense of humor brightens the darker moments. The novel is also about hope and a young man who prevails in the face of insurmountable challeges. *Breaking Glass* is an impressive debut from Lisa Amowitz."
—*USA Today*

"This book is a suspenseful mystery and you'll find yourself trying to figure it out before you actually do. There are tons of twists and turns and you won't put the book down until you solve it all."
—*Just Jared Jr.*

"Every character has a secret in this intricately plotted YA paranormal mystery that delivers a wild and rewarding ride for teen readers."
—*ForeWord Reviews*

"Betrayal, addiction, murder…and of course, a ghost…Just when you think you know what's happening, *Breaking Glass* punches you in the gut and leaves you breathless!"
—**Jennifer Murgia, author of the** *Angel Star* **series &** *Between These Lines*

"A dark romance that will keep you up at night with its twists and turns, *Breaking Glass* is a must-read debut. Lisa Amowitz has burst onto the YA scene with this intriguing novel. You'll be hooked from the first page - I certainly was! The characters are drawn with depth and sensitivity, and the plot is heart-pounding. Don't miss this one."
—**Christine Johnson, author of** *Claire de Lune, Nocturne* **and** *The Gathering Dark*

"*Breaking Glass* was a surprise addition to my reading list for July…definitely a book that will keep you guessing right until the very end. It wasn't a matter of if I was going to read the book, but when and how much I would like it."
—**Shelley Romano,** *Gizmo Reviews,* **gizmosreviews.blogspot.com**

"From the first page I was hooked. Lisa Amowitz has a writing style that made me feel sad I had social engagements because all I wanted to do was sit down and read this book from start to end."
–**Emily Trunko,** *On Emily's Bookshelf,* **www.onemilysbookshelf.com**

Spencer Hill Press

Contact: Spencer Hill Press
27 West 20th Street, Suite 1102
New York, NY 10011

Please visit our website at www.spencerhillpress.com

First Edition: September 2015
Lisa Amowitz
Until Beth/by Lisa Amowitz—1st ed.
p. cm.
Description: A teenaged girl starts to see darkness around
those about to die and soon finds herself in more danger
at a school for the talented.

The author acknowledges the copyrighted or trademarked
status and trademark owners of the following wordmarks
mentioned in this fiction: BMW, Coke, Disney Channel, Duke,
Facebook, Green Day, Hello Kitty, Janis Joplin, Jell-O,
Styrofoam, Q-tip, Vaseline, VW, Yoda.

Cover design by Lisa Amowitz
Interior layout by Errick A. Nunnally

978-1-63392-033-0 (paperback)
978-1-63392-034-7 (e-book)

Printed in the United States of America

UNTIL BETH

LISA AMOWITZ

SPENCER
HILL
PRESS

For my children, who've set out on journeys of their own.

1

OUTSIDE THE CAR WINDOW, BARREN TREES VEINED the pale flesh of the horizon. I fingered the Blast Mahoney button on my jacket and tried not to think about that night after the concert, and how Sam Bernstein's long slow kiss had tasted of cotton candy and popcorn. How he'd pressed the button into my palm and breathed in my ear that he believed in me. That, no matter what, my guitar and me were going places. And I'd believed him.

That was five months ago.

I'd been to every one of his favorite indie clubs, every dive bar where he'd ever used a fake ID. I'd posted flyers. Even made a Facebook page. I'd looked until there was no place left to look, but Sam Bernstein hadn't been seen since.

After Sam went missing, another teen from the Greater Linford area vanished without a trace. Five kids in five months. The town held candlelight vigils. The police searched in vain. The talk lately was that there was nothing more to be done. Everyone was starting to think Sam and the other kids were dead.

I wasn't sure what I thought anymore.

I glanced at the dashboard clock, shaking off the memory. "Crap. I'm gonna be late. Can't you drive any faster?"

Mom had made my brother Carson drive me everywhere

since my VW bug went belly up. "Driving Miss Crazy," he called it.

"The roads are icy." Carson steered the car in a slow crawl down the twisty road to Linford High. "It's just a band slam, Beth."

"Yeah. And your state championship match next week is just another game." I tapped my boot against the car floor, knowing how much it annoyed him.

Carson's jaw twitched. "Maybe if you put less time into your band and studied for a change, you'd have more going for you."

"Maybe you should just shut up." Ten months my senior, with a lacrosse scholarship to Duke under his belt, *he* never got calls home about a poor attitude.

The truth was that, lately, I'd even let my music slip. I tried to keep Sam from my thoughts, but every time the news of another disappearance hit the papers, the wound would split open. Sam had been my friend longer than he'd been my boyfriend. He was my muse, my manager, my coach, my drill sergeant, driving my skills to new heights.

His absence had ripped a hole in the heart of my music.

There was a tingling sensation inside my chest, as if my heart had a case of pins and needles, and I wondered if I was becoming immune to the anxiety med cocktail the doctors had had me on since Sam went missing.

Carson turned into the school parking lot, pulled into a spot, and cut the engine. Scowling, he rubbed at an invisible smear on his fuel gauge.

Flipping down the sun visor, I looked in the mirror and smoothed the blue-tipped strands of hair that peeked out from under my logger's cap. The Band Slam competition was in three hours. August Rebellion's first without Sam on keyboards.

The scarlet blur of a Linford lacrosse jacket moved between the rows of cars. Weaving around piles of soot-darkened snow, Luke Gleason zigzagged his way across the parking lot, drawing closer.

"Shit." I jiggled the door handle. "C'mon. Open this. I've got to go."

Carson stared at me, a twisted smile on his face. "What's with you? Give the guy a chance."

"I don't have time for this." I shook my coffee cup at him. "If you don't let me out, this latte is going all over your rug."

Carson blanched. "Luke's really into you, is all I'm trying to say."

In some past life I'd had a thing for my brother's best friend, Luke. He was Disney Channel adorable with honey-colored hair that fell in his dreamy eyes, but all Luke ever talked about was Carson and lacrosse, lacrosse and Carson, like he had some kind of man crush. Plus, his breath always smelled like bacon, except when the bacon smell was overpowered by beer fumes.

"I gathered that after he pinned me under the mistletoe at Shelly's Christmas party and slobbered all over my dress. Maybe a little too much eggnog?" *But not enough to drown out the eau de bacon,* I almost added.

"Sometimes Luke gets kind of carried away. But he's a good guy." Carson paused, eyeballing me. "It's been five months since Sam, Beth."

The pins and needles rose to my throat. I tried and failed to swallow them down. The latte sloshed around in my stomach.

"I'm well aware of how long it's been. Every single second." I pantomimed tipping my cup sideways and leaned on the door handle. "Open this damn door, now, or say goodbye to the pretty rug."

Carson's Achilles' heel was the fourteen-year-old BMW he'd saved up to buy. Threatening its wellbeing was the quickest way to get the temporary upper hand with my brother. Key word: temporary. But satisfying.

Carson shrugged. The handle gave way and the door

opened. The latte and I nearly tumbled into a snow bank. I righted myself and opened the back door to retrieve my guitar. "Thanks for the ride. A pleasure, as always," I said through clenched teeth. "Can you pop open the trunk?"

Raw wind stabbed at my cheeks and shoved my guitar against my thighs. Luke sauntered over, swishing the windblown hair from his eyes with his trademark neck twitch.

"Hey. Let me help with that," he said, reaching inside the trunk for my amp.

I grabbed it first. "It's okay. I'm used to lugging this thing around." As I struggled with my things, the winter-gray sky darkened and the ground lurched under my feet. I set down the guitar and amp and leaned against the car.

Luke frowned at me and scratched his head. "You okay, Beth?"

I rubbed at my temples. Zero sleep, too much coffee, and competition jitters were canceling out my meds. "Just nerves, I guess. Gotta run. I'm late for set-up. See you, Luke."

I hefted the guitar and amp and struggled across the parking lot, cursing myself for not accepting his help.

"No prob. See you later, babe," he called after me with a wave.

Babe. In a pig's eye, he'd see me.

My bandmate and best friend, Shelly Brandt, scrambled toward me over the snow piles, all striped tights and spindly legs under an obscenely short plaid skirt. She reached me, flushed and breathless. "Hey! This is it! You ready?"

Carson, who had not lifted a finger to help, was out of the car and gesturing for Luke to hurry. I exhaled, winded from hauling the heavy amp. "Yeah. All set."

Shelly took my guitar, glancing at Luke's and Carson's receding figures. "You and Carson have another fight?"

"I *so* need my own car. The idiot thinks he can pimp me out to his friends."

Shelly laughed. "You are pure evil, Collins. Luke Gleason

is really cute, though. Maybe it's time you—"

"Don't go there, okay?" I muttered as we entered the building through the gymnasium entrance. "I think it's because Carson's sick of driving me everywhere. He wants to outsource."

We pushed through the double doors to the gym. Rows of chairs had been set up to face a raised platform stage. The overhead lights were headache bright. The other band members were already there, shifting mic stands around. I shivered even though the gym was stuffy and hot. "Got any food in your bag?"

Shelly rummaged around in her bag again, this time pulling out a crushed package of crackers. She studied me as I ripped the package open, her head tilted. "You're a lousy actress, Beth. You're not fooling me for a second. Do you want to talk or not?"

As if on cue, Andre Serrano, our drummer and Sam's best friend, strolled up the aisle between the chairs, followed by Brett Davis, the new keyboard player. Andre planted a kiss on Shelly's nose. I couldn't get myself to look Brett in the eye. "Talk about what? That I'm nervous as shit about this slam? Last year we won but we still had—"

Shelly finished for me. "We still had Sam."

I still had Sam.

"Beth." Shelly placed her hand on my shoulder. My breath caught as my gaze wandered to Brett. He was slim and lithe, with a mop of brown curls. In the light's glare he could have been—

It hit me like a punch in the stomach—a memory of Sam striding toward me last year, wavy brown hair framing his face, his dark-lashed gray eyes crinkled up in a smile.

Suddenly I couldn't stay. I dropped the crackers and ran from the gym, combat boots clonking against the hard wood.

Outside, I gripped the rail for balance and gulped in the cold air. Music was how we met. How we related. How we loved. Sam drove me to play better and better.

With him gone the music was all bottled up, twisted inside me like a gnarled tree root. Shelly wanted me to accept that Sam was gone and move on.

Our fight that last night had been stupid. We'd argued about the band, and where our relationship was going, while in the dark of Sam's idling car, my chest had prickled with a strange tingling sensation. Thinking back, I knew now that it had meant something. Something ominous. But I'd said nothing.

Instead, I'd gotten out of the car, slammed the door and watched Sam drive away, never to be seen again.

2

NDRE BURST THROUGH THE GYM DOORS, AS bare-shouldered as always, graceful tattoos coiling up one of his muscled brown arms. Though his breath came in misty puffs, his hands were warm when he took my cold ones in his.

"Come inside, Beth," he said, a hint of a smile in his dark eyes. "You're gonna freeze your ass off out here."

At Andre's touch I felt my tension ebb, and the sob that was trapped inside my ribs dissolve. Andre, respectfully distant, was always just close enough when I needed him. I pressed my head against his chest and let him hold me.

"Not a day goes by when I don't feel it, too," he murmured. Andre was the only one who understood what it was like to breathe when your lungs were gone. Sam had been his best friend, the rock he could hang on to when things at home got to be too much for him. "But standing here in the cold isn't going to bring him back. Besides, it's time for the sound check."

And just like that, I felt better. *Andre's touch*, as I called it to myself, had the power to calm me. It wasn't attraction. Andre and Shelly had been together even longer than Sam and I. It was shared pain. And somehow, Andre had the ability to take mine away. I was in too much pain to wonder what he did with his own.

Squeezed into a black satin bustier over a cobalt tulle skirt and black fishnets, I waited in the wings backstage. I couldn't see past the glare of the lights, but judging from the crowd's roar, the whole town had shown up for the Band Slam Semi-Finals. August Rebellion was pitted against eight other bands. The winner wouldn't be chosen until the Grand Finale next week.

At last, our turn came and I tried to kick it into gear. I belted out Blast Mahoney's "Like Never," hoping to incinerate my nerves with the screaming licks of my guitar. Shelly scorched on bass. Andre hammered the beat. We sounded good, but inside I was hollow, the keyboard chords ringing in my ears. I wanted them to be Sam's notes. And they weren't.

When it was over the crowd went nuts. Long-time Slam tradition required the audience to throw random junk at their favorite band. They flung crazy stuff at us—coins, confetti, flowers, rubber chickens. Even someone's bra and underpants landed on the stage. I figured, as far as the crowd was concerned, we'd rocked the house.

When the spotlight dimmed, I glimpsed Luke and Carson standing on their chairs and pumping their fists. My chest tingled and I felt the roots of my hair, as if I was about to be struck by lightning. I had to get out of there.

Pushing past the kids who crowded the backstage, I fled to the dressing room behind the auditorium.

A boy with a halo of blond curls and mirrored sunglasses slouched against the door.

"Hi," he said, walking up to me, hand extended. "I'm Vincent Rousseau. Your bandmate Andre asked me to come to the Band Slam tonight to hear you play."

"What? Andre didn't tell me anyone was coming." Shivering in my skimpy costume, I scanned the empty corridor. The next band, Wails from the Crypt, was already tuning up. My phone was in the dressing room drawer. If Vincent Rousseau planned to kidnap me, no one would hear my screams.

"What do you want?"

The boy's surprisingly deep voice was colored by a trace of an accent. French, I decided, from the way he emphasized the second syllable in his first name—Vin-*cent*. I couldn't help but notice how his dusky skin contrasted pleasingly with his mop of bright curls. "I'm a scout for a high school residency program for talented youth. Andre speaks very well of you."

I twirled a strand of damp hair. "Huh? Where is this program?"

"We're allied with many colleges nationwide."

"Yeah? Never heard of something like that. Does it have a name?"

"HSTYP, or High Step as we call it. Your friend Andre thought you'd be a good candidate."

"Oh, did he?" I glared at the poor guy. I was in a crummy mood and had no problem taking it out on him. "I'm not leaving Linford."

"No matter, then," said Vincent Rousseau, shrugging. "I am just a student at one of the local affiliates. I will leave you with my card in case you have a change of heart." He smiled again, and despite myself, I felt my guard slip just a notch. Still, I wasn't sure if I could trust someone who wore mirrored sunglasses indoors in the middle of winter.

"Look, I've got to change," I said, taking his card. "It was nice to meet you—Vin*cent*."

I was pretty sure I didn't mean it, but if Vincent cared, he didn't show it. He smiled broadly and said, "It's been a pleasure to make your acquaintance, Bethany Collins."

I shook my head and watched him go. Strange guy. But polite. And oddly hot. I was going to have to chew out Andre for his well-meaning but lame attempt to shake me from my gloom. But first I had to get out of my ridiculous get-up.

Fumbling for the dressing-room key I'd stuck inside my bustier, I pushed open the heavy door. It swung inward with surprising force.

I turned and a bouquet of flowers was thrust in my face. Behind it, Luke twitched the hair from his eyes. "You guys brought down the roof, babe."

"Luke! You scared the crap out of me."

He glanced down the hall. "Hey, sorry. Who was that guy?"

"Just a kid from some music school—uh—somewhere."

Luke's eyes were glazed and bloodshot. "Well, you shouldn't be alone. These days, you never know what kinds of creeps are lurking around."

Arms aching, my adrenaline wave finally ebbed. I was spent, too exhausted to feel much of anything. "Thanks for the flowers and your concern. The door has a lock, so I'm safe in here."

Luke let the door close gently behind him. "Good. I wouldn't want anyone to barge in here and steal you away. Don't you want to put these pretty flowers in water?"

I caught a whiff of something under the heavy perfume of the flowers. And it wasn't bacon. It was cheap beer.

Luke was plastered.

"You looked so awesome out there, Beth. Like a rocking blue-haired angel." Luke smiled, his gaze dropping to my bustier. "Close up you look even better."

"Uh, thanks." I backed into the room, a smile pasted on my face. "I'm kind of tired."

Luke tossed aside the flowers and lumbered toward me. "Carson says you need someone to take your mind off your dead boyfriend."

"Carson should stay the hell out of my business." My cheeks burned. "And you should leave."

"What's the matter with you? It's not like Sam Bernstein's

gonna come back from the dead and beat the crap out of me."
Luke staggered closer.

Dead. I didn't want to hear that word. Not out of Luke's mouth. Not in the same sentence with Sam.

"Shut up, Luke! Get out of here. Now."

"What you need is someone who can protect you from the monsters in this town." Luke grabbed me and crushed me against him, his itchy wool lacrosse jacket scraping my skin.

His beer breath made my eyes tear. I shoved at him with both palms but couldn't pry myself loose from his grip. "Let go of me. I can protect myself."

Luke pushed me onto the couch and lunged on top of me, one hand thrust under my skirt, the other clamped over my mouth to muffle my shouts.

"Why don't you give me a try?" he breathed in my ear.

Suffocated by his sweaty palm, I clawed and scratched but couldn't budge his hard-muscled bulk off of me. His free hand went for the buttons of my bustier, which he yanked and ripped loose, exposing my strapless bra. I bit at his hand, my teeth digging into the flesh of his palm.

"Hey! What's wrong with you? I was just—"

"Asshole!" I squirmed and managed to knee him in the groin.

Luke rolled onto the floor, holding his crotch. Scrambling to my feet, I rushed for the door and managed to get it open, but Luke lunged, grabbed me, and slammed me onto the floor. Pinning me, he dug his fingers into my breasts.

I thought I might have been sobbing. Or I might have been screaming.

The door crashed open. "Omigod! Get off her!" Shelly shrieked.

I struggled; the world dimmed. My chest burned with trapped current. Luke lifted his mouth from my neck and snarled, "Fuck off, bitch."

"I said, get off her!" Shelly screamed. A folding metal chair made contact with the back of Luke's skull. Luke yelled and rolled away from me, rubbing his head. Shelly stood frozen, holding the chair as a shield.

I crawled away and grabbed a can of extra-hold hairspray from the dressing table. Pointing the nozzle at Luke's face, I could barely spit the words past the sizzling heat in my throat. "I'll blind you if you take one step closer."

Luke wobbled to his feet. "Isn't it time you tried a real guy?"

Depressing the nozzle, I unleashed a toxic cloud. Luke howled, knuckles pressed to his eyes.

In the same moment, Shelly swung the chair again, cracking it across Luke's face. He reeled and sank whimpering to his knees, blood gushing from his nose.

The room darkened to grainy tones of black and gray. The blood on Luke's face glistened like an oil spill.

Shelly tossed me her jacket. A moment later, Carson stormed into the dressing room and yanked the dazed and bleeding Luke to an upright position. My brother's glassy-eyed gaze shifted from me to Shelly. "What the hell? You two did this to him?"

"He did this to *me!*" Shaking with fury, I glared at Carson, my finger trembling over my phone screen. "Get him out of here before I call the police! Better yet, *you* call the police and tell them your drunk best friend tried to rape your sister!"

"Beth." Carson shot a look at Shelly, who paced a few feet away like she wanted to hit him over the head with a chair, too. "Don't make a scene. He's just a little drunk, that's all. He didn't mean—"

I snorted and flopped onto the couch, disgusted. "Fuck you, Carson. Just. Fuck. You. Take him and go!"

Carson kept an eye on Shelly as he dragged the limp Luke into the hallway. I shoved my phone into my bag. A night-dark haze drifted languidly above Carson's head. My lungs burned as if I'd inhaled a roomful of acrid smoke. I wanted to tell him not to go. He was drunk too. But I was way too angry.

Only when they were both out of sight did Shelly set down the chair.

"Shit. What did I do?"

"Saved my ass, basically," I said, trying to breathe past the lingering burn in my throat.

Shelly helped me out of my torn costume and back into my own clothes, then plopped beside me on the couch and wrapped me in her arms.

"It's okay. It's over."

Andre came skidding into the room, fury in his eyes. "What the hell? I just saw Carson and Luke. Don't tell me that asshole—he didn't, did he?"

I shook my head. "I just want to go home, guys." Mom was out of town. And there was no way I wanted to ride home with Carson.

"We'll drive you," Shelly said. "Why don't we just hang a little until the crowd thins out?"

Sitting between my two best friends in the world, wrung out and shaken, all I could do was nod in agreement. I don't remember how long I sat on the couch with my head nestled against Shelly's shoulder or how they managed to get me to the car.

I slumped against the back seat of Andre's beat-up old van as we exited the school driveway. From the corner of my eye I spied a lone figure standing at the edge of the woods across the road. When I turned my head for a better look, it was gone.

We turned off the winding road to the school and pulled onto Route 292. By the time we reached the notorious patch of Skilling Highway where the road snaked in hairpin turns, my eyes were slipping closed. I'd seen so many accidents on that stretch, I barely flinched at the red and blue alternating flashes that pulsed through the light snowfall. Smoke curled from the chassis of a car that had skidded into a ditch and flipped over. White-coated people swarmed the wreck like maggots, carefully extracting a bloody tangle of arms and legs. Tingling heat spread from my chest into my throat as I recognized the upside-down Duke Lacrosse sticker on the bumper.

"Stop the car, Andre!"

Andre jammed on the brakes. We spilled out of the van, me scrambling across the slippery ground. A white sheet, already accumulating a crust of snow, had been draped over a motionless body on a gurney. One red-sleeved arm dangled from under the sheet. Luke wore that damn lacrosse jacket everywhere.

The snowy air dimmed and twirled into an inky pinwheel of jet-black smoke that hovered, then sank onto the sheet-covered body.

I wasn't sure how I knew. But I was more than certain.

Luke was dead.

The EMTs hoisted a body, the head braced and secured on a backboard, onto a second gurney. I cried out. The face was beyond recognition, but I knew that bloodstained Duke jersey was Carson's.

The darkness emerged from Luke's still body and lingered near Carson, negative space against the falling snow and flashing lights.

The ground fell away. My chest inflated with so much crackling pain that I felt it behind my eyes as I wished the swirling disturbance away with all my strength.

The patch of darkness, as if it had responded to my will, brushed against Carson's blood-spattered chest. Hesitating for only a moment, it rose and dissipated into the night sky.

3

CARSON MADE IT THROUGH THE NIGHT. It was mid-afternoon of the next day when Mom, who'd flown back home on the red-eye, finally allowed me in to see him. Entwined in tubes and wires, he was outfitted with a neck brace, his face bruised and swollen, his head swathed in white. If the nurse hadn't walked me to his bedside, I would not have recognized my own brother.

He wheezed, each breath an effort.

"Carson?" I whispered, leaning in close to his ear. His eyelids flickered and opened, his gaze fixing on me for a second before drifting out of focus. The room darkened slightly, a vague electric tingle working its way up the back of my neck.

Mom sat upright in one of the chairs, knitting needles flying. Before she'd opened her gallery selling antique paintings, jewelry, and artifacts, she'd had a business knitting baby clothes for her rich customers. She could knit and crochet at the speed of a drum solo, her needles clacking out rhythmic paradiddles. The more upset she was, the faster she knitted. The year before Dad died, when the signs of his cheating were impossible to ignore, she'd knitted hats for every new baby in Linford.

I couldn't fathom what she was creating, but her needles were about to break the sound barrier.

Mom set aside her needles and whispered. "There was a blood clot in one of his lungs, Beth. They think they've resolved that, but—" she swallowed hard, "—his spine has a C8 fracture... It's at the base of his neck. It means he'll be... Carson will be in a wheelchair for certain. If he—" Mom broke off in a sob.

I looked away, my gaze dropping to Carson's hands resting still at his side, the palms flexed unnaturally backward, the fingers curled in. He moaned, his lids fluttering. The room darkened another notch. "Mom, why don't you take a break and get some food? I'll stay with him."

Mom hesitated, her brows forming a crease. "You sure, honey?"

"You need to eat," I insisted. "You can't afford to get sick."

"Okay." She rose to her feet with a sigh.

I waited until she was in the hall to lean over my brother again and say, "Can you hear me, Carson?"

His eyelids fluttered but remained closed.

"Are you in pain?"

A soft gasp. The darkness thickened around Carson. My chest flared with heat, but the room was chill and damp. I didn't understand what was going on, but it sure was a lousy time for an anxiety attack.

Carson and I had always fought. No squabble was too trivial. After Dad died it had only gotten worse, with him trying to prove he could do the "man of the house" thing better than Dad had. Which wasn't such a lofty goal to begin with, given the less than stellar example Dad had set.

Now, I wanted to take back every bad thing I'd ever said or thought about him.

What kind of sister would let her brother drive in the state Carson had been in? Even if he *had* wanted to set me up with a guy who'd tried to rape me.

Carson's eyes snapped open and locked on mine. He

mumbled something through the giant tube stuffed in his mouth, but I couldn't understand. His eyelids slid closed again.

I squeezed his hand tighter and watched the rise and fall of his chest, each breath like liquid slurped through a straw.

Carson shuddered. The green line on the wall monitor next to his bed went from sharp zigzags to lapping waves. The red light above the bed flashed. A shrill alarm blared. In seconds feet pounded the tile floors, headed our way.

Time slowed to a crawl. The room dimmed further, darkness pooling over Carson like ink stirred in water. My vision constricted to a tunnel of brightness and my chest screamed with pain as though my heart was literally on fire.

I closed my eyes and focused on a single thought.

Please don't let my brother die.

A pack of grim-faced medical staff hurtled into the room, backing me into a corner. Engulfing his bed, they clapped my brother's chest with metal paddles. The monitor's wiggly green line flattened out, accompanied by a terrifyingly long beep.

My labored breaths were like gulps of scalding steam. Blood roared in my ears. I was too afraid to open my eyes as I whispered, *You can't die, you can't die, you can't die.*

The electric heat in my chest had flared out. My fingers ached from squeezing them together. I opened one eye to look, not sure what I would find—a corpse, or a living brother?

Carson coughed and the monitor hiccuped back to life.

The thin green line on the monitor resumed its steady pace.

Carson was alive.

For now.

4

LUKE WAS BURIED THE MONDAY AFTER THE accident. Mom sent flowers. At least no one expected us to attend the funeral with Carson barely clinging to life. I was relieved not to have to face Luke's family.

I kept a bedside vigil with Mom, praying and begging the powers that be to let my brother live.

Over the next few days, Carson began to breathe easier. My dark anxiety had dissipated and with Carson out of the woods for now, Mom insisted that I return to my normal routine. Spent from my weirdly focused efforts, I finally agreed.

Carson's accident had had one positive side effect.

It had taken my mind off Sam.

I woke the following Monday morning to a silent house. Gray dawn seeped through my partly open blinds. While I'd prayed for Carson to live, I'd barely had time to think about much else.

I flopped onto the bed and reached for my guitar, but there was no solace to be found. My fingers were blunt slabs of meat, the music that used to burn inside me trapped under a layer of permafrost. The only thing I could feel anymore was the current of heat that had nearly consumed me in Carson's hospital room.

Mom had already left for the hospital. With Carson stabilized for now, I'd promised her I'd return to school. But I wasn't ready to face anyone yet, not even Shelly or Andre, who'd both offered to drive me around for the foreseeable future. I'd texted them to say I'd be staying home today. My phone rang a moment after my message was sent.

"C'mon, Beth, sitting home and wallowing isn't healthy," Shelly said.

"I just can't face everyone yet, Shel. It's like overnight I've become the poster child for tragedy."

"You've been working on that for a while now."

"What do you mean by that?"

There was a pause on the other end of the line. "Look, Beth—I've been meaning to talk to you. Life has kicked you in the butt, but you're not the one who's missing—Sam is. And he would want you to have fun, not turn into a zombie. You've just been going through the mo—"

I cut her off. "My brother is hovering between life and death, Shelly, and you think I care about *fun?*"

Silence crackled on the other end of the line. After a hesitation Shelly said, "Beth, you know Sam and I were friends since, like, forever, way before you two hooked up. I miss him, too. And I'm so sorry about everything else. But you have to keep living. You can't just curl up in a ball and die."

"I know you mean well," I said finally. "But your timing's a little off. Have a good day at school. I promise I'll be there tomorrow."

I stared at my guitar and tried to imagine strumming Blast Mahoney's "Like Never." It was our unofficial theme song. In a year would I still be sitting here staring at my guitar, missing Sam and praying for Carson to live?

Though I couldn't bring myself to play it, thinking about

the music calmed me, the memory of those ringing chords transporting me back in time—Sam smiling at me, brushing the hair from my eyes. When he looked at me in that certain way of his, my doubts fled.

Then I heard it. Soft tinkling notes like rain on a roof. Or was it the distant notes of "Like Never?"

I ran to the window. Outside, it was as though a dark curtain had been thrown over the sun. I squinted and looked down. A figure made of shadow stood in our driveway. It turned away and cut to the other side of the street, disappearing into the woods opposite our house. My heart pumping, something compelled me to see if I was imagining this or not.

If I was, I might need something much stronger than anti-anxiety meds.

I slipped into my sheepskin boots, bounded down the steps and out the front door. Crossing to where the weeds bordered the road, I peered down the snowy incline that ended in a rushing stream. No visible tracks.

Shivering and spooked, my feet numb from the cold, I hurried home, bolted the door, and ran up the stairs to my room.

It must have been hours later when I woke and peered out the window. Mom's car was in the driveway.

Mom always had classical music playing whenever she was home, so the utter silence in the house was eerie. I followed the faint clicking sound into the den where she sat with the shades drawn, knitting furiously, the TV on with the sound turned down. "Hi, honey," she said without looking up. "The school said you never showed today."

"Mom—I—"

"It's okay, Beth. Sit down, please." She patted the seat

beside her.

The whispery librarian quality of her voice sent a chill through me. The more quietly Mom spoke, the more upset you knew she was. In the spectrum of things I'd done to piss her off, ditching school would probably only rate a four—and under the circumstances, probably not even a two. But her voice was at level ten soft.

She set her knitting aside. "Carson's doing much better today. They took the tube out this morning and he was able to talk to me a bit and even eat a little Jell-O."

I nodded, my heart thumping. The news sounded upbeat, but Mom's voice maintained its level tone. I shivered. That's how she always did it. Start with the positive. Except when we found out about Dad. There was no appropriate segue for that.

"Beth, his spine was injured at the C8 level. An incomplete fracture. The doctors hope after the swelling goes down he'll have more use of his—" Mom stopped, swallowed several times, then continued. "He can move his arms somewhat, but he'll never walk. And he needs months and months of rehab before he can come home to stay."

I studied her mouth as she enunciated each word, the sounds looping and reverberating in my ears.

Quadriplegic, I heard her say. My lacrosse-playing brother would never walk, or possibly even move his arms, again.

I'd spent so much energy praying for him not to die, I'd overlooked what living would mean for him.

I thought of the moment when he'd dragged Luke from the dressing room. My fury. Not just at Luke, but at Carson for not protecting me from that pig. It reminded me of another moment—the bitterness that had swelled up inside me when I'd found the note to Dad from "Rhonda" in his office trashcan.

When I'd bid Dad goodbye before what would prove to be his last business trip, all I could think about was hurting him for hurting Mom.

My chest had tingled then, too.

I breathed in sharply and exhaled a shuddering sob. Mom pulled me closer to her. "We have to do what we can for him, Beth. And that's going to mean changes. Changes in the way we all live."

I pressed my head to her chest and listened to the rapid flutter of her heart. She took me by the shoulders. Carefully prying me away, she lifted my chin with a finger and gently swiped at my damp cheek with the back of her hand. Mom's eyes, rimmed in red, shone feverishly. "I've put the house up for sale. We're going to move to Gram's old lake house in New York, Beth. It's got only one story and it will be easy to outfit for Carson."

"You've got to be kidding." The news hit me like a body blow. In all my grieving, all my prayers, all my anxieties, I'd never imagined being uprooted from the place where my memories lived.

Mom smiled at me expectantly. "There's a good school nearby with a great music program."

"You want me to switch schools in the middle of junior year?"

"We really have little choice, Beth. Financially, we've been hanging on by a thread. Now with the medical bills and Carson's needs on top of everything else, we can't afford to live here. Besides, there are too many steps."

I stood and paced the floor. Hot tears burned my cheeks. Any objection would be purely selfish, so I said nothing.

Mom rose and walked over to me. "Beth. Your friends and I all know you haven't been in a good place since—Sam. Maybe this is for the best." She stopped and looked away. "It's a great opportunity for you to start over."

I walked to the window and gazed across our yard. No shadow figure. I resumed pacing, then stopped to stare at the bland face that filled the muted TV. An alert scrolled along the bottom of the screen. The camera switched to an aerial view of the woods around Linford, and that old sour taste climbed into my throat. Reverend Barclay Smith, the guy who always came to the school to speak to us after another kid vanished, was being interviewed by a reporter. Turning up the volume, I was no longer listening as Mom continued to speak. She took the remote from my hand and muted the TV again.

"Beth," she said softly. "Carson is going to be in a wheelchair."

I squinted, still trying to read the scrolling newsreel. Mom's voice trailed off as she pointed the remote at the TV and turned the sound back up. Our eyes met as her hand flew to her mouth.

Another missing kid. Jessie Bradley. A freshman. She'd disappeared on her way home from school just the day before. I walked backward and sank onto the couch.

"Another reason it's best to get out of Linford," Mom said. "I don't want—I can't be worried every minute of the day. I'm going to need to focus on your brother."

I wasn't really listening, my own thoughts going in circles. "He probably won't want me around."

Mom shook her head. "Why would you think that, Beth?"

"We had a fight that night. I-I should never have let him leave, Mom. He—"

"Carson had been drinking. I know that, Beth. And he's paying a terrible price for his mistake."

My eyes stung. Mom had turned down the sound on the TV again and I stared at a silent infomercial. "I should have stopped him. I *could* have stopped him. And I didn't."

"Beth," Mom said. "It's not your fault that he—" Mom began to cry, her hand clamped over her mouth. "Oh, I'm sorry, honey. It's just so hard."

I rubbed Mom's back, my own eyes dry. If we left Linford, I wouldn't have to face constant reminders of Sam. The wound would close and I could finally try to accept what everyone else seemed to have decided.

That Sam, along with the now five other missing kids, were all dead.

Either way, I didn't really want to leave my memories of him.

But I didn't want to stay either.

Later, in my room, I called Andre.

"So, dude. Did I totally mess up with that freak you sent to spy on me at the slam?"

Andre sounded sleepy. After all, it was past midnight. I'd spent the hours between strumming the opening chords to "Like Never" until my fingertips had gone numb.

"Huh? Oh. You mean Vincent Rousseau from the High Step Program?"

"I was kind of a shit. You don't think I screwed up my chances, do you?"

Andre yawned. "Nah. He's used to crazy musicians. I'm sure I can smooth over any rough spots. Vin is cool."

"So, I'm good? I can still audition?"

"Sure. You know it means you'll have to live there, right?"

"Yeah."

"What about your mom and brother?"

"She's putting the house on the market and moving us to Finley Lake. I just—I can't live with... I just can't live in that miserable little town."

"Well, okay then. But you'll need your mom's permission eventually."

"Sure, whatever," I said. "I'll figure it out."

5

AWEEK PASSED AND ANDRE HAD YET TO SET UP the audition with Vincent Rousseau. I'd returned to school, trying to act as if everything was back to normal while Mom split her time between visiting Carson and having our house shown by real estate agents. I just tried to stay out of the way.

After Carson was moved to the rehab wing, I'd stopped visiting. I hadn't spoken with him since his feeding tube came out. It didn't seem like he wanted to see anyone anyway, especially me. But today, Mom was waiting in the kitchen. Carson had developed a bronchial infection. And he did want to see me. Immediately.

My insides rolled with dread. I knew I couldn't avoid him forever, but I couldn't bear the thought of his accusing eyes and his immobilized body.

I sent Andre a quick text asking yet again when the audition was going to be, but there was no response.

The rehab unit lobby was modern and surprisingly homey. Decorated in warm oranges and browns, it reminded me of a ski lodge, though no resident of that place would be hitting the slopes anytime soon.

Carson was asleep in his bed. The tubes were gone, the bruises faded to pale green and yellow. He looked more like my brother again. I could almost convince myself that he was going to wake with a start, sing a Green Day song at the top of his lungs in the world's hottest shower, then hustle off to lacrosse practice.

Mom hummed softly, positioning some cards from well-wishers on the dresser. I settled onto a chair beside the bed. One of Carson's flaccid legs poked from under the blanket, his firm athlete's muscles already going soft. His hands were fastened with plastic supports, the fingers flexed in rigid claws. I wanted to run, but forced myself to sit stiffly, glued to my chair.

"He said to wake him if he dozed off," Mom whispered. "But I don't have the heart."

The tension ebbed from my body. It would be so much easier to just sit and listen to the gentle wheeze of his chest and not have to face him.

At that moment, a portly man in a suit walked into the room bearing flowers. I recognized him instantly as the man from the TV news, Reverend Barclay Smith.

Mom jumped to her feet and shook his hand vigorously. "Reverend! What a lovely surprise."

The man nodded, his lips pursed. He spoke in a hushed tone that reminded me of an undertaker. "I came as soon as I could get away, Mrs. Collins, what with the latest disappearance. I hope I can provide some comfort." His earnest gaze shifted to Carson, who was still asleep.

Mom turned to me. "Beth? This is Reverend Smith. He—"

"Yeah. I know him. He's, like, on TV or in our school every other day."

Mom's cheeks flushed pink. "Beth! Apologize for being so rude!"

The Reverend smiled and chuckled softly. "No offense

taken, Mrs. Collins. I completely understand what the young
lady is going through." The man closed his eyes as if fighting
back a painful memory. "Due to my own loss."

I exhaled. Mom shot me the evil eye. "How about you get
us all some coffee, Bethany?"

I scowled. "Sure. Fine." A few years before, the Reverend's
oldest son had been killed in a freak boating accident and, if
you asked me, he'd been milking the sympathy factor to turn
himself into the county's Comforter in Chief.

It took me a while to find my way to the cafeteria. By the
time I came back with three coffees, they were cold and I was
annoyed to find the Reverend had already left. But Mom was
flushed and looking satisfied with herself. "What a lovely man.
He couldn't stay long. You do know about his son, right?"

I sighed and set the coffees down. "Yeah, yeah. I may have
known someone who was a friend of his. What was his name?"

Mom took one of the coffees, sat and sipped at it. "I don't
know, William or something? It was a terrible tragedy. I think
the boy was about fourteen, a year or so older than you at the
time. Anyway, since Reverend Smith is no stranger to tragedy,
I found his insights very comforting."

"They must be real pearls. He was here, what, ten minutes?"

Mom glared at me over the rim of the Styrofoam cup. Her
voice dropped to its softest register and I knew I was in trouble.
"That's enough, Beth."

Carson had begun to stir, moaning softly and thrashing his
head from side to side, the only part he seemed to be able to
move.

"Honey?" Coffee still in hand, Mom leapt to his side and
spoke softly into his ear.

Still flailing, Carson's eyes flickered open. He coughed, a
dry deep rumble, and craned his neck to look at me. His eyes
were glazed, the pale hair clinging to his forehead in damp
clumps. "Mom. Hey, Beth."

Mom laid a hand on his brow. "Oh, my. Honey, you're

27

burning up. I'm going to get the nurse." She hurried out, leaving us alone.

Carson smiled at me, eyes slitted. "Didn't think I'd miss you, but I actually do."

I think the corners of my lips curled up in a pained approximation of a smile. I hoped it looked more convincing then it felt. "I missed you, too."

I started to reach for his hand and then stopped. Carson's jaw clenched as he lifted his arms a few trembling inches off the blanket, his hands immobile and stiff in their plastic supports. He coughed and said, "The doctor says I'll be able to do more as the injury heals."

I stared. My lips moved. "That's, uh, great, Carson."

He let his arms drop. "Yeah. Great." His breath sputtered and he began to cough even more, his face turning red.

I stood and paced the room in frantic strides. "I should get someone in here."

"No. Stay. Mom is taking care of it," he said, wheezing. "Hug me, Beth. Squeeze me as hard as you can."

I froze. "I don't know."

"I'm not made of glass." He stopped to gulp in air. "I just want— Please, just do it."

I glanced around the room, praying Mom would come back with the nurse. My gaze was drawn upward and I gasped. Darkness pooled on the ceiling, a whirlpool made of shadow.

"Please, Beth," Carson said, his voice straining from his diaphragm.

"Okay. Let me know if I hurt you."

He chuckled softly. "That would be something. Below my collarbone I can't feel squat. Except for the tiny tingle at the tips of my fingers."

I slipped my arms gently around him. Tears swam in my eyes. I was frightened. As much as I'd clashed with him, I didn't want to lose my brother.

After a few painfully long moments, I pulled away.

"Jeez. Don't cry, Beth."

"Sorry."

"Why are you apologizing? I'm the jerk who tried to set you up when you were still grieving for Sam. I'm the idiot who didn't get what a creeper Luke was."

"Carson, I—"

"It's not your fault he died. And maybe it's not so terrible he did, the bastard. It's not your fault I'm…like this. But you can't just hang on to me, like you're doing with Sam, so will you please just let me go now?"

"Let you go?" Heat flashed to my cheeks. I sprang away from his bed. "What are you talking about?" The whirling darkness dipped lower. The temperature in the room dropped as it grew dark at the edges. My chest prickled with electric heat.

Carson gestured toward the ceiling with his chin. "That."

A shiver quaked its way up my spine. "I have no idea what you're talking about, Carson."

"Liar," he said, staring at me.

The *click-clack* of Mom's footsteps drew closer, accompanied by the padding of the nurse's soft heels. I rushed from the room, raced down the hall, and stumbled off.

Dazed and exhausted beyond thinking, I wandered aimlessly until I found an empty room, curled into the fetal position on the made-up bed, and fell into a deep dreamless sleep.

Mom shook me awake.

"How could you run off like that? Carson's temperature spiked to 105, but they've got it under control now. They're putting him on an antibiotic drip, which will hopefully knock out this infection or he'll have to be moved back to intensive care. I don't have time for this behavior of yours."

"I'm sorry. I shouldn't have bolted. You have enough to deal with."

Mom drew me to her, folded her arms around me, and held me tight. "It's okay, honey. We'll get through this."

I let her hold me and drank in the scent of her tasteful perfume, listened to her steady heartbeat, and prayed it never faltered.

Mom pulled away and pushed the hair back from my forehead. "Did Carson say anything to you while I was gone?"

"No."

"Good." Mom closed her eyes. Tears trickled out from the corners. "He told me to let him die, Beth. But how could I do that? I could never...."

I was still in Mom's embrace when my phone vibrated with a text message.

When I finally got a chance to look, I saw that Andre had set up the audition for that Friday.

Once we got home, I remained outside on the driveway and stared up at the full moon. I thought of all the times that Sam and I had kissed out there under the same moon and my hand reached reflexively for the Blast Mahoney button he'd given me on our last night together.

I looked down at the empty spot on my jacket in disbelief. It was gone.

ON WEDNESDAY, OUR HOUSE WENT UNDER contract. Moving day was in a month.

Now that it seemed likely Carson would survive, Mom swung into action. She'd already hired contractors to build ramps and outfit the old lake house to accommodate the needs of a quadriplegic. The following Monday she'd scheduled a tour of my new school.

With Mom in full upheaval mode, I threw myself into practicing for the audition. Sam had written a song for me a few months before he'd vanished, called "Fragile Forever." and I planned to sing it in his honor.

It took many attempts before I could get through the song, and when I finally did, I strummed for hours, pouring my heartbreak into each note. I'd searched everywhere for that missing Blast Mahoney button, but it hadn't turned up.

This song was all I had left of Sam. I had to get it right.

I'd done my research and found only praise for the High Step Program online. Even my music teacher had heard of it. Apparently, High Step's exclusivity was legendary. Many had tried, but few succeeded in gaining a coveted spot.

By Friday, numb and shaky, I was cautiously confident

about my prospects. Andre advised me to pack an overnight bag and had graciously agreed to drive me to the audition site, two hours north over the Massachusetts border. If there were a lot of other contenders auditioning with me, we might have a long wait. The High Step Program had guest rooms available just in case.

I told Mom that the band and I were going to play a showcase at a school in Massachusetts and that we would be staying at the home of the music teacher. My lie had as many holes as a window screen, but as distracted as Mom was, she bought it.

We left mid-afternoon. On the long ride, Andre and I were mostly silent, absorbed in our own thoughts. Andre didn't talk much about his home life, but Shelly had hinted about how the father who had beaten him as a child was now ill with heart disease. How he was his family's main support. I couldn't waste his time with my problems

My insides curdled with guilt, I decided that I had no choice but to push ahead with my plans. It was self-preservation. Moving to that lake house would get me away from memories of Sam but also take me away from the band. It would wreck me and then I'd be of no use to anyone.

While Andre focused on driving, I hummed "Fragile Forever" under my breath, my fingers compulsively strumming a phantom guitar. I'd been told to leave my amp at home, as the audition would be strictly acoustic.

Though I was tensed into a tight little ball, as always, the steady heat of Andre's strength kept me centered.

I nodded off. When I opened my eyes, dusk shrouded the remote woods in hazy mist. A narrow road cut through trees and emptied to a field of pristine snow. Behind us, the woods vanished into grey fog. In the distance, gold light burned from the windows of a hulking stone building.

"Here we are," Andre said, pulling into a small parking area. There was only one other car.

Once outside, the icy wind smacked us hard. Wet snow fell in horizontal sheets, obscuring the contours of the building. If there was a sign or marking to identify what kind of place this was, it was probably covered over as well.

Andre carried my guitar and held my arm as we crunched across the slippery path to the entrance. Not for the first time, I considered how nice it would be to feel this protected and cared for all the time. Sam and I had had a different kind of relationship—we were usually too deep in discussion to even hold hands. But Shelly and Andre were a permanent item, and if I were to be totally honest with myself I had no real attraction to Andre, even if he was smoking-hot gorgeous.

As we got closer, I noticed that the old stone building was run-down and ancient. Snow-caked ivy clung to its sides. "What kind of place is this, anyway? I thought we'd be at a school."

Andre shrugged. "Vincent claims it's an old brewery that was in the family of the director. The acoustics are great, so they turned it into a retreat and audition space. I think they have concerts here or something."

"Wow," I said. "Pretty cool."

"Don't be fooled by the shabby exterior. I hear it's amazing inside."

A scarred wooden door opened to a toasty warm foyer. Candlelight washed the space in honey-gold light and cast dancing shadows on the brick walls. The scent of hot cider and fresh flowers wafted toward me. With Andre's hand pressed against the small of my back, I felt my twisted nerves untangle.

Coming here was probably insane. But at least I was doing something to pull myself out of my funk. With my anxiety symptoms escalating, I had no doubt that I stood at the edge of a bottomless pit. One more push and down the rabbit hole I went.

A tall woman in a dark, gauzy gown opened the door and motioned us in. Her jet-black hair was swept off her long neck in an artfully careless updo. I noted that she was entirely too dressed up for an audition, but whatever.

"Hello, Andre! And you must be Bethany Collins! I'm Monica DeWitt, head of recruitment for the High Step Program."

I flashed Andre a questioning look, but the woman answered before he could respond. "Didn't he tell you? Andre is a part-time student with High Step."

The wind rushed out of my lungs. "Huh? Why didn't you say?"

Andre shrugged and smiled sheepishly. "I wanted you to feel like you did this on your own."

"That's silly. It would have made me a lot less nervous. But why only part-time, dude?"

"You know the score. With Dad's pacemaker and all," Andre said, "and Mom can't really handle much."

"Oh, right." I felt like an idiot all over again. It had never occurred to me to ask why he hadn't tried out himself.

I wondered if I would take that option, too—if I'd want to split my time between the program and home. Carson's desperate gaze and limp body flashed in my mind, and I reaffirmed my resolve to escape. I had to.

Monica DeWitt's eyes glittered like pale blue opals set in ivory; her face crinkled in a luminous smile. Her lyrical alto set me instantly at ease, though I felt small and mousy in her breathtaking presence. "Please, both of you, come in quickly! It's frigid out there. We are *so* pleased that you have decided to try out for the program, Bethany. Vincent has spoken very highly of your performance at your high school."

At the mention of Vincent, the beautiful boy with the

French accent, a fleeting chill chased up my spine. The pressure of Andre's hand on my shoulder steadied me.

Monica DeWitt led us through hammered-copper double doors to a huge room with polished wood floors, arched ceilings, and plush couches arranged around two massive fireplaces. Stone walls rose around us, cresting in a vaulted brick ceiling.

"Wow," was all I could manage.

"Lovely, isn't it?" Monica gestured to a raised platform where an array of musical equipment had been set up. "It's now our state-of-the-art music space. We hold concerts here as well."

"Cool," I said, completely awestruck and a little weak-kneed.

"Why don't you both make yourselves at home at one of those couches around the fire? I'll get some hot cider and scones after I make a quick phone call. Vincent was supposed to have been here by now."

Monica glided from the room, gown trailing behind her.

"I thought they'd be auditioning other candidates," I said to Andre once she was gone.

"It's mid-semester. You should be honored they've arranged for this."

"I am," I muttered. Andre's phone rang and he answered, brow furrowed with concern. He ended the call, looking distressed.

"Crap. Dad's had another heart episode and Mom's freaking. I'm going to have to leave."

"That sucks. They can reschedule this, right?"

Monica DeWitt reentered with a tray of steaming mugs and a bowl of scones. She set them on a table, but we were both standing.

"Is something wrong?"

Andre explained the situation.

"I'm so sorry about your father, Andre, dear. But Beth,

there's no need for you to leave. We have lovely accommodations here, and Vincent can take you home tomorrow."

"Or I can come back tomorrow to get you," Andre offered.

Monica turned to me. I was skeptical about the offer, but something told me that if I let this chance slip by, I'd end up warehoused forever in that backwoods town, my mind turning slowly to mush, my nerves shot. Not to mention having to face my helpless brother's pleading eyes every day.

"It's fine," I said, hesitantly. "If I can get a ride with Vincent, I guess. You don't need to do all that driving. Or maybe I should just leave with you and come back?"

"No! Don't do that. I'll come back for you."

"You sure?" I asked. "Just get going, then. Your parents need you. We'll figure something out."

Andre hugged me hard and left. In his absence, the chill swept through me again until Vincent walked in, shaking snow from his headful of springy curls.

"Oh, hello. Bethany Collins, right?" Vincent shook my hand gently, as if it was made of eggshells, his broad smile lighting up the room. He'd lost the sunglasses and I could see that his eyes were the startling light blue of phosphorescent undersea creatures, eerily vivid against his tawny skin. The shock of his beauty rippled through me.

Monica glanced pointedly at her watch. "It's high time we get started, Vincent, isn't it? Miss Collins has been waiting patiently for you to get here."

"My apologies. Very sorry for the delay."

For the audition, it was just me, Monica DeWitt, Vincent Rousseau, and my guitar. I climbed onto the platform, and though I was trembling and knock-kneed, my fingers found their places on the frets. By some miracle, I fell easily into the rhythm of the song. My voice built, forcing past the layers of pain and grief I'd let accumulate, and exploded into a wail of anguish. My cheeks blazed, and Monica's and Vincent's rapt expressions fueled my performance. I knew I was killing it.

While I played, I could have sworn I saw something shift in a dark corner of the room. I soldiered on, determined to ignore it.

When it was over, I suppressed the smile that twitched on my lips. I couldn't help but think that I'd nailed this. That I had actually clinched a place in the super-exclusive High Step Program.

When Monica and Vincent erupted in applause, I knew I was right. I'd rocked it.

I was in. I had to be. For the first time since Sam vanished, I had truly brought it.

But neither Monica nor Vincent confirmed my acceptance or rejection. Instead, I was led to a sumptuous guest room upstairs, served hot tea, and wished a good night's sleep. Votive candles flickered on the mantel of the cozy fireplace.

Sipping at the tea, I stared into the quivering shadows, expecting to see something move. There was nothing. But the possibility that a mouse might be lurking in one of the dark corners lodged itself in my mind and I could not get it out. Rapists I could handle, but those tiny disgusting little things were my Achilles' heel.

Too wound up to sleep, I paced the room and considered calling Shelly to admit where I really was or at least checking in with Andre. I felt too guilty about having lied to call Mom, so I'd come clean once I knew the score.

Turned out I wasn't calling anyone. My cell phone had no reception.

The refrain of "Fragile Forever" still echoing in my head, I couldn't stop thinking of Sam, his memory a thick pressure in my lungs. Suffocating and claustrophobic, I pulled back the heavy drapes. Moonlight had broken through the cloud cover and streamed across the snow like spilled silver.

Glinting in the moonlight on the ledge of the windowsill was a button. A Blast Mahoney button. The small scratch and dent under the name identified it as the one Sam had given me. I had no doubt it was mine.

I grabbed for the button and clutched it tightly in my fist, tears squeezing between my lashes. I was lonely and hollow, and without Andre to soothe me, the jagged pain of loss stabbed me like a thousand blades.

I had no idea how the button got there, but I had to talk to someone before I exploded. I'd been to a shrink a few times, but after Carson's accident there was no money for that. Now it was obvious the meds she'd prescribed weren't cutting it either. I was starting to doubt the solution to my troubles would come from a prescription or from entering the High Step Program.

I wasn't going to let it out of my sight this time, so I tucked the button into my overnight bag's outer pocket, and then paced the room searching for reception on my cell. It was a dead zone. No service.

The call to Andre had gotten through downstairs, so I slipped into the hall in search of reception. The wall sconces had been snuffed out and the corridors were dark, with only the thin strips of moonlight that filtered through the a few slitted windows to guide me.

I stumbled along, hand trailing the cold walls, in search of the staircase to the ground floor. Then my foot caught and I lost my balance, falling forward into darkness. My head smacked into something hard on the way down and I fell flat onto my stomach, disoriented, engulfed by spinning darkness. There was the scuffle of feet, then concerned voices.

Strong arms lifted me before it all went silent.

7

BRIGHT SUNLIGHT SEARED MY EYELIDS; A HEADACHE reverberated inside my sinuses. I was sitting in a chair, the world revolving too quickly behind my closed eyes.

"Bethany? Were you listening?" asked a voice inflected with a crisp upper-crust British accent.

My lashes were crusted together, so it took a few seconds to pry them open. "What?"

My eyes blinked open. If this was a dream, it was a vivid one.

A strange man smiled at me from behind a massive oak desk. He was handsome and elegant, shoulder-length auburn waves falling over the collar of what appeared to be a very expensive suit. To the side of the desk, Vincent Rousseau's gold curls gleamed like the sun's corona. He gazed intently at me, his forehead creased. Everything was blurred and fuzzy, as if I was looking through a Vaseline-smeared lens.

"How did I get here?"

The man sighed. "Bethany, dear, it may take some time for your mind to clear after that nasty fall you had. We feel terrible that your time with us has been marred by your injury. But you are healing fast. You'll be up to speed in no time."

"My time with you? What do you mean? I only just came for an audition last night."

The man's dark eyes were warm and concerned. "You

don't remember what happened after that? Oh, my. Our doctors said you merely had a slight concussion. Perhaps it was more severe than we'd suspected."

Watery light poured in from the floor to ceiling windows and hurt my eyes. "I really don't know what the fu—what the heck you're talking about. Last thing I remember was that I fell, and—"

"Yes," Vincent interjected softly, his voice reassuring and resonant. Between the two European accents, I wondered if I was even still in the US. "I heard the crash. I ran from my room and found you barely conscious on the floor."

I squinted and tried to focus my thoughts and vision, but my brain was sponge cake—porous and empty. Anger flared in the pit of my stomach. A dark smear hovered vaguely above the man's head and tickled the back of my throat. "I remember that, but nothing else. Someone better tell me what's going on."

The man glanced at Vincent, then nodded, stood, and extended a hand to me. I was momentarily fixated by the antique ring set with a massive ruby on the man's finger. Bits and impressions floated aimlessly in the soup of my mind, but I couldn't really make sense of them.

"I'm sorry for how this must seem to you, Bethany. I'm Gideon Ross, the Director of the High Step Talented Youth Program or just High Step, as we like to call it. We had already decided to offer you acceptance into the Program when you fell and hit your head. Under the circumstances, we had to inform your mother of the accident and learned about your situation at home. Given the demands of caring for your disabled brother, your mother, once she got over her initial anger at your deception, agreed it would be best if you entered the High Step Program without delay."

I jumped to my feet. "But—but—my friends. My *things*. I didn't get to say goodbye to anyone."

"But you did, Beth," Vincent said, brow furrowed. "You

don't remember that either? Your friend Andre came for you.
You had two days to get your things together. The audition
was a week ago." He took my hand. I desperately wanted to
believe him. I strained to remember, but came up blank.

"I lost an entire week? How is this possible?"

"Brain injuries are strange that way," Gideon Ross said.
"We've had you evaluated by the school doctor and he gave
you the all-clear. But I guess this means you don't remember
anyone here at the Program, so we'll just start all over."

"Not a problem," Vincent said with smile. He rested a
hand on my shoulder and warm comfort rushed over me.
Patchy memories seeped in to fill in the blank spaces until I
wasn't sure what I'd actually forgotten. Wispy memories of
packing, tearful goodbyes floated through my mind.

I gazed at Gideon Ross and realized that, somehow, I was
pretty sure I did know him.

And did it matter? Wasn't acceptance to the High Step
Program the answer to all my problems?

Gideon was beaming at me. "Very well, then. It just so
happens that each week the Program showcases the talents of
our extraordinarily gifted students, and one showcase is just
about to begin. Vincent will be happy to take you there, if
you feel up to it."

Vincent offered me his arm. "It would be an honor."

I slipped my arm into Vincent's, unsure if I could actually
stand and walk on my own. My legs were weak and wobbly;
my vision still blurred at the edges. I wasn't wearing the
clothes I'd auditioned in, so apparently time *had* passed.

No matter. I'd done it. I'd escaped the fate of the lake
house, escaped being a witness to Carson's suffering. I told
myself that he'd adjust to life better without me around to
remind him how I could have prevented his tragedy in the
first place. And I was one less body for Mom to worry about.

And maybe, here, I wouldn't need those meds anymore.

Vincent led me out of Gideon's study and my brain hiccuped. The halls of this building did look familiar, even though we were clearly not at the old brewery. Pale light streamed through tall arched windows. I peered out to the snow-covered fields and the birch forest beyond, both clouded in mist. The sense that I'd forgotten something important crept up and gnawed at me.

Vincent's hold on my arm kept me steady as we strolled slowly through the halls. "Where exactly are we, Vincent?"

"The Program compound is not far from the Brewery," Vincent said. He gestured toward the windows. "We are in the state of Massachusetts. Lovely, isn't it?"

"Yeah. Pretty foggy out there, though."

"It's usually this way. We are in a low-lying valley."

"It's always foggy? Even when the sun shines?"

Vincent nodded.

"Weird."

"You get used to it."

"Where are you from originally, Vincent?" I blurted.

"I was born in Normandy in northern France. But this country is my home now."

When I realized his answer was not quite what I'd hoped, I decided to press him a bit.

"So what's your talent?"

Vincent scowled for a moment, then broke into a bright smile. "You mean why I'm in the High Step Program? I play violin."

"Neat. I'd love to hear you play."

"You most assuredly will," he whispered as we entered the darkened auditorium. The place was full and hushed, the aisles sloping down to the spotlit stage, bare except for a single stool and a mic stand.

"It's packed. We'll have to sit in the back," he said.

We took our seats in the last row just as a tall boy with longish black hair that fell in his eyes walked onto the stage. I couldn't see his features too clearly from this distance with my still slightly blurred vision, but something about his bearing sparked recognition. I wondered if he was one of the people I'd met this past week and forgotten.

"Who's that?" I whispered to Vincent. "Did I meet him?"

In the dark of the auditorium I couldn't be sure, but I thought I saw Vincent's lips curl into a sneer. "I doubt it. Xavier doesn't socialize much."

I was about to press him when the boy mumbled something into the microphone. If there was whispering before, the place became quieter as the boy named Xavier began to sing what sounded like an ancient folk song without instrumentation.

I'd been around a lot of singers. I'd been told my own voice was powerful and raw, like a baby Janis Joplin, one of the great female rock singers of the twentieth century. But this kid's voice was like nothing I'd ever heard. Unearthly in its range and purity, at first it dropped to its lowest registers, breathy yet vibrant, then climbed steadily to majestic heights of fiery fury. I felt the vibration in my teeth—in the marrow of my bones, as though I were a human tuning fork.

The audience was dead silent, apparently as enthralled as I was.

When he finished, Xavier appeared exhausted and limp and needed to be led from the stage. The crowd was up on their feet and going wild.

"Wow," I said. "This guy's amazing. It's no wonder he's here."

"Yes," Vincent said without a trace of a smile. "Everyone adores Xavier's singing. But I should get you back to your room. You're not quite yourself yet."

"But the concert was only just getting started."

"It can get quite wild in here once things heat up. You've

had a serious head injury with memory loss. The medical staff wants to have a look at you again. You need to rest."

My head did throb, but apparently it had healed during the lost week. There was no bump or cut, though my scalp was still a bit tender to the touch.

Reluctantly, I let Vincent lead me out of the auditorium. Questions rattled around in my mind, and I was strangely wired, as if I'd just had my batteries recharged. The last thing I wanted to do was go back to my room. I wanted to explore and see what the High Step compound was all about.

But I was tired. And I realized I had no actual recollection of my room. Obviously my things were there, since I'd been living here for a week. I wondered if it would seem familiar.

We meandered through the halls, my arm in Vincent's, and I was amazed how comfortable I felt striding beside him. It suddenly dawned on me that I might have known him better than I thought. I cleared my throat, color rushing to my cheeks.

"Vincent. How well do we know each other?"

The vibrant eyes went wide. "Pardon?"

"I mean, the stuff I forgot. Did we spend a lot of time together? Because…" I stumbled over my words, embarrassed and confused. "You feel so…like I know you. But I can't for the life of me remember a single minute we've spent together beside the audition and when I met you at Linford."

Vincent smiled and looked down. "I've been showing you around. That is all."

"Oh," I said, and wondered if I was disappointed. If I wished there was more.

We walked through the sconce-lit stone halls, paned windows overlooking endless drifts of mist-shrouded snow. The sun had gone down while we were in the showcase and now the moon peeked from behind wispy clouds. The High Step compound was vast, and since I didn't remember seeing it from the outside, the interior seemed endless and changeable, an opulent labyrinth of halls and staircases.

We stopped at an unfamiliar door in an unfamiliar hall. Nothing was recognizable except the pain that was slowly resurfacing in my awareness. Without warning, the song I'd auditioned with, "Forever Fragile," sprang into my mind and the anguish returned full-force.

Sam. How on earth could I have forgotten Sam?

My expression must have registered my thoughts, because Vincent's brow wrinkled. "Is something wrong, Bethany?"

"No," I said. "Nothing. I'm just tired."

"This week has been hard on you." Vincent leaned toward me, lips parted, and I was suddenly not so sure that touring the High Step grounds was all we'd been doing. In the amber light, his eyes glowed like blue lava lamps.

I turned away and Vincent stepped back, rebuffed. I felt as though I'd been dropped into someone else's part in a play and was expected to know the lines. In fact, this whole experience had been surreal. I wondered again if maybe I was still unconscious and dreaming the whole thing up, Dorothy-style.

"Good night then, Bethany," he said curtly, nodded in his quaintly formal manner, then left.

I entered my room to find my suitcases open, my amp plugged in, and my makeup collection and medication bottles strewn across the vanity in my usual slapdash style. The messy bed had been slept in. Obviously, I'd been here before. I'd left my stamp—utter chaos.

Besides the mess, it was a beautiful room with vintage floral drapes, a marble hearth with a crackling fire, and a floral hooked rug over the stone floor. There were botanical prints on the whitewashed walls and the bed was an antique four-poster beauty.

A powerful wave of longing grabbed me by the throat, choking me with its violence. The pain of loss crowded out all other thoughts. Hot tears sprang into my eyes.

I tore at the curtains to get to the window so I could breathe. Just like the night in the Brewery, moonlight streamed across a pristine blanket of snow. I pried open the ancient casement windows and sucked in a lungful of the winter air, letting the razor-sharp cold cut into my lungs. But there was no escaping the emptiness that threatened to swallow me whole.

Through my tears, I saw a figure made of shadow move at the edge of the woods. I blinked and it was gone. There was nothing there at all.

I pulled the window closed. I wanted this, I told myself. I wanted to run away and make a new start. My memories of the past week were Swiss cheese, but the pain was fresh and raw as always. Talk about baggage. If anything, Sam felt closer than ever in this place, the guilt over abandoning my disabled brother and harried mother as sharp as an open wound.

I drew the curtains closed. There would be no wandering around tonight, though. I had no urge to call anyone. I wanted to escape the pain, not pull it closer. In fact, I realized, I had no idea where my phone was.

I turned to face the fire, and let the dancing flames soothe my tattered nerves.

And there, lying on the braided rug where I was dead certain it hadn't been a minute before, was Sam's Blast Mahoney button.

I WOKE BEFORE SUNRISE, DRAWN TO THE WINDOW where predawn light had cast the woods in a bluish haze. I pressed my face to the glass. Tree trunks faded into grey-blue nothingness. Though the property was bounded by mist, the sky above the woods was a deep clear blue, with a shimmer of pink fringing the horizon.

I stared at the woods, heartache and loneliness crashing down on me, and wondered if escape had been such a good idea. I missed Shelly and wished I could remember our goodbyes, how she and the band had reacted to my sudden departure. But it was all a blank. I clutched the Blast Mahoney button hard, until it made an indentation in the flesh of my palm, determined not to lose track of it again.

The figure made of shadow slipped between the trees at the edge of the woods, then went still. I swore it was looking straight at me.

Without hesitation, I threw a coat over my pajamas and tugged my sheepskin boots over my bare feet. Beneath my window there was a narrow ledge, then a drop to the sloping roof of the floor below. I didn't remember seeing the compound from the outside, but I'd glimpsed a large wraparound porch through some windows, and I hoped it was also directly under mine.

I pinned the button to my jacket, pushed open the casement

windows, and slipped out to the ledge. The cold bit viciously into my face and hands. I told myself that I wouldn't get in trouble for this because they'd figure my head injury was making me do nutty things. Maybe it was.

Easing myself down, I landed on the roof of the lower floor, but there was no traction and I skidded gracelessly to the edge. Clinging to the gutter, I prayed it was too early for anyone on other side of those curtained windows to witness my idiot moves.

My hands were frozen by the time I dangled from the roof's ledge and found my footing on the porch rails. I fell to the snow with a soft *thud*, the cold already invading every crevice of my body. I didn't know what I was thinking, or how I'd get back inside if the front entrance was locked. I quickly realized that I could freeze out there because of my stupidity.

At the edge of the woods, the shadow figure was gone. I waded through knee-high snow that caked the insides of my non-waterproof boots. Shivering, I made a circuitous path to the woods so my tracks weren't so obvious to a casual observer. Sunlight streamed through the thick fog, turning the woods into a mystic wonderland. Beyond the fringe of trees, the fog was dense, the trunks obscured in a solid haze. If I wandered into that, I might never find my way back. The figure had vanished without a trace and I had to wonder if this, too, was a result of the head injury or a hallucination. Maybe the stress really was causing me to lose my mind.

There was no point in going any further. The icy air crystallized in my lungs, and my feet and fingers were numb. The sun was up and soon someone would notice I'd sneaked out of the building by way of the roof. I had worked hard to get into the High Step Program. I didn't want to get kicked out before I'd even started.

I turned to go, but something made me pin the Blast Mahoney button to the trunk of a gnarly old oak whose bare branches grasped for the sky like arthritic fingers. I'd remember that tree, I was sure of it. And I was certain my precious button would be safer outside. It was crazy, I knew. But I was sure no one would disturb it there.

Frozen to the bone, I trudged back to the High Step building, finally able to see it from the outside. It was a sprawling fieldstone mansion, one that had probably once belonged to some robber baron family from the Gilded Age. It stood about four stories high with turrets and a widow's watch at the top, a stately porch wrapped around its full length. Beautiful. I was momentarily filled with pride to be a member of such an amazing establishment. That I was sought after and had been chosen to be here.

Then I remembered I was on the verge of hypothermia and probably breaking rules I wasn't even aware existed. I hurried across the snowfield, hoping desperately that the back entrance was unlocked.

Mercifully, there was a path cleared through the snowfall, so I trudged up to the back porch and told myself that, out here in the boonies, what would be the reason for locking a door in the first place? I jiggled the brass doorknob. It was locked. I was about to scurry around to the front entrance and beg for mercy when the door creaked open. Standing in the doorway in pajamas and a robe, tousled black hair in his eyes, the singer from last night regarded me sleepily.

"Who are you, and what the hell are you doing?" he snapped, twitching the messy hair from one startling blue eye. What was it with the blue eyes in this place? I was about to snark back at him when I realized how I must have seemed—a frozen stranger trying to break in at the crack of dawn.

"I—I'm Beth. Bethany Collins, the new girl? I woke up and I just got this—I don't know—urge to see the sunrise in the mountains. You're Xavier, right? I saw you perform last night."

The boy regarded me in silence. The one eye that I could

see was the dark cold blue of a winter lake, totally different from the warm glowing blue of Vincent's. A corner of his mouth curved into a sardonic smile. "I heard about you. People say you have brain damage."

I glared at him. "Very nice. Are you going to let me in, or let me to freeze to death out here?"

He stepped aside to let me pass. "I guess it's true, then. Only someone with brain damage would be out in the woods on a morning as cold as this."

I huffed past him. I was starting to understand Vincent's tone when I'd asked about this guy. On first impression, he really did seem like a rude prick. "Yeah? And what were you doing up at this ungodly hour?"

The single blue eye, fringed by dark lashes, regarded me. His gaze may have been hard, but his lips were soft and well formed. There was hint of dark stubble on his jaw. He was a little older, from the look of him. Eighteen, I figured, maybe nineteen. I wondered why he was here and not in college.

"I don't get much sleep," he said, his chin thrust forward. With one hand, he pushed the hair from his face again. Before it fell back, the silky strands parted to reveal the blotchy skin of scar tissue that started at the corner of his right eye and continued down along the side of his face, ending at the jawline. I tried not to stare, but I couldn't help noticing that the uneven skin continued along the side of his neck, disappearing under the collar of his robe. I knew he'd seen me staring, but all he said was, "You should get those wet things off," before he turned abruptly and strode away.

9

AS CURIOUS AS I WAS TO HAVE A LOOK AROUND the High Step grounds, I decided that the risk of getting caught was too great. I was already the girl with brain damage and I didn't want to add any fuel to that label.

Instead, I scurried back to my room to dress for breakfast. It wasn't long before Vincent came to get me, looking fresh and bright as the morning sunlight that streamed through my window. He greeted me with a sunny smile, and I returned it.

"I hope you are hungry. Breakfast at the compound is epic."

I smiled at his adorable attempt to sound American. It didn't quite work. "Hell yeah!" But my enthusiasm quickly gave way to apprehension. "Crap. The kids at breakfast all know me already. His Royal Highness called me brain-damaged."

Vincent's lips pulled into a scowl. "His Royal Highness?"

"You know, the singer guy? What a jerk."

"I tried to warn you. Xavier has no grasp of social etiquette, as you may have noticed. It's as if he carries a grudge against the world."

"If he's so miserable, why doesn't he leave or go to college or something? Isn't he old enough?"

Vincent sighed. "How I wish he would. But this *is* a college, Beth. High Step is not only a preparatory academy, but a world-class conservatory. And *His Royal Highness* is smart enough to know that he will never find a better education anywhere else."

I peered into the glowing blue eyes, so filled with conviction and spirit. "You don't care much for Xavier. But you really like *this* place, don't you? How much do they pay you for such loyalty?" I said, laughing. "And where are all the other college kids?"

"Mainly at another location. Xavier mostly just boards here." For a moment Vincent's eyes clouded with hurt before he brushed it away with a smile. "It's only a small stipend. But there is no place like this anywhere. For that, I am loyal and grateful. And no, I don't dislike Xavier, though I would not call us friends. There are reasons he is the way he is, I suppose."

"Does it have something to do with those scars?"

Vincent shrugged. "Possibly. It's said he does not sleep. Which would make anyone irritable, wouldn't it?"

We finally entered the dining room, a sprawling affair of floor to ceiling windows overlooking a lake I hadn't known was there. Above the seven or so round tables packed with students hung flying-saucer-sized chandeliers. Each table was heaped with steaming platters of food. Students busily talked and stuffed their faces.

"I don't recognize anyone," I said glumly. At my words, the din quieted and the students all turned to face me. As one, they stood and applauded. I felt my face heat to cherry red and fought the urge to run the other way.

"What are they doing?" I hissed between my teeth.

"I'm sorry. I should have warned you. Usually, we do this on a student's first day to welcome them. But because of your memory loss, we decided to start over."

"Great," I mumbled. "Now they all think I'm a freak."

Vincent took my arm and led me to an empty space on a bench. "No one thinks you are a freak. High Step is a tight and supportive community, as you will learn. We do not taunt or abuse each other. Anyone who does so faces severe punishment."

I rolled my eyes. "So they're being forced to be nice to me. That makes me feel so much better."

"That is not what I meant to imply," Vincent whispered into my ear. "We are charitable and forgiving. No one will judge or label you. It is not our way."

We squeezed onto the bench and my mouth watered at the plates of French toast, bacon, scrambled eggs, and muffins. There were also hash brown potatoes, five kinds of jam, dishes of whipped cream, and giant plates of sliced fruit with berries. I didn't know where to begin. My stomach growled like I hadn't eaten in weeks.

At the other end of the hall at a table, I spotted Xavier, eating in silence, hair hanging in his eyes. There was something strange about the way he was eating, but I made myself look away.

I turned to find the girl on the opposite side of the table staring intently at me, eyes sparkling, a half-formed smile flickering across her dark red lips. "You really don't remember me, do you? I'm Lila. We met the first day you were here."

Lila had a petite doll-like face with dark bird-bright eyes. Her milk-pale skin, black blunt-cut hair, and red lipstick gave her the look of a 1920s flapper. When her smile erupted full-strength, I knew I must have liked her right away, because I liked her now.

I reached over to shake her hand. "I don't remember you. But I'm sure we can catch up in no time. How well can you get to know a person in a week?"

Lila smiled and shrugged. "You'd be surprised at all the gossip I'll need to recap for you. Not a problem, though."

The breakfast was delicious, and I felt surprisingly comfortable with everyone. They were open and friendly and, like Vincent promised, seemed willing to accept me despite my blue hair and vacant mind. I was introduced to a Demetri Priskin, a Dawn Waverly, and a Roddy Zuber, as well as others in such rapid succession I could barely keep them all sorted out.

Again, because I couldn't really help myself, I glanced to where Xavier was sitting, and wondered what it was about him that intrigued me so much. Despite the scars, he was lithe and graceful and amazingly nice to look at. Still, I didn't understand why the sight of him stirred up so much emotion. Thoughts of Sam crept in and eroded my happiness. I thought of the button I'd left stuck to a tree. If the angst he radiated was not enough warning to steer clear, I didn't know what would be.

Yet, I looked back again. Xavier was gone.

If Vincent had noticed my fascination, he didn't let on. He leaned over and whispered in my ear, and my distress dissolved, his fingers warm where they brushed the skin on my arm. "Gideon wants to meet with you after breakfast to evaluate if you're ready to attend your classes."

I swallowed. Classes. What an idiot. I was at a school. Of course there would be classes.

I heaved a deep sigh. "Sure."

"Don't sweat it," Lila said. "Classes here are nothing like the kill-and-drill sessions you're used to. Everything at High Step is strictly hands-on, right, Vincent?"

But Vincent had leapt to his feet, bounding across the dining room to greet a slight figure in an electric wheelchair.

Lila sighed and rolled her eyes. "There goes Saint Vincent, at it again. The boy thinks it's his personal mission to heal the sick and give comfort to the needy. If I didn't know better I'd say he thinks he's…"

"The second coming?" Roddy Zuber deadpanned, one

eyebrow quirking up.

"Don't get me wrong," Lila continued, "Vincent is an amazing person with a heart of gold. But sometimes he carries the Mother Teresa thing a little too far."

I tried not to stare at the figure in the wheelchair, a slight girl with white-blonde hair, porcelain skin, and bent limbs. Vincent sank low to kiss her contorted hand. The girl jerked spastically in her chair. I was sickly fascinated but I couldn't look away. Nausea rolled into the back of my throat and I couldn't help but think of Carson.

"Wh-what's her talent?" I blurted.

"Try not to stare. Her name is Della Ferguson," Lila said briskly. "She's a composer. Apparently she was born like that and it took years before someone discovered she was a musical genius."

"How sad." I thought of Carson trapped inside his own body and wondered what talents he could draw upon with his talent for lacrosse, the only one he'd ever needed, now lost to him.

"She's the niece of some big shot on the Board of Directors. Which is most likely the reason she's here," Demitri Prishkin said. With his round cheeks and straw-colored curls, Demitri reminded me of an angry oversized cherub.

Vincent continued to fawn over the disabled girl. The cynical thought that he was just a shameless brown-nose, trying to garner favor with the powers that be, crept into my head. But as much as my instincts told me to think badly of someone so squeaky-clean perfect, I couldn't get myself to believe that Vincent's attention wasn't genuine.

"C'mon, Demetri. You've heard her work. It's amazing," Zuber said.

It was painful to watch the girl's lips twist into a twitchy parody of a smile as her body jerked and spasmed. If not for her affliction, she would have been delicately pretty.

"How," I muttered. "How can she do anything?"

"One finger works. Some brilliant teacher figured that out and the rest is history," Zuber said, his long face somber. "She attributes her work as One-Digit Della."

I cringed, the contents in my stomach churning. "That's tasteless."

"It's her name for herself," Lila said. "Girl's got a sense of humor, I guess."

When breakfast ended I said goodbye to my new friends, still surprised over how easy it was to fit in here. Vincent ushered me from the dining room to Gideon's office.

"No need to be nervous," he reassured me. "I'll be back for you after my class is finished." He smiled, ducked his curly mop in one of those ridiculously courtly nods of his, and took off.

Gideon was already waiting for me behind his monster desk. "Did you enjoy your breakfast, Bethany?"

"Yes, thanks, everything was delicious."

Gideon rose and walked around from behind his desk, the enormous ruby ring on his finger catching the morning light. Silver strands flecked his deep auburn waves. Though not tall, the man was imposing and important-looking, yet somehow not intimidating in the least.

"Perhaps you are feeling well enough to attend one class today? Our setup is quite unique. The high-schoolers take their academic classes together in the mornings, regardless of grade. Classes are small and instruction is tailored to address the particular needs of the individual. The college students leave for a central site for their studies. In the afternoon everyone gets one-on-one training in their concentration, so you'll be getting lessons tailored specifically to your needs."

Gideon paused and looked me over, clearly proud of the

program's breadth and scope. It dawned on me how little I really knew when I jumped headlong into this, despite all my research, but I wasn't put off. "How does that sound to you?"

"It sounds awesome. I'd love to start right away."

"We need to evaluate you first."

"Evaluate me?"

Gideon smiled and paced in front of the windows. "Just a series of routine placement tests, both academic and artistic, to determine your levels." He turned to face me, his figure silhouetted against the light. "I'll schedule your tests for tomorrow. Consider today a trial run."

I never liked tests much, nor excelled at them. And this was not presented as a choice.

"Uh. Okay. But are you sure I didn't take them already?" I rubbed my damp palms against the brocade arms of the antique upholstered chair. Every bit of furniture in the High Step compound looked as if it should be in a museum.

"No. Of course not. We would not subject you to them twice," Gideon said with a reassuring smile.

I cleared my throat. The encounter with One-Digit Della had stirred up my worries for Carson. I was overwhelmed by a sudden wave of homesickness.

"Okay. Cool. I, uh, was wondering when I'll be able to visit home."

Gideon reached for a pipe, which rested unlit in a glass ashtray on his desk. He chewed thoughtfully on the stem. "We have also found that visiting home too soon disrupts the creative flow. It is better to postpone visits until later, when the effects of your training bear fruit, rather than sooner."

I swallowed, my throat burning. "But, my brother. He's so—he's in such bad shape. I thought—"

"Bethany." Gideon walked over and knelt next to my chair so his face was level with mine. "Unless your mother makes a specific request to get a visitation policy waiver, I'm afraid it will be a while until you visit home."

I stared at his ring, my insides stiffening. "But what if—"

Gideon rested a hand on my arm, his voice mild and calming. "Your mother has expressed a very clear wish that you should remain here at the compound until your brother is completely stabilized. Between us, we agreed that this is for the best."

I was about to protest when Vincent entered, his sunny presence as reassuring as ever. I felt my shaken nerves settle and understood that Gideon meant me no harm. That he only had my best interests at heart.

"Nothing worth having comes easily, Bethany," Gideon continued. "Our program is intensive, our good name built on our efforts. The time will pass so quickly, you will barely notice."

He smiled warmly and returned to his seat behind the huge desk.

Vincent nodded and placed a hand on my shoulder. "Let's go. I'll walk you to your first class. It's Literature. The teacher, Mrs. Halcott, is expecting you."

I studied the fine stubble on his chin, like a powdering of gold dust against his tawny skin. He leaned in slightly. "Getting used to this place can be quite an adjustment, Beth. But I promise you, you will not regret your decision in the least." His blue eyes glowed with conviction.

"What was it like for you, Vincent?" I blurted. "How long have you been here?"

Vincent straightened, his cheeks tinged pink. "Long enough. This is my home. The best one I've ever had. Class is starting soon. We should hurry along."

He led me through meandering halls, lit by glowing sconces and lined with oil portraits, to the academic wing. Students chattered and walked by in pairs.

Once we arrived at our destination, Vincent smiled and nodded toward my classroom.

"It's easy to find your way back," he said, as if he understood my need to exert my independence. "Make a left, a left, and a right, and that will take you to the grand foyer. You know your way from there, right?"

"Yep," I said.

I watched him stride purposefully away. Beautiful as he was, Vincent was an enigma I was no closer to understanding now than the first moment we'd met. Yet being around him flooded the hollow places inside me with comfortable warmth.

My Literature class had only six other students, including Roddy Zuber, who smirked and winked at me the entire time. The mood was intimate and casual, like no class I'd ever been in before. We read out loud from Dickens's *Great Expectations*, debating each passage. There was laughter and quips, and Mrs. Halcott, who taught in a conversational manner, joined in the fun. Still, it was all business as we worked our way through the text. I was more engaged in learning than I could ever recall and before I knew it, the class ended.

Exhilarated by the experience, I said goodbye to Zuber and slipped into the hall, following Vincent's directions back to the grand foyer. From there, finding my room was a snap. I had reached the massive circular double staircase and started to climb when I heard soft footsteps.

"Yo."

I whirled around. Xavier stood at the base of the stairs gazing up at me, a half-grin quirking his lips. He strode up the stairs to stand beside me. "Hey. Just wanted to apologize for being a jerkoff this morning. It was a bad night."

I studied the way the nearly blue-black hair fell over the scar-ravaged eye. The smile suited him well. "It's okay. You had no idea who I was. I could have been a prowler or something."

Xavier nodded, the smile lingering, as if the sight of me amused him somehow. "So, I hear you're a killer guitar player and singer. I'm in room 324 if you ever get a midnight urge to—uh—jam, if you—" He rested a leather-gloved hand on the banister. I looked away, not wanting to stare. "If you ever can't sleep. Like me."

I was dying to ask what troubled his sleep and how he'd gotten his scars. Instead, I blurted, "You play guitar, too?"

"Used to," Xavier said casually, as if he was talking about the weather. He tugged off the leather glove to reveal the curled fingers of his left hand, the tightly stretched skin raw and patchy. He flexed it slightly, the range of motion clearly impaired. "Can't do much with this."

"Jeez. I'm so sorry."

"Don't be." Meeting my gaze, his eyes flared briefly then cooled, a red flush spreading across the sharp plane of the one visible cheekbone. He hesitated as if the words burned painfully in his mouth, yet he couldn't force them out. Finally, he stammered, "I-I k-kind of sucked, anyway." He pulled the glove back on the ruined hand and chuckled, the words once again flowing as smoothly as ever. "My thing has always been singing."

Xavier held me in his gaze and I shifted my weight uneasily. Something unspoken had passed between us, but it was hard to put my finger on precisely what it was. Attraction? Contempt? A warning? With my mind so muddled, he was no easier to read than the ambiguous Vincent.

"You have an amazing voice," I said and managed to look away. It was obvious he wasn't comfortable talking about his injuries and I'd put him on the spot.

Xavier exhaled and sighed. The tension released. "Yeah. Whatever. Everything is what it is. See you around then, Bethany."

Pivoting, I watched him lope down the steps in a few nimble strides. Then he was gone.

Somehow, on the way up the stairs, my energy drained to the point where I was too exhausted to drag my own weight around. When I got to my room, Vincent was already waiting, leaning against the wall.

"How was class?"

"Stimulating. Exhausting."

He nodded. "You look tired. We thought it would be a little much for you so soon. Perhaps you would like to rest until dinner. There's no point in rushing into your activities before you are fully well."

Though I'd been looking forward to meeting with my teachers, my head buzzed, my eyes heavy with the need to sleep. "I guess."

Without even undressing, I climbed into bed and buried myself under a warm nest of feather comforters. Before I could fully process the events of the morning, I was asleep.

But sleep was anything but restful. Vague images and half-formed impressions flitted through my dreams. I chased a shadowy figure. Carson's accusing eyes stared out at me, his body wasted and immobilized, his face bloated. For some reason Xavier was in my dream, too, unscarred and magnificent, whispering unintelligible things in my ear. His speaking set me on edge, though I had no clue what he said.

I bolted awake in my bed; the sun had already gone down. There was nothing tangible I could latch on to or remember in the dream, but I woke shaky and trembling, my head spinning with vague impressions, like the brush of invisible bird wings. I wondered if in all the excitement I'd missed a dose of my meds.

I was about to climb out of bed and hunt down my pills when I heard a light tapping at my window. Edgy, but still groggy with sleep, I pushed back the heavy drapes and cried out. A large crow perched on the sill. Its bright black eyes met mine for a flash of a second before it fluttered off, vanishing into the night.

I rubbed my eyes and wondered if this was one of those dreams when you think you're awake, but you're really sleeping. Midday naps could be so disorienting, I told myself. I glanced at the clock. I must have slept for hours.

But no, I wasn't dreaming. On the windowsill, again the Blast Mahoney button glinted in the moonlight.

Stunned, I staggered out of bed, and stumbled through the dark room to the vanity where my pills were scattered among my personal items. I flipped on a light switch and blinked. My eyeliner, glittery blue performance eyeshadow, makeup remover, and dirty Q-tips littered the vanity top.

But my three bottles of prescription anti-anxiety meds were gone.

10

OPENED THE WINDOW AND STARED AT THE BLAST Mahoney button, my heart pounding. There was no way I'd forgotten how I'd stuck it to that tree.

Either my mind was going or, more likely, someone was trying to mess with my head. If someone was playing tricks on me, I was going to have to wring their neck.

Setting the button on the sink basin, I ran the shower as hot as I could stand and stripped out of my clothes. The steam enveloped me, but without the meds to take the edge off, my anxieties quickly took hold. Sam's beautiful smile, his soft gray eyes, invaded my vision until I couldn't breathe around the memory. I felt him reach for me through the hot mist. And I saw Carson, his once-athletic body now a useless husk, eyes pleading. What was I thinking to leave my mother to care for him alone? Guilt swirled with the soapy water as it ran down the drain.

I squeezed my eyes closed, letting the hot water scald my skin. I talked myself into believing that the school nurse had my meds and it was just another thing I'd forgotten. That they probably wanted to evaluate my dosage, monitor my intake with all the painkillers I'd been on. Maybe they were worried I was having an adverse reaction. As for the button, I wasn't sure, but I figured that a logical explanation would eventually materialize.

By the time I'd toweled off, I'd convinced myself that it all made sense. That I was just being paranoid and my stressed mind was having a delayed reaction to past traumas.

Just as I slipped into a fuzzy terrycloth robe, apparently the High Step compound standard issue, a knock at the door startled me.

"Beth? It's Vincent."

Though I'd talked myself off the ledge, I was still edgy and skittish, nearly hyperventilating. I didn't want him to see me like that. I didn't want to be expelled from the High Step Program because I was having trouble holding myself together.

"Just a second." I scrambled to wedge the Blast Mahoney button under my mattress, swung the door open, and slapped on the best smile I could muster.

As always, the sight of Vincent left me just a little breathless. He wore a button-down shirt, a few lazy curls overlapping the collar. He was freshly shaven, the gold dust peppering his jaw gone.

"Are you feeling rested?"

"Uh, yeah."

He must have seen through my lie because he stepped inside, his expression wary. "Are you sure?"

"Why wouldn't I be sure?"

He reached for my arm, the warmth of his fingers penetrating my skin. I tracked the heat's climb through my nerve endings to the source of my jitters. My fears dissolved and vanished.

Vincent smiled, blue eyes glowing.

"How," I asked, incredulous, "do you do that?"

"Do what?"

"C'mon. You sent some kind of heat up my arm, then poof, everything that was bothering me melted away." And it was true. For the life of me I couldn't remember what I was so worked up about a few moments before.

"Something *was* bothering you, then." He leaned in closer

and cupped my face with one hand, his voice tender and low. "I knew it. I am so glad you feel better now."

The heat from his palm tingled on my jaw. I shivered and swallowed hard, my mouth dry. Vincent leaned in close enough for a feathery curl to brush against my cheek. He smelled delicious, an intoxicating blend of aftershave, baby powder, and some indefinable spice.

"But how did you know something was bothering me?" I murmured, wondering if what was keeping me close to him was a good thing or not. "I didn't say."

He framed my face with the other hand. Eyes like the open sea were all I saw. "Your pain is written all over your face, impossible to miss. I wanted," he said, so close now I feel his breath in my own mouth, "to take it away."

And then, as if tugged by invisible strings, he took a step back.

"I forget myself. I am sorry."

I rubbed the place on my jaw where he'd touched me. Tension had already begun to return to the muscles at the back of my neck.

"It's okay," I said.

Vincent straightened and spoke softly, his face serious, as though he was praying or taking an oath. "I promise to look out for your best interests. You have my word."

He pressed his hand to his heart and I struggled to stifle a laugh. Such a strange boy. But the sense that large chunks of understanding had faded out of my mind clouded my thinking. Through my own confusion, I felt the need to throw him a bone, to reassure him, somehow. "When am I going to hear you play violin? You said I would."

"Yes, yes," Vincent said, suddenly distracted. I wondered if I'd offended him by mocking his solemn duty to watch over me.

Instead of backing off, I tried to make another dent in that saintly demeanor of his, knowing this too would bother him.

"Xavier asked me to jam with him."

Vincent's eyes went wide. "Never. You should not…you should steer clear of him."

"But why?"

Vincent inhaled deeply, regaining his composure. "Bethany. I told you that I am looking out for your best interests. And Xavier is the furthest thing from your best interests."

In a swift motion, he reached for me, his expression strangely intense. Heat sizzled up my arm and I was woozy, then terribly tired. I shuffled to my bed, sat heavily, and yawned.

"Man. I don't know what's wrong with me."

"Life here is an adjustment," Vincent said kindly. But there was a slight strain to his voice. He looked tired and a little haunted, his bright eyes the tiniest bit glassy. "I will be back in a half-hour to escort you to dinner."

Thirty minutes was enough time to dress, but not nearly enough time to sort out my wobbly thoughts. My adrenaline-fueled heart beat double-time, as though I was on the verge of an anxiety attack. Phantom worries whirled around me, but couldn't seem to get a toehold or make themselves known. The net effect was numbness. I was as fuzzy inside as if my emotions had been shot up with novocaine.

I had to wonder if this was how a complete nervous breakdown begins.

As promised, Vincent returned to take me to dinner. None

of the tension from earlier darkened his mood. As we walked to the dining hall, he kept up a steady stream of banter, recounting the story of how he'd gotten his first violin when he was a boy in Normandy. Somehow, he managed to do this without giving away much factual detail, his tale carefully edited to reveal as little as possible. His ploy worked well. By the time we got to the dining room, I was relaxed, though no closer to understanding Vincent and what exactly made him tick than ever.

Once we were seated, all thoughts, formed and half-formed, fled my mind as the servers set steaming platters of roast chicken and vegetables on the tables in front of us. I loaded up my plate with the goods. I was ravenous.

I scanned the dining hall for a glimpse of Xavier, but he was nowhere in sight. Catching Vincent's wary gaze, I reached for my glass of sparkling cider to wash down the lump in my throat. I wanted to tell Vincent that he might be taking his watchdog thing a little too far. That I was feeling better and didn't need a bodyguard.

My drink tipped over, sending a waterfall of sparkling cider across the table and onto Vincent's lap. Everyone laughed and threw their napkins at him. Vincent, to his credit, smiled, taking it well. But his eyes were pinned to me. The odd thing was that they were not angry in the least.

They were worried.

After dinner, once again, Vincent walked me to my room. The courtly gentleman was back. There was no sign of the boy who had leaned in so close I could taste his aftershave.

"I hope you rest well tonight. They have decided to go ahead with your evaluation tomorrow." Vincent's brow was furrowed.

"Should I be worried? What's the big deal about some academic and music tests? I don't understand why they didn't do them the first week. Most likely I'll barely pass the academics and ace the music."

Vincent was still looking at me. More like through me. "It's a bit more intense than anything else you may have experienced in the past."

"C'mon. How bad can it be?"

"Get some rest." There was no tenderness in his gaze, but his touch on my arm was feather-soft.

He turned to go, leaving me shivering. Alone in my room, I was that same restless combination of vacant and hyper. I paced, strummed a few chords on the guitar, and hummed a new tune, but that only made me less able to sit still. I checked under the mattress to make sure the Blast Mahoney button was still there.

It was, but that did nothing to calm my restless energy. I peered out the window, half-expecting to see the shadowy figure, but the moon was hidden behind a thick covering of cloud. It was pure darkness out there.

Then I remembered Xavier's invitation and wondered if he really meant for me to come to him any time I wanted. The thought of his voice and my guitar brought a little heat to the back of my neck. I didn't give a crap what Vincent said. He wasn't my keeper.

I threw on some sweats and trod the silent halls to Xavier's room in the South Wing on the other side of the central staircase. I found my way easily, pleased by my stealth. Standing outside Xavier's door, my hand poised to knock, I heard a low moan from behind the door, followed by laughter. Xavier was not alone. Apparently, I wasn't the only invited guest.

Embarrassed, I slinked back to my room. Vincent had warned me to stay away from Xavier. Maybe it was time I started listening to him.

In the morning I woke from a sleep fractured by dreams of my brother and my mother scolding me. Guilt lingered as a bitter film in the back of my throat.

I pried my eyes open and was shocked to see Andre sitting at the edge of my bed, smiling. I was certain I'd locked my door.

"Morning, stranger. Bad dreams? You talk in your sleep, you know."

I rubbed my eyes, disoriented. I was so happy to see him, I threw off the covers and dive-bombed into his lap. "Andre!"

"Easy, mama! You're small, but shot out of a cannon you can still do some damage." He laughed and squeezed me into a bear hug.

I buried my nose in his shoulder. He smelled like wood-burning stoves and home. Tears sprang into my eyes. "How is my mom? Have you seen her?"

Andre massaged my rock-hard shoulders, the knots easing under his supple fingers. "She's coping. Your mom is a trooper."

It was not easy to pull away, but I got up and padded to the other side of my room, where my ache for Mom, for home, even for Carson deepened.

"How's your dad?"

"He's well enough to… Well. Let's just say the crisis has been averted and he's back in business. For now."

Another dodge. Why were all these guys so damn evasive? I let it drop. Andre was entitled to his privacy. I knew pity was the last thing he wanted. "Have you seen Carson? How is he doing?"

Andre's face took on a grayish cast. "He's stable now. He can lift his arms with effort, but hasn't regained much use of his hands. The doctors think it's as good as he's going to get. Carson's not—he's not in a good place mentally."

I pulled back the drapes to stare out at the bleak snowfield. Mist obscured the forest floor like a carpet of clouds. "I should be with them. I shouldn't be here."

Andre came up behind me and, gently pushing a tuft of hair behind my ear, said softly, "With you here, your mom has one less thing to worry about."

"But—" I whirled on him, a protest on my lips, but the worry had already lost its sharp edges. "I just want to see him."

Andre's mouth pulled tight. "Beth," he said. "With your brother's health so fragile, your mother agreed with the doctors that it's best for you to stay away."

"What?"

"Your mother asked me to tell you she doesn't want you to visit. Not for the foreseeable future."

The sob I'd been withholding for months thrust its way out of my chest in a great heaving gasp. First losing Sam. Then Carson's accident. Now my own mother didn't want me to come home.

"Doesn't she want me to call? Send an email?" Questions slammed against the inside of my skull, but died on my lips as Andre gathered me in his arms.

"Everything's going to be all right, Beth," he whispered, and shook his head. I leaned into a hug and let myself go limp against him. We stood that way for I don't know how long, just breathing.

Andre pulled away first, and met my gaze, eyes glimmering. I felt our bond as a physical connection, linking us in shared pain.

"If you say so, Andre," I said finally.

His dark eyes danced with relief. "You've been through so much, Beth. This is the best place for you to heal."

I nodded in agreement. It was a hard pill to swallow, but I knew he was right.

"Are you ready for your evaluation now?" he asked. "Because they're ready for you."

Andre escorted me down twisting halls to an unfamiliar wing of the school. We entered a magnificent library where shelves of old books lined the soaring curved walls. Upholstered chairs clustered around polished oak tables, the soft light from green table lamps reflected in their polished surfaces. Other than us, the place was empty.

Andre led me to a group of chairs in the center of the room and let go of my arm. "This is the library," he said.

"No duh," I snarked, but my jumpy nerves snapped into panic mode the moment he let go of my arm.

"Try to relax," he said. "They'll be here in a minute."

Fear tightened my throat. I had no idea what I was so afraid of. "You're not going to stay?"

"No," Andre touched my arm, but at the withdrawal of his touch, more anxiety poured in. He coaxed me into a seat.

"Please? Stay until they come?" I pleaded.

"I can't, Beth. No one is allowed to attend an evaluation. But I promise, you'll be fine. It's not like you'll fail and get kicked out of the program."

I studied the lock of glossy chestnut hair that slanted across his forehead, the elegant tattoos coiling gracefully up one ropy copper-skinned arm. Andre smiled his beautiful smile and I was warmed. Protected. Still, I couldn't help but wonder vaguely why my brain seemed unable to hold onto a single coherent thought these days.

"Can you wait outside? I'll feel better just knowing you're there."

He nodded. "Certainly."

As I waited alone in the silent library for what felt like an eternity, thoughts and impressions dead-ended in my mind. Time had become distorted in this place, with no beginning or end. Had I always been here? My memories of life before High Step were growing threadbare and thin.

Maybe it was true, I thought, that the best way to heal was to shed the painful memories like a snake sheds its skin.

The library doors whispered open. Monica DeWitt entered with three other people I didn't recognize. Treading softly across the carpeted room, they faced me in a semi-circle. Two blank-faced and beefy young men flanked a frail elderly man with Coke-bottle thick eyeglasses. The frail man carried a satchel that looked a little too heavy for his thin frame.

Monica DeWitt's porcelain face broke into a radiant smile. "How are you today, Beth?"

"A little nervous, I guess."

"There's no need to be. This is simply for placement. Your position and scholarship with the High Step Program are secure."

I sucked in a breath and told myself I'd be fine.

"This is Dr. Randall Wellington," Monica said. "He will be performing your evaluation."

"Performing?" There was something ominous to the sound of that. I eyed the door and wondered if Andre was really out there.

"This is all very routine, dear," Monica soothed.

Despite her reassurances my heart kicked into a wild gallop. My addled brain fired off a warning and I wondered if I should mention that I could really use a dose of my meds right about then.

The man, Dr. Wellington, reached into his bag and pulled out a gleaming contraption, some kind of steampunk offspring of a massive hypodermic needle and a pressure gauge. The greenish light reflected off his thick glasses so that I couldn't see his small eyes.

I sat ramrod straight, in full panic mode. "What the hell is that? How is this a test of my talent?"

"Please," the man said, his voice trembling and weak. "You must be still, my dear."

My heart thumped harder as Monica retreated into the shadows. I tried to stand, but it was as though I was tied to the chair by invisible cords. I wanted to scream for help, for Andre to rescue me, but the words sat unsaid in my mind as if I'd lost the ability to speak.

I was wordless and frozen, but my vision was laser-clear. The contraption loomed closer. Beads of sweat dotted the man's wrinkled forehead as he placed the thing against my neck. He licked his dry lips with a bluish tongue as I tried to scream for Andre.

And couldn't.

My heart was a runaway train, but even my eyes were paralyzed and locked into position. I couldn't even blink.

Oh God, oh God. I'd never had a panic attack this intense before. Darkness rolled in like thunderheads until I was completely paralyzed and in the dark. I could hear the man's raspy breath.

"This will only sting for a moment, my dear," the man said.

The needle pierced my neck with a bite of frigid cold. Icy

shock spread from my spine to my head. My tongue swelled, crowding the back of my throat, blocking my airway. I couldn't breathe. Colors swam in darkness as bright clear pain shot through every nerve in my body.

There were muffled shouts, the scuffling of feet as I slumped over and fell out of the chair. My body began to jerk crazily as violent spasms rocked my limbs, slamming my head against the floor again and again.

As quickly as it started, the fit ended.

I freefell into black nothingness.

11

I WAS IN A BED, MY BODY TICKING WITH NERVOUS energy, my bones made of lead. My eyelids were too heavy to open, so I sat in darkness and wondered if I was still alive.

A cool cloth pressed against my forehead. I moaned and tried to say something, but my voice came out as a strained croak.

"Don't try to speak."

It was Vincent. "Where's Andre?" I rasped. "What happened?"

"It's okay, Beth," he said. "You're fine. You had a bad reaction to the Evaluation. It happens sometimes."

I tried to sit, still unable to fully open my eyes. Through my slitted lids the room was a blur of light and shadow, and I wondered if I'd been drugged.

"What did they do to me?"

"It's okay, Beth," Vincent whispered. "Everything is okay."

Cool fingers brushed against my temple, pushing away clumps of damp hair. I clung to consciousness, but it was no use—my grip failed and I returned to thick black sleep.

I had no idea what time it was when I finally woke, but my heart was pounding. I was weak and drained yet restless.

I checked under my mattress for the Blast Mahoney button and found it was still there. The room was stuffy and hot. I thought about escaping to the woods where I could breathe, but as soon as I threw on my robe I realized that was a bad idea, since I could barely stand on my wobbly legs.

But I didn't want to be alone with my formless fears. I wanted someone to talk to.

I staggered through the darkened halls like a drunk and found myself in Xavier's wing, not quite sure how I'd gotten there. A clear thought sliced through the layers of my confusion. I needed to know exactly what the Evaluation was and what had been done to me.

I was pretty sure, though I couldn't say why, that Xavier was the only person who would tell it to me straight. Maybe it was because of how eager Vincent was to keep me away from him.

I pressed my ear to his door and listened carefully to make sure he didn't have another nocturnal visitor. It was all silence in there. I was about to knock when the door crashed open and a slight girl with a corona of white-blonde curls glared at me before flouncing away. I knew I'd seen her before, but with my mind all fuzzed up, I couldn't say where.

Maybe talking to Xavier was a bad idea, I decided. But the door was ajar, beckoning. It wasn't like I wanted to date him. All I wanted was a few answers about what the hell was really going on.

I slipped in. The room was pitch dark and silent. It felt empty.

"Hey, Xavier? Sorry to barge in like this."

There was no response. Maybe, for once, he was actually asleep. I was about to leave when a barely audible moan issued from near the bed.

"Xavier? You okay?"

Another weak moan. I was sure he was sleep-talking, but it struck me as odd for a guy who suffered so famously from insomnia to be in such a deep sleep.

I pulled back the drapes to let in some scant moonlight. Xavier was sprawled flat on his back, covers off, eyes closed, like a body on a morgue slab.

"Xavier?"

His eyelids fluttered but didn't open. Moonlight threw the patchy skin of his scars in sharp relief. Still, he was beautiful, like an ancient statue that had been damaged by vandals but not enough to destroy its grandeur. I felt like an idiot watching him sleep, like I was violating his privacy at the basest level. I was about to leave when a faint murmur slipped from between his lips.

"Beth," Xavier said, so softly it could have been a breath. But he didn't move at all.

I drew closer, intrigued that he recognized his intruder in his sleep.

"Beth," he repeated with a tiny shudder. Still, he didn't wake.

I nudged his shoulder gently. "Xavier? Is something wrong?"

His lips trembled. The word came out as a soft hiss. "Help."

It was then that I remembered where I'd seen the girl who'd fled his room.

I was almost certain she was One-Digit Della, the severely disabled girl I'd seen at lunch two days before.

But that couldn't be possible.

I raced from the room, operating on gut instinct. There was something abnormal about the way Xavier wouldn't or couldn't wake. He seemed to be in some kind of pain.

I barreled through the halls, not sure where to go for help. There had to be a school nurse or doctor on call somewhere in this place. I'd heard about a medical team examining me, but couldn't recall any of it.

I had the wind knocked out of me when I slammed into an immovable object. I was momentarily stunned, but not entirely surprised, to find myself gazing up into Vincent's concerned eyes.

"What's the hurry?"

I backed up so he couldn't touch me. I wanted to hold onto the raw clarity of my emotions before Vincent's strange touch clouded them over.

"I-I—" I knew I had to come out with it because Xavier was in trouble, but I hesitated to admit I'd gone to visit him in the middle of the night. "Something's wrong with Xavier."

Vincent stepped closer, arms extended. I ducked and slipped out of his reach. A shadow passed over his bright gaze. "I doubt that. Were you in his room?"

"So what if I was? I'm telling you there's something wrong with the guy. I think he's having a seizure."

Vincent's arms dropped to his sides. "He's fine."

Again, Vincent reached for me and I darted out of his way. "Don't touch me," I snapped with more venom than I intended.

"Are you angry, Beth?" Vincent asked softly. He stepped closer and I realized that I'd backed myself into a corner. He stood gazing at me as if he was debating whether to sock me in the jaw or kiss me on the lips.

"Forget me," I pleaded. "Xavier needs help. Jeez. I know you don't like him, but he was in a bad way."

Vincent stood his ground, but didn't advance. His posture was relaxed, but the intensity in his eyes made my stomach flutter. "I warned you that Xavier is troubled. And those troubles manifest in unusual ways."

"I can swear I saw the handicapped girl, Della, walk out of his room. How is that possible?"

Vincent squinted just a fraction, but his composure held, his voice measured and even. "It must have been her twin, Evangeline."

"No one ever said Della had a twin."

Vincent shrugged, but the intensity of his gaze hadn't softened. "It never came up."

I was breathing fast, my heart clacking like a metronome on speed. My fight or flight mechanism had been activated, and suddenly, despite the warm blue eyes and golden curls, I wanted to get away from Vincent very badly.

He moved closer. "You're agitated, Beth."

Throat dry, my pulse pounded in my neck. "Don't touch me."

Another step closer. "Are you afraid of me?"

The walls were closing in, transforming from a protective enclosure to the bars of a cage. A dark shadow hovered vaguely over Vincent's head. "There's something weird about the way you touch me."

One corner of his mouth twitched up, but Vincent didn't move any closer. "It's only because I care about you."

"You barely know me."

In a blur of motion, Vincent lunged for me and enfolded me in his arms. His grip was shockingly tight, yet gentle all at the same time, cool silk over steel. At his touch, my anger melted, and the tension leaked from my tight muscles. I slumped against his chest, exhausted and defeated. The shadow was gone.

Whatever power he had over me, I thought, in my last clear moment, I couldn't fight it.

And I wasn't sure I wanted to.

Back in my room, I eased the Blast Mahoney button from under my mattress, and, clutching it to my chest, fell asleep.

I dreamt about Sam. He was running through the woods, calling to me, but I didn't stop. I was running, too, from the massive shadowy figure that chased us both.

12

FIRST THING IN THE MORNING, VINCENT CAME TO escort me to breakfast, and for just a moment, I recoiled at his presence. But my initial reaction was tempered by the need for him to touch me. To settle my swirling thoughts.

Since I'd come to the High Step compound it was as if my brain's frequency had been scrambled. I wondered if they'd let me stay when they realized that I was a two-fingered grip away from slipping down the rabbit hole for good.

Vincent's blue eyes were bright against the creamy tan of his freshly shaven face. He smiled as if seeing me was the peak moment of his day. In the morning light that streamed through my window and glinted on his curls, he was more beautiful than ever.

"How are you feeling this morning? Better? The aftereffects of the Evaluation did a number on you."

"Much."

"I'm very happy to hear that." Vincent leaned over and kissed me lightly on my cheekbone. My heart stuttered, and I admitted to myself that I'd begun to crave his touch. That, with my meds gone, it might have been the only thing holding me together. When he reached for me, the heat from his fingers bathed me in the sweet reassurance that I was fine. That the longer I was here at the compound, the better I would feel. That the paranoia was only the last of my depression sloughing off as I healed.

Yes. I believed this as we walked arm in arm to the dining hall.

In the noisy hall we found our places at the table with Lila and the others. The teasing and happy banter felt normal and routine as we dug into overstuffed omelets with sides of bacon and sausage. I belonged there, I told myself.

I was smiled at. I smiled back, but still, it was a blur, as if I was on autopilot, one Beth carrying on the social niceties, the other Beth lost in a distant labyrinth of forgotten thoughts and emotions.

"Hey," Lila said, interrupting my silence. "We have second period History together. Isn't that cool?"

"That's awesome," I answered, but my gaze wandered to the entrance where someone had wheeled in One-Digit Della. There was no sign of the flouncy blonde who looked like her, just the frail girl with the stiff unyielding body.

The question about Della still tingling on my lips, I stabbed a sausage with a fork. It was heavy and greasy in my mouth. Chewing mechanically, I felt the bad thoughts start to sift in again, staining my mood, dragging me under. I had to fight this darkness that wanted to overtake me. If High Step kicked me out, what would become of me?

I made myself smile and thought of something to add to the conversation that flowed around me like water over rock. I grasped at a hopeful thought, something I really was looking forward to. "Maybe today I'll get my individual instruction assignment."

Everyone smiled and nodded, then broke off into happy chatter. My ears rang with the sound, like rain hitting a tin roof. My gaze drifted back to Della. She was parked at a table, her head jerking in rolling spasms while someone spooned cereal into her mouth.

That someone, I realized with a shock, was Xavier. As if he'd noticed me watching, he turned toward me. Our eyes locked. His look was piercing, accusing. I scanned the memory of my midnight break-in and blushed. I'd probably imagined that he was as stiff and frozen as a corpse. He was just pissed I'd barged in on him in the middle of the night like a crazy woman who watched him sleep, and rightfully so. Or maybe he thought it was a dream.

Yet beneath the hostility, there was something else. Something that reached across the room, grabbed me by the throat, and told me that I would venture to his room again.

My heart raced as fear pumped to my nerve endings. I tore my gaze away and glanced at Vincent. His expression was stern, lips pressed together in a thin line. In a quick motion he rested his arm on my forearm and my thoughts stilled as the distress dissipated and broke apart.

"Gideon and Monica want to meet with you after breakfast," he whispered. Despite his calming touch, remnants of worry still lingered. What if they'd discovered I was a nut job and didn't want the trouble of dealing with me? Maybe I'd failed my Evaluation.

Vincent must have recognized the panic in my eyes, because he tightened his grip. It helped, but not enough to wipe away the fear that there was something really, really wrong with me.

"There's nothing to worry about," he said. "They're just going to set you up with your individual instruction today."

I frowned briefly, then smiled hopefully. "I passed my Evaluation?"

"I've told you a million times. It's not a pass/fail situation, Beth. It's all about placement. You know that. Acceptance here is highly selective. Once you're in, you're in."

Vincent informed me that I'd be missing my first period Literature, but would be able to get to second period History. He said goodbye after breakfast to go to his first class. I was left to find my way to Gideon's office alone.

Intellectually, I knew I shouldn't be scared. I told myself that it was just the years of ingrained trauma from my poor academic track record, and that here at High Step, I had the chance to change my ways and make a new start. But that didn't help quiet my galloping heartbeat.

In the moment that I hesitated outside the dining hall, someone grabbed my shoulder. I spun around to find Xavier's face just a few inches from mine.

His voice silken, he flashed me a lopsided smile. "Why were you in my room last night?"

My heart pounded, yet I kept my tone even. "You invited me, didn't you?"

"I guess I did." He stepped back. "I'm sorry if I wasn't exactly welcoming."

"You were asleep. I didn't want to wake you."

"I wasn't asle—" Xavier's words cut off as if they'd gotten stuck in his teeth. His jaw clamped shut, his expression strangely fierce, as if he was fighting to pry them apart. His lids fluttered and his eyes, the haunted dark blue of a forlorn winter lake, seemed to lose focus briefly before his gaze reclaimed its usual intensity. Finally, he managed to spit out very, very softly, "I would like it if you would...if you would visit again."

Xavier stared into my eyes for a beat, then flipped his hair so a dark curtain sheathed the scarred side of his face. His easy smile returned and he turned, strolling away as if we hadn't just had the strangest non-conversation ever.

Watching him go, I couldn't help but admire his languid grace, so at odds with the weird stuttering fit. It was so impossible to reconcile the two Xaviers that I had to wonder if his mysterious injuries had also left him with some kind of neurological damage. Either way, messed up as he apparently was, nothing diminished his incredible hotness.

Then I remembered I was due in Gideon's office for my placement conference. I stopped to adjust myself in a mirror, expecting to see something pale and bedraggled, but was shocked to find that I actually looked pretty good.

Since I'd been at the compound, I'd barely glanced in a mirror. I hadn't bothered with my usual dramatic eyeliner and extreme eyebrow definition, but my cheeks had color and my dark eyes shone. Even my skin looked clearer. Radiant, almost.

I barely knew this girl.

It made no sense that the lack of sleep and meds along with the stress hadn't taken their toll. Maybe they'd been jacking our food supply with some kind of mega-vitamin supplement. Nothing would surprise me about High Step, but to be honest, I was pretty happy with my new *au naturel* self.

I walked to Gideon's office with a little bounce in my stride, resolved to untangle the mystique of Vincent and Xavier another time. Meanwhile, basking in my own awesomeness was enough. Maybe, despite the rough start, this place agreed with me after all.

I was so enveloped in my unfamiliar daze of self-appreciation that I barely noticed when Xavier fell in step beside me.

"Huh? What now?"

Again, his eyes rolled up and he choked on his words. It couldn't be that I made him that uncomfortable, I thought, not when he'd been so cocky at other times. "I-I'm s-sorry," he stammered.

"What the hell for?"

"F-for being an ass."

I kept walking and found that, despite my initial attraction, my patience for his games and weirdness was quickly wearing thin. "I don't know what you're talking about. You didn't do anything. If you have something to tell me, just come out with it."

He stopped walking abruptly. His face drained of color and his eyes took on that glazed look again. For a minute it seemed like he was about to keel over. "I-I *can't.*"

"Should I get the nurse? Are you okay?"

"No." Xavier sighed and leaned against the wall, eyes closed. He breathed heavily in and out a few times before he managed to speak again. "I have—a lot of problems." Then his eyes flashed open, the laser-hot blue washed out. With his usual swagger gone, Xavier seemed deflated, vulnerable, and very young.

"I know y-you'll think I'm nuts," he blurted. "But d-do you have something from—from before you came here? S-something important to you?" Struck by a sudden bout of coughing, he bent over.

"I'm going to get help," I said.

"No!" He straightened and leaned against the wall, eyes closed and head tilted up. "Please. Listen," he whispered, not looking at me. "What is it? What do you have?"

I wiped a hand across my brow. My heart thudded. There was an ominous turn to our conversation and it was stirring up strange emotions and memories I'd tried so hard to bury. "I have a button."

Xavier's eyes snapped open. "Keep it close," he whispered. "Always close."

He stared at me for a beat, then buckled over slightly and dashed away down the hall without looking back.

My palm burned with the thought of the Blast Mahoney button, my throat aching with the memory of Sam. How could Xavier know, and why would he want me to hold onto so much pain?

13

I CLOSED MY EYES AND WILLED MYSELF THE STRENGTH to walk to Gideon's office.

But Xavier's words, those haunted eyes, struck a chord deep inside of me, and I knew he was far from crazy. Still, I had no idea what he was trying to tell me.

When I entered his office, Gideon stood and directed me to the chair opposite his desk. His shoulder-length auburn waves caught the sunlight streaming through the floor-to-ceiling windows and his dark eyes glittered, warm and friendly. Proud, almost. I settled in the chair, feeling instantly reassured that everything would be all right. That I wouldn't be sent packing from the High Step compound.

It was only after I sat that the frail old guy and the goons from my Evaluation entered through a concealed door in the paneled wall. My heart began to flutter like a trapped bird. I flashed Gideon an alarmed look, but his smile hadn't wavered.

"There's nothing to fear, Beth."

"I thought I was just going to be assessed to determine my level of training."

"Absolutely," Gideon said. "You tested very well. Outstanding, in fact."

"I don't understand. The Evaluation wasn't about music at all. How can you—?"

My throat was dry. The walls of the opulent office seemed to move in closer, crowding me. Beyond the gauzy curtains, the snow-bound woods were hazy and white.

"You are correct, Beth. The Evaluation has very little to do with music. Your musical ability is a side effect of your true ability. And for that you tested very, very high. Astronomically high, to be precise."

I gripped the arms of the chair. "I don't know what you're talking about."

Gideon's smile faded, his deep voice vibrating inside my skull. "I think you've known there's something different about you for a very long time, haven't you, Beth?"

There was a scream trapped in my throat.

The frail man with the glinting glasses smiled too, but the goons behind him did not. Closing ranks around him, they braced as if a masked gunman was about to burst through the office doors and mow us down in mob-hit style.

I tried to speak, but my words were gone, my vocal cords useless.

"You're angry, Beth, aren't you?" Gideon asked mildly. "Angry because it's starting to dawn on you that you haven't been told the whole truth?"

I nodded wildly, unable to move from the chair. Angry wasn't the word for it. Rage crackled through my nerve endings.

"And you're also angry because you fear to face who you are. *What* you are."

I closed my eyes. Traveling through my bloodstream, searching for release, the heat that built inside me was a physical pain.

"Focus on that anger. On your fear. Let it build. You are very powerful, Beth."

Shaking and sweating, I watched as the frail man set a black box on Gideon's desk. He slid up the side and a very frightened white mouse skittered onto the polished surface.

My pulse jackhammered insanely in my ears. Carson had once threatened to drop a dead mouse on me as I slept, and I'd lain awake the entire night keeping watch. I'd been phobic ever since.

The mouse leapt into my lap. I was paralyzed and desperate, unable to act, convinced that I was going to die of a stroke right on that chair.

"Use your ability, Beth. The one you've tried so hard to deny. Do what it is you do best. Channel your energy and destroy the thing you hate."

The words rattled through me like chains. The mouse clawed its way up my shirt as if I was a rodent wall-climbing challenge. I shuddered, my hysteria a reservoir of molten lava boiling inside of me. A cocoon of shadow enveloped the mouse as it climbed. The back of my neck and scalp prickled with an electric tingle.

I needed this mouse to die before it reached my face.

I exhaled, letting go of the anger and fear in a rush of need for this creature to be gone.

As though my breath was spring-loaded, something heavy released from my chest. The air split with a sharp crack, the shadowy cocoon exploding in black cinders. The goons crowded in front of the frail man and Gideon as if I'd aimed an AK-47 assault rifle at them.

There was moment when I was in darkness, numb and floating, a thing out of time and space.

Then noise and color come pounding back and my chair was thrust backward. Gideon, the frail man, and his goons were clapping as if I'd just scored the winning goal in a soccer match. I had a split second to take this in before I hit the floor. Once I did, the shaking and convulsing started, my eyes shuttering open and closed. I got a glimpse of the dead mouse on the carpet before a shot jabbed into my arm and everything went dark again.

The first thing I was aware of was the warmth coiling up my arm. My eyes blinked open to find Vincent gazing down at me.

"You did great," he said, beaming.

His hand felt so good on my arm, so natural, that I dreaded what would happen when he removed it. The terror of the past few moments was still fresh in my mind, but softened, the rough edges smoothed down.

I glanced at the dead mouse. "Did I do that?" Despite the soothing heat that spread from Vincent's fingers through the rest of my body, horror tightened my throat. I was certain I was going to be sick.

Gideon stood, leaning forward on his desk. "Indeed you did, Beth."

A tiny thorn of anger still throbbed beneath Vincent's gentle touch. "I'm not here because of my musical ability, am I?"

"High Step is first and foremost an accredited school, Beth," Gideon said, "and we do provide a top-notch education in the arts and humanities, focusing on our student body's diverse artistic gifts. However, we also specialize in a curriculum you won't find anywhere else."

I pushed Vincent's hand off of my arm, and the avalanche of shock knocked the breath from me.

It was coming back to me. The shadow that had followed Luke and Carson the night of the accident. The same shadow that had hovered in Carson's hospital room. The dead mouse.

"What am I?" I shouted, staggering backward toward the

door. Vincent followed me and, though I put up a lame resistance, pulled me back into his arms. The fight drained out of me, and I sank against him, the relief like stepping into a warm bath.

Vincent guided me back to my chair and, gently coaxing me to sit, rested a hand on my shoulder. Calm returned in lapping waves. My rage was tamed, an angry bull shot with a tranquilizer dart.

Gideon came around from behind his desk and knelt to look me in the eye. His voice was soft, the crisp accent precise and pleasant. I admired how the stream of sunlight lit the strands of red fire and pure silver in his auburn hair and I listened as Gideon's words dropped around me, feather-soft.

"You are special, Beth. So special that we had to devise a unique strategy to read you into the Program."

"Read me in?"

"I'm going to try to help clear things up for you," Gideon said. "But you have to promise that once Vincent lets go of you again, you will try your best to restrain yourself."

Vincent lifted his hand from my shoulder and the fury of confusion bombarded me. The room darkened and my neck tingled with pins and needles. I whirled on him, my anger tempered with the aching need for him to touch me again.

"Never mind me. What the hell are *you*?"

"I'm your control," Vincent said calmly, pale eyes burning. "Remember, I have only your best interests at heart."

"What does that mean?"

"It means," Gideon said, "that this valiant young man has volunteered to work with you at great risk to his personal safety and well-being."

Vincent extended a hand and pulled me to my feet. My ears were ringing. Darkness swirled around the room like a shadowy whirlpool. I grabbed hold of Vincent like a drowning woman caught in a rushing current. Silence dropped over the chaos and the darkness dissipated. Vincent pulled me closer and pressed me against the hard muscle beneath his flannel shirt. "We are two working components of a greater whole, Beth. In our world, certain Talents work in pairs."

My head against his chest, I listened to the vibration of his voice inside his ribcage. I had no idea what he meant, but as he guided me back to my seat, Vincent did not leave my side.

"The weeks ahead will be challenging, Beth," said Gideon. "But here, under the tutelage of the High Step Program, you will learn to master your abilities. Taking you in to the compound has been a great risk for all of us. With each newfound Talent comes a unique set of circumstances. Sadly, integration is not always successful."

I closed my eyes and shook my head. I was still missing something.

"Beth," Gideon said, "this school trains abilities that differ from the norm—talented people who, if left to their own devices, uncontrolled and untamed, can endanger society as a whole. It's our duty here at High Step to manage that situation. It's a contract we signed long ago."

I opened my eyes and gazed into Gideon's dark pools. Vincent's hand on my shoulder felt like all that was anchoring me to this earth.

"I know this is hard to take in," Gideon said "but if we didn't discover you, read you in, and commit to teaching you how to master your Talent, it would only be a matter of time before you would have been tagged, hunted down, and eliminated. There are uninformed and fearful segments of society who offer a generous bounty on the capture and execution of those like us. It's a fate other, less fortunate, members of our kind have been suffering for centuries.

"Your town of Linford, Connecticut, seems to be a nexus for this activity, but the dangers are everywhere. They will follow you," Gideon added. "Which is why, Beth, it's not safe for you to ever go home again."

14

DESPITE BOTH OF VINCENT'S HANDS PRESSED TO my shoulders, the floor seemed to drop away from beneath me. I couldn't believe what I was hearing. A cloud of darkness blotted out the sunlight and lowered over Gideon's head. I choked out the words, "You don't understand. I have to see my mother. My brother is—he's severely disabled. She needs me. I need to go home. *Now.*"

Gideon clasped and unclasped his hands. "I'm afraid that's not possible. Not for the foreseeable future."

I was on my feet, fists clenched. I leaned over the desk so my face was right up close to Gideon's. The darkness was as thick as smoke between us. My neck and throat pulsed with electric energy. Gideon pulled away and for a moment I saw the fear that flashed across his serene features. He glanced to the side panel door, as if he expected his goons to come rushing to his rescue.

"Settle down, Beth," Gideon said, backing up, forcing his voice to sound calm. But I wasn't fooled. Vincent's grasp on my shoulders did nothing to dampen my outrage.

"Settle down? Don't you think my mother is going to get a little suspicious when I somehow forget to come home?"

The panel on the wall opened and Monica DeWitt glided in, flanked by the same goons from earlier.

"That's all been taken care of, Beth," Gideon said. "Your

mother signed an agreement that you will remain on our premises for a full year, until your training is complete. Given her overwhelming circumstances, she felt she had no choice."

Monica stepped between Gideon and me and pushed me back into my seat. "The funny thing is that gradually, over the course of the year, she will simply forget that you exist."

"What?"

Vincent's fingers dug into my shoulders, but nothing could quiet the shuddering grief that pushed its way out of my lungs. "How is that possible? My mother would never forget me!"

Vincent nuzzled my neck and my emotions twisted and pulled, caught between psychotic rage and the sudden desire to attach myself to his lips.

"Please, Beth. Get a hold of yourself for your own sake," he pleaded quietly.

Monica smiled, opal eyes like sun on ice. "Here, the impossible is possible." She backed away. Twirling around to face Gideon, she added, "*If* your dear little pet can control her. Is it worth putting the safety of this entire compound at risk over a single girl?"

For only a moment, Gideon seemed to shrink into himself, then straightened, regal back erect, and glared back at Monica. "That will be enough, Ms. DeWitt. I am the Headmaster here, and my decisions overrule all others. Bethany is worth our efforts. Isn't that right, Vincent?"

Vincent whispered in my ear and I felt my outrage ebb and cool. "Absolutely, sir."

Monica faced us, her delicate features pulled into a scowl. "Worth dying for, Rousseau? I told you from the start, the girl is too unstable to be managed. And you're too weak either way." She whipped around and stormed through the main office exit, filmy gown trailing. The goons remained and glared at me like they'd like to crack open my skull with their bare hands.

Vincent gathered me in his arms and held me close and

tight, our electric connection heating me. I was soothed, but I felt his tension in my pores.

I understood it now. As he'd been from the start, Vincent was petrified of me. I was vaguely aware of Gideon and the goons watching us tentatively.

"Leave me with her," Vincent said.

"Is that wise?" Gideon asked.

"I don't believe she'll hurt me."

If not for the warm haze of Vincent's embrace, I'd have been outraged about the way they were talking about me, as if I were a stray dog with rabies. I stared into Vincent's eyes, blue and serene as the Caribbean, but I recognized the fear that he'd worked so hard to disguise.

They were all afraid of me.

Vincent squeezed me tighter. "Leave us alone. Please. I can handle this."

Gideon motioned to the goons, who exited through the side panel door. Once they'd gone, he rubbed his chin thoughtfully. "I hope I don't regret this."

"She's fine," Vincent snapped. "We're fine."

I was fine. Totally. There was no place I would rather have been than wrapped in Vincent Rousseau's arms.

With a worried glance back at us, Gideon left through the side door. We were alone in his office.

"Beth," Vincent whispered. "I'm going to let go of you."

"Why?" I laid my cheek against his chest and listened to the steady thump of his heart.

"We need to talk."

Slowly, Vincent peeled me off of him. A black emptiness, as if I was a small child abandoned in the winter woods, engulfed me, but the room remained bright. My own mother had turned her back on me. I wondered if they had messed with her mind, too.

"Beth," Vincent said, softly. "I took a big chance on you."

I wanted to leap into his arms to stop the stampede of

thoughts, but I needed to think clearly to understand my circumstances. Part of me wondered if I was still trapped inside a waking dream from the fall I'd taken on the night of the audition. If I was lying comatose in a hospital bed with a cracked skull and irreparable brain injuries.

The desperate look in Vincent's eyes told me I was not.

"I didn't ask you to."

Vincent looked down at his hands, the fingers long and elegant. I imagined them sliding across my skin, raising goosebumps. I gave myself a mental smack. What was wrong with me?

Vincent looked up again, his eyes immeasurably sad. "Not everything we do is a choice. Our life—this life—is not easy. But, believe me, the alternative is far, far worse."

Agitation rose inside me. I stepped closer. A vague shadow fell across Vincent's face and I noticed him flinch. "You're not making a whole lot of sense. Give it to me straight. What am I? What are you? Why are we prisoners of this sick excuse for a school?"

Vincent remained still, but I could smell the fear on him. The coldness in his voice wounded me. The shadows around him deepened. "I will tell you everything if you will sit in that chair and not come a step closer."

I obeyed and settled into the chair, anger crackling in my chest. "Do you even like me at all? Or is this your sacred duty? Some kind of penance? Is this a cult or something?"

Vincent's stiff posture softened, but the wariness did not leave him. He was still on high alert, ready for me to do anything. "I like you very much. Much more than I ever expected to."

"Then why are you so afraid of me?"

Vincent closed his eyes. Maybe he'd hoped I wouldn't notice. Maybe the weird connection we had made me hyper-aware of his feelings.

"You are," I pressed. "Admit it or I won't believe another

word out of your mouth."

He sighed. "I took a huge personal risk reading you in. It was an unpopular decision. A Talent like yours is dangerous and exceedingly hard to control. Many think—they think I'm not up to the task. That I'm not strong enough because of my... But I just—I just couldn't walk away."

My cheeks heated as I was swept by a fresh wave of anger. Darkness fell like ash around us. My voice boomed unnaturally in my ears. "Who asked you to rip me out of my life and install me in this nuthouse? You should have just left me alone. I can take care of myself."

"I don't doubt that, Beth," Vincent whispered, taking a tentative step closer. "But in time you'll understand our world and the terrible risks our kind face. Have always faced. That you face."

"I'm not a freak like the rest of you here, hiding away from the world like some fanatic cult."

"This isn't a cult, Beth. There have been Talented since the early days of the Druids, and probably before that. We have been crucified, burnt at the stake, drowned, hanged— you name it. I didn't ask for this life either. No one asks for this, Beth."

Vincent's arms hung loose at his sides, his radiant eyes sparking. "Do you want to know my story?"

I nodded. Cinders of shadow orbited around me. I was afraid that one wrong word would shut him up for good.

"We'd just moved from Normandy to Paris and I loved it. I never wanted to leave. But..." He sank to the floor and sat cross-legged across from me. "There are many prominent families in the Talented world, Beth. I come from an old family, a dynasty of Talented. But my father was rebellious. He married a Regular and wanted to raise me apart from this life. To train me to master my Talents his way."

"And?"

"That didn't work out so well."

"What exactly," I blurted, "is your Talent?"

Vincent closed his eyes. "I'm afraid that, if you haven't realized it yet, you are going to hate me even more when I explain it you. And that may have fatal consequences for me."

When Vincent reopened his eyes, they were shiny and full of pain. "Please, Beth, promise you'll try to understand that I've meant you no harm. I've only wanted to help you."

My heart started to pound. "You make me feel what you want me to feel. That's your Talent, isn't it? You've been messing with my mind from the minute I got here."

"It's called Weaving," he said after a pause. "Weavers knit, embroider, braid, and untangle emotions. We can cut cords that are inconvenient, thereby shifting your memories so they have no emotional resonance. We can braid in new emotions and alter your moods and thoughts. Some do it by touch, others by thought. I'm a Tactile." Vincent looked away. "I'm sorry. I know it's hard to understand, but I had to work you. You could have killed me. You could have done a lot of harm. You don't understand your power."

"This sucks." I lowered my head. There was no waking up from this dream. I was a captive of the freaks, locked away from society so I could do no further harm. "So, what do they call this lovely Talent of mine?"

After an uncomfortable pause where Vincent looked everywhere except straight at me, he finally spoke. "We call your kind Liferenders." He stopped, and a slight shiver rippled across his shoulders. "Liferending is the rarest form of Talent. It only appears once or twice in a generation, usually to a Regular family."

Edgy as I was, I couldn't pass up the opportunity for a lame joke. "It sounds like some twisted kind of leisure sport."

Vincent did not return my smile. "It's anything but a joke, Beth. Liferending is, simply put, the ability to stall death, detect death, and in its most lethal form, bring death, at will, to as many souls as desired with simply a thought. And like

Weaving, it is either Tactile or Psych-based. You are a Psych."

I stared at him. To hear those words spoken so plainly confirmed my greatest fear. "Are you saying I'm Death itself? Teen Grim Reaper?"

Vincent gazed at me, his expression mingled with concern, fear, and an obvious desire to hightail it out of there. "Your Talent may be the basis of some well-known legends. But it's not your job to collect souls. You simply can kill with a thought."

I stared at the intricate floral pattern on Gideon's rug and shuddered. "If you didn't offer to, uh, read me in, what would they have done with me?"

Vincent looked away again, unable to meet my gaze. "I-I don't honestly know. It's just that when they bring in a new Talent, not all of them adjust. I guess maybe there are other training centers that are better equipped to deal with difficult and dangerous Talents."

"And you decided to take it upon yourself to fix me because the idea of playing with death in girl form was fun. Is that the only reason?"

Vincent looked at me, perplexed. "No, it's—no. I just felt—I felt I could help you, despite everyone's lack of faith in me. That I understood you."

"Do you?"

"Maybe." Finally, a smile swept across his face, darkness banished. Light finally reached his eyes. "Or maybe I just like flirting with death."

"What if I blow it? Like, let's say I lose control and kill someone?"

He drew closer, so I could feel his breath warm my face, but he didn't touch me. "You won't. But you do understand why it's too dangerous for you to go home, don't you?"

I let the words hover between us. I didn't mention that I had already decided there was no way I was going to let this confederacy of wackos keep me from visiting my family.

"What about your family? Isn't it okay to see them, since they're part of this giant freak show?"

"It's better not to speak about our homes, Beth. When your training begins you'll understand fully."

Vincent edged closer, his lips near mine. The space between us was no longer shadowed but charged with electricity. Vincent's breathing quickened. Maybe, I thought idly, the possibility that I could strike him dead was an aphrodisiac. Because neither of us seemed able to break free of each other's gravitational pull.

"This weird bond we have," I whispered. "Where does your Talent leave off and the real us begin?"

Vincent murmured, his cheek brushing against mine, "Only time will tell, won't it?"

15

GIDEON ENTERED SO QUIETLY THAT WE BOTH cried out and sprang apart when he spoke.

"I trust you actually know what you're doing, Vincent. I've put my reputation on the line for you."

Vincent flashed me a panicked look before he regained his composure. "Everything is fine, sir. Right, Beth?"

"Peachy-keen dandy," I chirped, and then rolled my eyes.

Gideon eyed me coolly. "Tomorrow we will have a meeting to discuss your education in earnest, Beth. For now, you should get plenty of rest. It will be a rigorous and demanding training, but quite rewarding, should you achieve the goals set out for you."

"Sounds great." I didn't ask what would happen should I not meet those goals. I'd caused enough excitement for one day.

Gideon frowned and cut a sideways look at Vincent. "I'll be
monitoring the situation carefully. Any slip-up or incident and you will be held accountable, Vincent."

Just as a black smudge began to form in the space above Gideon's head, Vincent grabbed me around the middle with both arms.

"Lucky for me I enjoy the work, sir," he said. I shivered at the electric tendrils of heat that radiated up my spine. My back arched as my knees turned to water.

"I should take you back to your room now, I think," he said, in my ear.

Despite the intensity when we touched, the atmosphere between us when we were apart had cooled. Walking back to my room, anger filled the empty spaces after the withdrawal of his touch, but I didn't let on. I didn't want Vincent doing any more macramé with my feelings tonight. I wanted to keep my rage, and hold it close to me. Without the meds to dull my emotions, I had no plans to replace them with a dose of Vincent.

"The problem is, Beth," he said suddenly, as if we'd been talking all along, "that you can't really hide how you're feeling from me. Once I've Woven someone, I'm attuned to their frequencies. I can feel the anger emanating from you. To be very clear, I can *see* it, and it's kind of blinding me right now."

I turned on him, thinking I'd like to sock him in the jaw, but there was no fear in his eyes, only a glimmer of a smile. A very sexy one. My anger softened like butter in the sun. "What? What in creation are you talking about?"

"Your anger is visible to me, like threads in a loom. Right now, it's pretty dense and it's getting in my way. I can barely see around it."

"That's a pain in the butt. What does it look like?"

"It's hard to describe. But I can tell that you're already beginning to master your reactions. Probably because your Talent manifested only recently, it's still easy to separate emotion from the killing impulse. That's why it's important to bring in Talented while we're young."

I was breathing fast, trying to stoke the bottled-up emotion that had rippled through my tendons only seconds before. But

I was losing steam. Vincent smiled. Apparently he could see that, too.

"No fair, Yoda. You infected me with this craving for you, so no matter how angry I get, you know I won't harm a single curl on your pretty head."

"Since you put it that way. It's one of the first things a Weaver learns—to neutralize his subject so dangerous Talents won't lash out at us. But it's always touch and go at first. Like playing with fire."

"You could have died at any moment in the past few weeks. Bet you got a sick thrill out of that."

Vincent laughed. "I wouldn't call it a sick thrill. But it was kind of invigorating."

"You've got a death wish."

"Not at all. More like how a lion tamer enjoys the challenge."

I glanced at him sideways. "It's not like you're out of the woods yet. I don't really know you that well. I may find something to hate and strike you while you sleep."

"I'm prepared to take my chances."

We walked in silence, until I blurted, "So does this mean everyone in this school has some kind of freaky Talent with a capital T?"

"We really all do have legitimate artistic and musical abilities," Vincent answered thoughtfully. "But to answer your question—yes. That's why we are here. It's kind of uncanny how the two kinds of Talent go hand in hand. And we get excellent training for those talents as well. High Step really does have annual performances for the public at the concert venue where your audition was held."

I thought back to the night when Andre and I drove the two hours to Massachusetts and realized that I had no idea where the hell I was. Which might make getting home a little difficult.

"Crap. Fucking Andre! Does he—"

Vincent nodded slowly. "I'm betting you can guess what it is."

I thought of Andre's hand on my back, how the knots and tension always released at his touch. Andre's touch. "His touch is magic."

Vincent smiled. "Better than any high-priced massage."

"Jeez. I always knew there was something supernatural about that boy. He's way too good-looking to be human."

"But we're all human, Beth. Think of us as enhanced humanity."

"Sounds like a great tagline. We should use it in our infomercials."

Vincent chuckled, and I felt the tension between us ease up a little.

"What about Xavier? What's his?"

Vincent stopped short, his brow furrowed. I laughed at him. "C'mon. Tell me you didn't see that one coming. What is it? What's Xavier's freaky thing?"

Vincent grimaced, as if speaking about Xavier gave him indigestion. "His voice. It's—it does things to people."

"He's a great singer, but how is that freaky? Does his singing make people rip off their clothes and run shrieking naked into the woods?"

Vincent laughed weakly. "As you might have heard, Talented who do not gain control over their abilities get sent elsewhere. And none of us knows where elsewhere is. Except Xavier. He was sent away. He came back changed. No one knows what was done to him or where he went. Just suffice it to say that before he left, he was a royal pain in the ass. Once again, I'm urging you to stay away from him and I hope you'll listen."

"So that's where he got those scars."

"No," Vincent said. "He had those already."

"How can a crazy-good voice be dangerous?"

Vincent did not smile, but instead tucked a stray strand of

hair behind my ear. "In our world, Beth, even the most innocent thing can be deadly."

We walked in silence. The people we passed smiled at us, waving in a strangely enthusiastic manner. It dawned on me that they'd all been in on the secret from the start. Anger began to build inside me again, but I swallowed it down. I promised myself that no matter how hot Xavier was, and no matter how much I was drawn to Vincent, there was no way in hell I was spending my life as a prisoner in this compound.

Because if I was really that dangerous, who on earth was going to stop me?

16

WHEN WE GOT TO MY DOOR, LILA WAS THERE waiting, fighting to suppress a fit of giggles.

"So?" she said, hand over her mouth.

I glanced at Vincent and he shrugged.

"Everyone knows, Beth. We've been playing along. We all know the drill."

"Nice," I said flatly.

"A few of us come from Talented families. But most of us come from the Regular population, and integration is always a little touchy in those cases."

"In my case, that may be the understatement of the century."

Lila frowned slightly as if she'd just noticed Vincent glaring at her. "You can go now, Saint Vincent. I'm sure Beth can breathe perfectly well on her own. We have some girl business to attend to."

Vincent stiffened. "I know what you're thinking and I don't recommend you try it."

"You're a poop, Rousseau. Go attend to the sick and the poor and leave Miss Collins to me."

Vincent looked from Lila to me, clearly not happy with the situation. Someone called his name from down the hall and he waved. "Don't make me regret this."

Lila pursed her lips as we watched Vincent dash over to his

waiting friend. "Such a kiss–up. Always trying to prove something to everyone. Kid's got a complex," she said, then turned to me and smiled impishly. "But he sure does have a cute butt."

We giggled together. If I was going to be stuck in this place for the foreseeable future, I was going to need as many friends as I could get. Besides, it was probably not a good idea to make enemies when they could potentially turn you into a toad.

"What's got Vincent's undies in a twist?"

"Never mind him. He worries about everything." Lila ushered me into her room, which was directly across the hall. It was identical to mine, only neater. Instead of electric guitars there were an easel and paints. "Anyway," Lila said. "In honor of your 'coming out,' I have a surprise for you!"

"Huh?"

Lila laughed. "As a Talented. We usually have a party called a Reveal to mark the occasion. So just close your eyes and sit at my desk. Don't say another word. And no peeking!"

I sat, hands over my eyes and heard Lila pull back the drapes. A draft of bitter air swept into the room.

"Okay! Open wide!"

Flapping before me were four crows holding a teal silk dress in mid–air, the straps and hems in their beaks. They gazed at me brightly, as if waiting for my delighted approval, but I was too stunned to speak.

"Do you like it?" Lila asked, bouncing on her bed. "I wore it at my Reveal."

"I-I—jeez. I don't know what to say. I've been to some strange-ass clothing stores, but never one with flying hangers."

Lila broke into peals of laughter. "I thought I'd show you the dress and my Talent all in one fell swoop."

I was still staring at the birds. They blinked back at me, flapping mightily. My teeth started to chatter from the arctic blast. Lila nodded her head and the birds dropped the dress at my feet and winged out the window, diving off into the woods.

"Well?"

"The dress or the Talent?"

"Both," said Lila, scooping the dress from the floor and dangling it in front of me. "I'm all about animals. They answer my call. Always have. It's a handy skill."

"Bet it is," I said, still a little numb with shock. It was going to take a while to get used to this nuthouse, I thought. I was about to reach for the dress when the wall appeared to liquefy. A human form took shape in the liquid mass, and a boy materialized, then walked toward us. My hand flew to my chest. Roddy Zuber nodded approvingly at the dress dangling from Lila's finger.

"Teal is definitely her color. But don't get me wrong. You looked great in that dress, Lila."

"Yeah, I did, right?"

I glanced from Lila to Zuber, saucer-eyed. "Wow," I said. "You guys are insane."

"Nah," said Lila. "We're just like everyone else. Just slightly modified. C'mon. Try it on. They haven't officially announced your Reveal, but at least you'll be prepared."

I swallowed hard. "Not to disappoint, but I put my clothes on the old-fashioned way." I hooked the dress with one finger and headed for the bathroom, heart pounding wildly. It turned out the dress fit like it was made for me, hugging my curves in all the right ways.

"Whoa," Zuber said.

Lila looked me up and down approvingly. "Very nice. But Lord knows what we're going to do about shoes."

"Isn't there anyone here who can pull stuff out of thin air? That would be a handy skill."

"That's called a Fabricator," Lila said. "They're very rare. I hear there's one of them somewhere. I'm guessing they fetch a pretty high salary."

"Salary? You mean Talented get hired out?"

Both Lila and Zuber looked at me like I'd grown a horn in the middle of my forehead. "What'd you think? You'd just stay here playing school forever? There are tons of jobs for our kind. We are in high demand. Unemployment is at zero percent."

"What kind of employment agencies place *our kind*?"

Lila smiled her cat smile. "Very discreet ones."

I was back in my room, still wearing the dress at Lila's insistence. She'd promised to either find a pair of matching shoes or get permission to take me shopping, a perk I wasn't aware the inmates of the High Step Program were privy to.

I was about to unzip when there was a tentative tap, different from Vincent's firm, determined knock. I opened the door to Xavier, who baldly looked me up and down. "That's one hot nightgown."

"It's not a nightgown."

"Yeah, yeah," he said. "I know all about it. Party Girl is already planning your Reveal so she can smuggle in drinks and get Demetri Prishkin wasted."

I stepped out of his way. He entered and plopped on my desk chair. "Drunk Talented are a scary thought," I said.

"Which is why it's not allowed. The punishment is pretty harsh if you get caught," he added, his voice catching slightly.

"Is that what happened to you?"

Xavier didn't answer. Instead, he wandered around my room and stopped to admire my three guitars. He lovingly stroked the sleek body of the blue electric with his good hand. "Nah," he said. "That's kid stuff to me."

"So," I said, conversationally, "It'll be dinnertime in an hour and I've got to get out of this dress."

Xavier turned to me, lips crooked up in a half-grin. "I can help with that."

"Very funny. Tell me why you're really here. There's something on your mind. What is it?"

Xavier's expression changed, the cockiness replaced by the briefest flash of longing. He closed his eyes, and when he opened them the darkness I'd glimpsed was gone. "I just want to hear you play. Rumor has it that you're amazing."

I narrowed my gaze. "Who's been spreading that around?"

"No idea. But if you play, maybe I'll sing a little." Xavier's hands were on his hips, his head tilted.

"Okay. Sure. Kind of weird timing, but why not?"

"It's the perfect time for me," Xavier said, one cobalt eye burning into mine.

His hungry gaze scared me a little, and I questioned my judgment for ignoring Vincent's repeated warnings. But here in my dorm I couldn't imagine a guy with a super-powered voice as a threat.

I got my acoustic and plopped on the bed. "What do you want to hear?"

Xavier dragged over his chair. The sheaf of jet-black hair covered half his face as usual, and again I wanted to ask how he got those scars and what he'd done to get sent away. But I didn't expect to get a straight answer, so there was no point in bothering.

"Something that matters to you."

I shrugged. It had been a few weeks, but something made me want to play "Fragile Forever." Ever since coming here, my memories of Sam had been steadily fading. It was almost like he'd died twice. I strummed the first chord and a tear escaped and slipped down my cheek. I wiped it away quickly so Xavier wouldn't see.

If he'd noticed, he showed no sign of it. He watched intently as I sang and picked at the strings, my voice hoarse from disuse. I was pretty sure I sounded like crap, but Xavier barely blinked, either to show approval or to show that I sucked.

Without warning, he joined in, the miraculous tenor curling around my raw soprano like tendrils of sunlight. I didn't want to stop playing to ask how he knew this song. I just wanted to let the ethereal intensity of his voice hum inside every cell of my body.

The hard lines of Xavier's face smoothed out as he sang. He was transformed, angelic in his rapt concentration. I was so weak with the beauty and majesty of his voice, I almost forgot to keep playing. But I forced myself to continue so he didn't stop, wondering what exactly the true power of his voice was, other than being the most beautiful sound on earth.

Shadows like smoke filled the space between us, but I didn't want to stop. They thickened, growing more distinct, and took on the shape of something tiny and winged. We kept singing, though Xavier's face showed signs of strain.

He stopped abruptly, the color drained from his face. The winged shadow vanished.

"What on earth was that?"

Xavier's visible eye was glassy, darting wildly. I wasn't sure what he was looking at.

"D-do you have that button? Here in the room?" he choked out, his voice strained and raspy.

I frowned. "Yeah. Why? Are you okay?"

Xavier's eye fluttered and rolled up into his lid so I saw the white. "Shit," he murmured. "I didn't think it would…" He stopped midsentence, interrupted by a hacking cough. Pulling a white handkerchief from his back pocket, he pressed it to his mouth. Bright crimson bloomed around his lips. Eyes closing, Xavier looked like he was about to keel over.

"Oh, God," I shouted. I rushed for the door, but Xavier flailed out and managed to grab me by the wrist.

"Please," he begged. His eyes were unfocused and fluttering as though he was fighting to stay conscious. And losing. "Get

Zuber," he whispered.

By the time I got back with Zuber, Xavier was sprawled on the floor, eyes glazed over and unseeing, coughing softly. Blood trickled from the corner of his slack mouth.

I was in full panic mode, ready to run for the nurse or whatever, but Zuber stopped me. "Don't. I can handle this. It's nothing new. I just don't get why he risked this."

"What the hell are you talking about?"

"His punishment for misuse of a regulated Talent. He knew this would happen. Other than his performance at the weekly review and his daily lessons, he's forbidden to sing. His voice has been classified as a lethal weapon. It's why he was sent away in the first place."

"How can something so beautiful be lethal? He didn't hurt me."

Zuber patted the blood away from Xavier's mouth with the deft motions of someone who'd done it before. "The effects aren't obvious at first. But I'm not sure why he'd want to subject himself to this."

I gazed at Xavier. He rolled to his side, moaning softly.

"This is cruel. It looks like he's in pain."

"He is. That's the point," Zuber said gravely. "But I know what to do."

Though Xavier was much bigger than he was, Zuber hefted his limp body over his shoulder and disappeared through my wall.

17

I SLIPPED OUT OF LILA'S DRESS AND INTO MY SWEATS. I had only a half-hour to clean up Xavier's bloodstains from my carpet and make it down to dinner on time. I was on my hands and knees scrubbing and had gotten the worst of it out when there was a firm rap on my door. I knew in my gut it was Vincent.

"Crap," I muttered. "Just a second!"

I swung open the door, smiling innocently.

Vincent didn't return my smile. "There's no point in trying to hide what happened from me. Even if you could, it's all over the school that Xavier violated his disciplinary contract."

"Jeez. I didn't know he wasn't allowed to *sing*. You just said to stay away from him."

"And did you?" His voice was measured and gentle, but it didn't take a psychic link to see that Vincent was fuming.

"He just showed up. I thought—"

"You thought I make arbitrary rules. Or that I'm just jealous. Neither is true." A tendon in Vincent's jaw twitched. He was gambling that I couldn't really get mad at him, but he wasn't totally sure, I thought. "There are good reasons why certain Talents are strictly regulated. Yours, for one. They are not only dangerous to the Regular public but carry great risk to the Talented world as well. Xavier is one of the lucky ones. He's still allowed to stay here, though I have no idea why."

Vincent brushed past me, pacing back and forth across my carpet, treading over the damp spot where Xavier's blood had only just been scrubbed clean.

"He doesn't seem that lucky to me," I said. "According to your crazy rules, it's okay to make someone so ill they cough up blood. That seems pretty inhumane, no matter what he's done in the past. What will they do to him now?"

Vincent stopped pacing to glare at me. "You have no idea of the stakes involved in managing Talents. It's like defusing land mines every day. You never know when one will blow up in your face."

I folded my arms, mildly pleased to have my own anger in check. If anything, I was upset at myself for disappointing him. "I still don't see how a beautiful singing voice can be classified as a lethal weapon."

"Xavier knows exactly what his voice can do. You walked right into his trap."

I rolled my eyes. "You make him sound like an archvillain. If you ask me, he's just a lonely lost soul looking for a friend, since everyone around here treats him like a leper."

Vincent whirled on me, eyes flaring. "Think what you want, but be careful. Xavier's more slippery than you can imagine. And, just so you know, if *your* deadly Talent is manipulated by another to commit a crime, *you* can be held accountable as well. The punishment for that will make Xavier's look like a slap on the wrist."

I checked my watch. "Is that all you wanted to tell me? Because we have five minutes to get to dinner."

Vincent stood by the window, staring absently, and ran a hand through his hair. The orange light of late afternoon cast blue shadows on the snow, slicing through the window and catching gold fire in his curls. Even sullen and pissy, Vincent was still achingly beautiful. I stepped closer to him, resisting the urge to reach out and touch one of those silky locks.

"Actually," he said, letting out a long sigh, but still refusing to look me in the eye, "Gideon and Monica have decided that you should have your Reveal after all. They concluded that *not* having one will cause even more speculation about you. They've even come up with a fictitious Talent for you. Since all new students are forbidden to use their Talents, no matter how tame, until they've passed their second-level training, no one is going to ask for a demonstration. Except at the Reveal."

I moved in closer. The air between us heated with a tangible charge. "Which means?"

Vincent inhaled sharply and sidestepped me to get further away, but instead found himself wedged into a corner between the floral drapes and my desk. "They'll say your Talent is to disguise yourself chameleon-style and no one will question it. Adaptation is one of the most common Talents."

I rolled my eyes, enjoying his obvious unease. "Pfffft. So what happens to Xavier now?"

"He deserves whatever they dish out. Too much time and money has been wasted on him already, and to be honest, I have no idea why they don't just ship him out of here for good."

"Harsh. But what will they do for an encore? Draw and quarter him? Lock him up in a stockade? What other medieval torture devices do they keep in the basement?"

"House arrest for a week. He'll get food, but he won't be let out of his room."

I shuddered to think of the state I'd found Xavier in when I'd barged into his room the last time, and wondered if that strange frozen state was a part of his punishment.

A stray thought bubbled up from somewhere deep in my mind. The moment I blurted it, judging by Vincent's reaction, I knew it was true. "What they've been doing to him is real torture, isn't it, Vincent? High Step thinks it's above the law, doesn't it?"

Vincent's eyes ignited. He wrenched me by the wrist and twisted hard, hissing in my ear. "Never talk like that."

As if surprised by the violence of his reaction, he let go of me quickly. I was breathing heavily, trying to force down the bile of my anger, but the ceiling over Vincent's head had already started to dim. My throat tingled as a shadowy pool of darkness collected over his head. Vincent looked up as if he could see Death gathering in the air above him.

"Please. Get a grip on yourself," he whispered. "I-I'm sorry. Give me your hand."

I was hyperventilating, choking down my anger, swept up in my outrage over Xavier's treatment and Vincent's sanctioning of it, but reluctantly placed my hand in his.

Vincent closed his eyes. Sandwiching my hand between his two, he slowly lifted my fingertips to his lips, kissed them, then pulled me into his arms. At first I was stiff and resistant, but it only took a second for his heat to sweep through me, dismantling my fury.

"You wanted to know where the Talent leaves off and the real us begins," he whispered, raising shivers up the back of my neck. "Right here."

My knees buckled as I leaned in toward his lips. We kissed, softly, tentatively, his breath sweet with cinnamon and oranges. Vincent pulled me hard against him, the kiss deepening, his heart hammering against his ribcage. Caught up in the want of him, I could still sense him working me, his thoughts probing mine, searching, softening knots, rebraiding my emotions to diffuse my anger and anxiety.

But if it felt this good, I didn't care.

I relaxed, languid and boneless, yet with all of his efforts Vincent couldn't reach the crystalline kernel of my anger over Xavier's treatment. It remained untouched and safe, as cold and sharp as the edge of a blade.

Vincent cupped my face in his hands and studied me, his eyes pale fire shot through with the gold and russet glow of the setting sun. "I never expected to feel this way about you.

If I had, I would have turned the job down."

I let him hold me, hoping he really meant those words; and that how happy and protected I felt in his arms was not just another lie.

18

THE NOISY CHATTER WENT SILENT THE MOMENT I entered the dining hall, then erupted in earsplitting applause. I thought back to my first day there. From the start, this room full of cheering students had played along with the ruse that High Step was simply a school for artists and musicians. I knew I should be angry, but there was no denying the fact that I was as strange as the rest of them. That I really did belong here.

I bowed and nodded to the admiring crowd. The talk was all about my impending Reveal, leaving me to conclude that High Step's oddball student body didn't need much of an excuse to throw a party. Vincent worked the crowd, stopping to chat at every table like the maître d' of the dining hall.

At Xavier's usual table across the dining hall, a red-haired boy spooned food into One-Digit Della's twisting mouth. A flicker of sorrow shuddered through me. No one said a thing about Xavier's absence.

My sorrow was quickly drenched by Lila's full frontal assault. "People, people! We need to discuss decorations. Themes. We need a theme to end all themes. Any ideas?" Zuber, Prishkin, and Dawn stared at her blankly.

"I like magenta," I ventured.

Lila grimaced. "Yeesh. How imaginative. Plus it will clash with your dress. Why are all of you so brain-dead?"

"Not to mention your blue hair," Zuber quipped. Everyone laughed, except Lila, who drummed her fingers impatiently on the table. My gaze locked briefly with Zuber, worry for Xavier shimmering in his dark eyes. I vowed to check in on him later, no matter what Vincent said. It was my fault he'd gotten into this mess in the first place.

My attention returned to the ongoing debate. Lila was not pleased by the lackluster pool of ideas. I was at a loss over what would be a winning theme at a party for freaks.

"Circus!" Dawn blurted. The girl spoke so infrequently that it was easy to forget she was there.

"Hmmm," Lila said, a finger pressed to her scarlet lips. "Not too shabby, Waverly. What if it's a *haunted* circus? We could have ghost clowns, zombie jugglers, and a vampire ringmaster."

"I call Vampire Ringmaster!" bellowed Demetri Prishkin, shoving the shock of straw-colored hair from his sleepy blue eyes. Lila colored a deep rose and Zuber smirked. I snickered behind my hand over how blissfully oblivious Prishkin was to Lila's obvious infatuation with him.

The conversation bounced back and forth at breakneck speed until an actual idea popped into my head. "Wait, I think I have it. Zombie rock concert!"

"That's perfect, Beth," Lila said, clapping. "Finally!" Then everyone started talking at once at high volume. It was decided that I'd perform with my zombie band to an audience of zombies. I found that I was actually excited to play some pure shrieking rock and roll in front of a live group. It seemed like it had been forever since I had.

Vincent returned to the table and reluctantly agreed to be a zombie violinist in my band. Before I knew it, dinner was over and we all shuffled back to our rooms.

Vincent walked me back, his touch respectful and distant, the earlier intensity between us muted. Tomorrow was my first full day of classes and lessons and I found that, though I was a little nervous, I was actually looking forward to it.

Vincent kissed me chastely outside my door and bid me goodnight. I was disappointed that it was nothing more than a peck, but I was getting used to his mercurial moods. And if I was really honest with myself, I knew I wasn't ready. Even with all the forgetting I'd done since coming to High Step, the loss of Sam still weighed heavily on me. Maybe I could let go, I told myself, if I knew what had happened to him. But with each passing day, that seemed less and less likely.

My high spirits crashed and burned the minute I closed the door and I was alone in my room. A fire crackled in the hearth, shadows dancing crazily on the walls, but it did nothing to warm me. I crawled into bed, slipped under the heavy down comforters, and tried to read one of the books I'd apparently brought from home, but unwelcome thoughts crowded out my focus.

As if a dam had burst, a deep ache for home rushed in. Remembering Xavier's repeated reminders to keep my Blast Mahoney button close, I dug it out from under the mattress and clenched it so hard the metal point punched through the skin of my palm. Sucking on the small wound, I pressed my face to the cold window and peered into the night woods. I had no idea why, but the simple act of clutching that button helped keep my thoughts in focus.

It could have been the wind whistling, but I swore I heard the tinkling notes of a piano solo echoing through the trees. Could I be Talented, yet still be losing my mind?

The hours ticked by, but I was too wired for sleep. I knew I probably wouldn't get away with it, but I couldn't stand it anymore. Maybe it was displaced energy over the lingering mystery of Sam's disappearance, but I decided to check in on Xavier.

Nobody stopped me as I glided through the darkened corridors, but when I rounded the corner to Xavier's hall, I spotted one of the massive guards from Gideon's office leaning against the door. I lingered in the shadows, watching, knowing this was pointless. Then the door opened. The One-Digit Della lookalike strolled out, smiled coquettishly at the guard, and flounced right past me.

It made no sense for her to be allowed in there if Xavier was under house arrest. I had to get into that room somehow to see what was really going on. Maybe there was another way in.

From where I hid, I could still hear the howl of the wind in the rafters, beckoning me outside. Bristling with restless energy, I hurried back to my room, grabbed my down coat and a pair of waterproof boots, and found my way through the bowels of the compound to the same back door that Xavier had opened for me the first time I'd gone out prowling.

Exiting through the student kitchen, I stood on the back porch, gazing up at the sky. The stars were a spray of silver dust across an ink-dark sky, the moon a crescent of gold. Wind bit through my jacket. I thought of Carson trapped in his useless body and wondered if he thought I'd abandoned him, or if he'd forgotten me like Monica said.

A streak of shadow, an almost imperceptible smear, darkened the mist that coated the forest floor. And as soft as a trickling stream, the tinkle of piano keys rode the wind, calling to me.

I traipsed through the snow to the edge of the woods, the pinprick on my palm burning. The snow-covered forest floor glowed eerily through the mist that curled around my ankles. A shaft of moonlight broke through the roof of skeletal branches and fell across the trunk of a great old oak. In the scant light, I could barely make out how the bark had been peeled away to form a clear spot. Something had been scraped into the wood. Squinting, I peered closer, operating more by touch than by sight.

It was a crude heart, worn by age, with the words "Fragile Forever" carved inside of it.

The shock of the familiar words knocked the breath from me. I ran my fingers over the grooved wood. It was real. Weathered and gray, it wasn't recent, which meant it was probably there long before I got to High Step.

I had no idea what this meant, but I was totally spooked. Trudging across the snow to the compound as fast as my legs could go, I noticed something that gave me pause. The building was dark, but two stories above the back exit a dim light glowed. I was certain, from its nearness to the stairwell, which came out by the back exit, that this was Xavier's room.

If I could haul myself onto the roof of the wraparound porch and up to the ledge that bordered the third story, there was a chance I could peer in. If I didn't kill myself, that is.

I already knew I was going to try.

Standing on the porch rails, I reached for the ornate gingerbread woodwork overhead and, gaining a foothold on the cornice of the porch column, heaved myself up onto the porch roof. It was slightly sloped and caked with snow, so on my hands and knees, I carefully shimmied up to where the roof met the side of the building. Under the third-story windows was a narrow ledge, just wide enough for me to stand on if I could climb that high. Wedging my feet on the sill of one of the second-story windows, I grabbed for the lintel, using the windowpanes for foot grips. One slip and I was dead, but since I was already this far, why stop now? With a massive push, I pulled myself up onto the third-story ledge and prayed it wasn't coated with ice.

It was, but somehow, teetering three stories off the ground, I managed to find a foothold. I was okay, as long as I didn't look down. There was a small crack in the heavy drapes through which I could see only a sliver of room. A dim nightlight on the table by the door had been left turned on. There was zero activity in there. If Xavier was in his bed, which was right beside the window, I wouldn't be able to see him with my limited range. I pressed my face to the glass, not sure if I was seeing what I thought I was seeing—One-Digit Della's empty electric wheelchair.

I hadn't really given much thought to how I was going to get back down. If I could shimmy a few yards to the small second-story porch, it would be simple enough to ease myself to the main porch roof and slip down from there.

I was pondering this when a rush of flapping black feathers startled me. My foot slipped and suddenly I was dangling off the ledge, holding on by one numb hand. My grip gave way. I fell, hitting the porch roof hard. Skidding, I rolled clear off of the ledge and landed in the snow, my left ankle bent in a way no ankle should bend.

White-hot pain sliced through my leg; the slightest movement was agony. I pulled off my boot and was sick at the sight of the splinter of bone that had broken through the skin. I sank backward into the snow, dizzy with shock. Stupid, stupid, stupid. A crow landed on my chest and cocked its head, bright pebble eyes blinking. I wanted to tell the crow that this was all its fault, but I was too delirious to form the words.

19

OPENED MY EYES TO THE SILHOUETTES OF THREE people huddled around me.

"Lila?"

"Shh. Quiet. I have no idea what on earth you were doing out here, but it was pretty dumb of you to go and break your ankle four days before your Reveal."

"I—" I stopped myself, because I had no appropriate defense. Meanwhile, my entire leg throbbed insanely. I glanced at my foot, which was dark purple and swollen like an eggplant. "How did you guys know?"

Lila slanted her head. "Pluto, my bird. I was—"

"Pluto was doing a remote fly-by on poor clueless Demetri and she spotted you lying out here in the snow," Zuber cut in.

"I was not spying on Demetri. I was taking Pluto out for some exercise."

"My eye," Zuber snorted.

Why hadn't I thought of that? I wanted to find out more about Pluto and what exactly Lila was doing, but my leg hurt too much. Meanwhile, silent Dawn bent over me, poking and prodding the injured ankle. I whimpered, biting back a yowl.

"I can fix this," Dawn whispered, so library-soft that I wasn't sure I'd heard what she'd said. "But it's going to hurt."

"What?"

"Lovely Dawn has a very convenient Talent," Zuber said. "She can melt and mend bones, among other things. You don't want to get her mad. Of course, like the rest of us, her Talent is highly restricted. Outside of training she's not allowed to use it."

"But we all do anyway," Lila added.

"But Xavier—" I stopped and grimaced with pain. "Why is Xavier the only one who gets in trouble?"

Lila shrugged. "Because he's the only one stupid enough to get caught?"

Dawn poked my leg again and I cried out.

"Let's get her inside," Zuber said.

He hefted me in his strong arms and in seconds I was swaddled in formless gray haze. Warmth and light returned with my next blink and I felt myself set gently onto my bed. Zuber padded across my room to open the door for Lila, Dawn, and a reed-thin younger kid with a mess of frizzy red hair. Lila dragged the kid toward us by a bony arm.

"This is Kevin," she said.

"Hello," Kevin said. In the dim of my room it took me a minute to notice that, under his shock of hair, the freckled lids were closed and sunken. "Nice to meet you," he said in a broad Southern accent. "I'm from Texas, a long way from home. And in case you're wondering, I'm not asleep. This is just how I am."

"Kevin was born without eyes," Lila said cheerfully. "But he has one wicked-ass Talent."

Kevin smiled and bowed. "That's right. I'm here to eat your screams."

I shuddered and groaned, hoping that I was asleep in my bed, dreaming. "My screams?"

"Kevin can absorb sound," Lila said helpfully.

"Did we mention that before Dawn can heal your bones, she needs to melt them?" Zuber interjected.

"And that's most likely gonna hurt," Kevin said, with a

little too much relish. "So I expect you'll be screaming some."

Dawn returned from my bathroom with a warm cloth and began to clean my ankle. Even her soft touch sent razor-sharp pain shooting up my leg.

Sweat broke out across my forehead. I gritted my teeth and swallowed down a howl. I didn't want to give Kevin an appetizer. "Do you get much work around here?"

"Some," Kevin said. "Job's a job. I'm not good for much else. 'Cept drumming, that is. Thing is, sound is like sonar for me. The louder the screams, the more I can feel my surroundings. Kind of like a dolphin. So it ain't half bad. Usually, I got no idea who does the screaming, so everyone is happy."

"Except the screamer." I clenched my jaw and closed my eyes.

"We're ready now." Dawn sat lightly on the side of my bed. Lila and Zuber each grabbed one of my hands and squeezed hard.

"I'm sorry," said Dawn. "But this will hurt. A lot."

Kevin smiled, his face tilted upward like a flower to the sun. I cringed.

Dawn waved both hands over my leg, as if she was strumming an invisible harp. At first, my leg went numb and all I felt was the gentle heat pulsing deep inside my leg. The sensation was almost pleasant. But the heat intensified rapidly to a furnace of molten agony. I peered at my leg and nearly fainted. The bottom half of the leg lay limp against the sheet like a sock filled with Jell-O. Nausea surged inside me, and with the next wave of pain I unleashed a massive roar.

I screamed and screamed, but the sound died as if I'd gone deaf. I glimpsed Kevin laughing like he was on the best high ever. I vowed to murder him in his sleep when I got my strength back.

Sharp edges poked and ground inside the empty sack that was my lower leg. Lila and Zuber squeezed my hands tighter.

It did nothing to stop the blinding pain that filled my entire body, only kept me from flailing around and punching them in the face.

Woozy and exhausted from screaming, I felt my chest tingle. I glanced upward through slitted lids. Shadow pooled at the ceiling.

"Stop!" I screamed. The sound of my voice was swallowed whole. Kevin's arms were extended wide as if to embrace the glorious noise. "You don't understand! You've got to stop!" I mouthed, my words silenced.

The mass of darkness dropped lower, and with it came the icy chill and pinprick tingles creeping up my spine. My leg was a lumpy mess, half-melted, half-whole.

I wanted to draw the cloud into me and be done with the pain. And everything else.

"Go!" I shouted. "All of you get out of here! Now! Leave!"

My silent shouts were ignored by everyone except Kevin, who basked in the vibrations like a kid dancing in a summer downpour.

My dorm door burst open and Vincent stormed in.

"What in hell is going on here?" he yelled, his shout snuffed out the moment it left his lips. Kevin's smile grew wider.

He stalked over to Kevin and pushed him into a chair. "Stop it. Right now."

Kevin folded his arms over his chest and frowned. My voice returned, but my screams had subsided to a series of whimpers.

Vincent leapt onto the bed and cradled me in his warm arms. My whimpers became sobs.

"Do you need someone to help you back to your room, Kevin?" Vincent asked, not unkindly.

Kevin stood. "I can find my way back on my own, thank you very much." He strode confidently across the room, opened the door, then slammed it behind him extra-hard, though it didn't make a sound.

"Guess he'll have to find his next fix somewhere else," Zuber said.

Vincent held me tightly, but there was nothing romantic about it. Still, I felt my brittle rage soften. My leg still screamed as if it had been packed up with glass shards.

"Finish with her. Now!" Vincent barked, his anger pulsing through my pores.

The rest of Dawn's treatment was so excruciating that Zuber needed to stick a cloth in my mouth to muffle my screams. Vincent hung on for dear life. Finally, as gray morning light spilled through the window, Dawn finished her work.

My leg was still bruised, but whole. It was incredibly sore, but before Dawn collapsed from exhaustion on my desk chair, she told me I should be able to walk on it with only a slight limp, which would be gone in a day.

I was too tired to properly thank her, and she was too tired to care. Zuber gathered her in his arms and vanished between blinks. Lila sleepwalked out of my room.

There were only a few hours until breakfast, and Vincent had fallen asleep, one arm flung across my chest. Breathing softly against me, his mouth partly open, he looked like one of those exquisite angels in a nineteenth-century painting. All he was missing were the halo and wings.

Vincent leapt out of my bed with a shout when he realized where he was.

"Please forgive me. That was inexcusable."

I smirked. "You make a very nice teddy bear."

He peered at my leg and shook his head, frowning. "I should report all of you. But I won't, because then I would have to explain why I assisted, rather than stopped, the illegal activity." He raked a hand through his curls and sighed. "How is the leg?"

I sat and eased my legs over the side of the bed. The injured ankle throbbed mildly. Slowly, I lowered myself to the floor and stood. It hurt, but the leg could bear weight. I limped over to him and he caught me in his arms.

"I do have to admit Dawn does nice work. She fixed the finger I broke once while shooting hoops and I was able to play my violin the same night."

I raised an eyebrow. "When am I going to hear that violin of yours, anyway?"

"You will. I'm going to get ready for breakfast, as should you. You've got a big day ahead. I'm not going to ask how you broke that ankle, but I do hope you will decide to tell me at some point." Vincent stared at me pointedly, then left.

I hobbled back to my bed, eyes gummy with exhaustion. I was going to have to limp through my day on two hours of sleep. Which was probably a much better day than Xavier was going to have as a prisoner in his dorm room.

My tired mind crept over the facts. An abandoned wheelchair. A blind boy who ate screams. Then I made the connection. I knew where I'd seen Kevin before. He was the same red-headed boy who had been feeding One-Digit Della at dinner last night.

20

BREAKFAST WAS QUIET AND SLUGGISH. DAWN'S eyes slipped closed, head nodding, her fork frozen in motion over her scrambled eggs. Zuber was haggard and drawn, and even Lila was quiet. Vincent, dark circles under his eyes, stabbed at his omelet like he was harpooning a fish.

I glanced across the dining hall and spotted Kevin confidently guiding Della's wheelchair to the table. I watched him spoon cereal into her gaping mouth, the utensil never faltering. Though he couldn't see a thing, Kevin got the food in without a spill. Apparently, he'd augmented his sound fix somewhere between last night and now.

I hurried through breakfast and limped after Kevin and Della as they left the dining hall. I realized there had to be an elevator somewhere in the building to accommodate the wheelchair, which was most likely where they were heading.

Turning down a rarely used hall outside the dining hall, I saw them waiting by a set of steel doors. Kevin whistled, stroking Della's hair. Della moaned and rolled her head, an arm flailing in his direction. Kevin grabbed her gnarled hand and kissed her finger.

I limped up to them and grabbed Kevin by the arm.

He whirled on me. "Hey! You're not supposed to grab at a blind person like they're a piece of fruit in a bin."

"Do you recognize my voice, or would you prefer if I screamed?"

A half-smile quirked Kevin's mouth. "Beth, is it?" He cocked his head. "I hear you're a singer. Singers make the best screamers, you know."

Kevin absently patted Della's blonde head. She craned her neck to look at me, eyes wide.

I studied Kevin. "You seem to have your dolphin sense in full working order today. Was our session last night that rewarding?"

"I have plenty of other resources."

"Do you, now?"

The elevator dinged and the doors slid open. "Well, then. Nice chatting. See ya around, Beth. Or should I say, hear ya?" Kevin snickered and pushed Della's wheelchair into the elevator chamber. I stuck my good foot in to block the doors from closing.

Kevin punched at the buttons. "Let it go! We have to be at class."

"Singers make great screamers, don't they? Been visiting any others lately?"

Kevin frowned. In the elevator light, shrouded by a swath of crazy red curls, he looked like a dust mop. "Ain't none of your business who I work. Not like I can see 'em, anyways."

Kevin scowled in my general direction. Della blinked at me. I let the elevator door close and headed to my first period class, my limp fading with each step.

As I walked to Literature, I thought about how I'd lost track of the date that I'd first entered High Step. A thick coat of snow still blanketed the grounds, so I figured it couldn't be more than two weeks ago. It was almost as if the part of my brain that kept time had been tampered with. Memories of my life from before were vague, the sharp edges faded and washed out.

The place where the Blast Mahoney pin had pricked the

skin of my palm began to burn. Xavier had said to keep the button close, and I couldn't help but wonder if it was somehow the key to understanding what really went on in this place. And if he had some similar object of his own to anchor his thoughts.

Sleep-deprived as I was, the morning classes whizzed by in a blitz of information and spirited debates. To my astonishment, I found that I was engaged in the class discussions like I'd never been before. After third period Physics, where I discovered I was beginning to grasp a subject that used to bore me to tears, I decided that High Step teachers had an uncanny ability for teaching. Lila's comment about Talented employment statistics struck a chord. I wondered what lay ahead in my own future as a controlled killing machine, how you wrote that on a resume, and what would become of me if I didn't learn to how to control my dangerous Talent.

As I was about to enter the dining hall, Monica DeWitt flowed out from the shadows and blocked my path. A glittering smile curved her lips, but I hadn't forgotten the frost in those opal eyes on the day of my Evaluation.

"Good afternoon, Beth! How are you enjoying your classes?"

"They're great," I answered honestly. "I've never had such amazing teachers."

Monica clasped her hands together. "We take pride in our exceptional teaching staff. We train individuals for the best match of Talent to vocation." She gazed at me expectantly, eyes burning with inner light. Swallowing hard, I pondered what exactly Monica DeWitt's Talent was.

"Cool."

Monica squinted at me, leaning in closer. "And you're not wondering what possible application there may be for your particular Talent?"

I took a step back. "Well, yeah. A little?"

"I'm going to take your training into my own hands, Beth.

A huge and rare Talent such as yours can become a dangerous liability if not handled properly. On the other hand, if it is honed and shaped to a fine point, it can become an asset, an instrument of great power."

I stared at her as wide-eyed and innocently as I could.

"You do understand how important proper training is, yes?" she pressed. "And what might happen if a Talent is left untended?"

I nodded vigorously. Under the scrutiny of Monica DeWitt's cool gaze, it occurred to me that High Step was only the smallest tip of an iceberg. That out there somewhere was an entire hidden world of Talented. I shivered.

"We'll start today, after lunch." She arched a finely shaped eyebrow, apparently expecting a more enthusiastic response than the blank stare I offered in return.

"What about my music education? Wasn't that what got me in here?" I blurted.

"Why, yes, of course. We have not forgotten that." Monica spoke gently, as if explaining to a small child. "You will get guitar and voice lessons, Beth. Our music instructors are experts in their particular areas, as well. Not only do they make music, but they can see it, smell it, or taste it. However, your true Talent, the real reason you are at High Step, takes precedence."

My stomach dropped, like I was on an elevator that had plunged between floors too quickly. I said nothing.

"After lunch, go directly to your room. The items you need for training will be there. Then, meet me in the library."

At lunch everyone was even more sluggish than at breakfast. Vincent, I decided, probably needed his beauty rest even more than the rest of us, because he was downright surly.

After wolfing down his food, he got up abruptly and left.

With my insides so taut over my impending lesson with Monica, I was too wound up to eat more than a few bites of my lunch. Noticing that neither Della nor Kevin was in the dining hall, I excused myself twenty minutes early and slipped out. My friends were too tired to call after me.

No guard was posted outside Xavier's door, which was slightly ajar. I crept closer and peered inside the room. Sunlight streamed through the window. Giggles came from the moving lumps that rocked and rolled under the blankets. I wanted to turn and run, but sick curiosity rooted me to where I stood. Then I saw the thicket of red hair, intertwined with a tangle of white-gold ringlets.

I rushed over and pulled back the covers.

"Why'd you do that, babe? It's wicked cold in here," Kevin murmured, his face still buried in the blonde's breasts. Pancaked under Kevin was a buck-naked girl, who was either a miraculously cured Della or her mythical twin. She glared at me, looking like she was about to breathe fire through her nostrils.

"Get the hell out of here!" the girl snarled.

Kevin sat up, searching her face with gentle fingertips. "What's wrong, sweetheart? Did I hurt you?"

"We have company," the Della lookalike hissed.

"Shit." Kevin tilted his head. "It's her, isn't it? She's been stalking us."

I stepped forward and grabbed the girl's wrist. "What are you two doing in Xavier's room? Where is he?"

"Not here, obviously," the girl said. Her words slurred slightly as if her jaw was hinged a little too tight. In the corner sat an empty wheelchair.

"How the hell——?"

Della's head jerked slightly. "Thanks a lot for wasting our time. We only get a few minutes to——" Her words were cut off by a snap of her jaw. "K-Kevin. I'm sorry," she stuttered, her limbs contorting and curling inward.

Kevin took Della's rigid hand and pressed it to his cheek, his voice choked. "Go! She doesn't like people to see her when she reverts."

"Just tell me what the hell is going on." A vague swath of darkness streaked across the ceiling. I tried to slow my breath, but my heart pounded like a tribal drum.

"Mostly she's trapped inside her own body, in terrible pain at all times. But Della can escape."

"How?"

Kevin lovingly drew the covers over Della, who had stiffened as if she'd been turned to stone. "Her Talent is Transference. She can claim the health of others. Now, I'd appreciate it if you'd just have some common decency and leave us in peace," Kevin said. Blushing pink under his freckles, he'd apparently remembered that he was stark naked himself.

"I get it. She shifts her disability onto someone else so she's free to screw you? How about you? Got your dolphin radar on?"

"We're in love," Kevin stated emphatically, as if that explained everything.

He gathered Della's bent form in his arms, hefted her to the wheelchair, and struggled to tug her clothes over her unyielding limbs.

"Who's paying the price for your fun?" I asked.

"Someone who deserves it." Kevin slipped on his own clothes and maneuvered Della's clunky wheelchair toward the door.

They blocked the doorway. Kevin caressed Della's cheek with the backs of his fingers and Della stared straight at me. A corner of her twitching mouth curved up in a smile.

The first spasm arched my back and knocked me heavily to the floor. My limbs curled in on themselves, my fingers contorting into stiff claws. The pain was a deep ache, a fire inside my bones. My jaw flexed painfully off its hinge. I lay there, in frozen agony, understanding instantly what it meant to be Della.

Della climbed out of the chair and pressed her body against Kevin's. They kissed slowly and passionately for my benefit. I was forced to watch, my body as rigid as a suit of armor.

"How does that feel?" Kevin asked, facing me. "What would you give for a few minutes to be able to move and be free of the constant pain?"

Della flipped her white-blonde hair behind her shoulder. Twisted and bent, I couldn't even grit my teeth. I held back the moans that wanted to escape through my constricted throat. I didn't want to give Kevin the satisfaction of my garbled screams.

I rolled my eyes upward. Even that simple movement was a great effort. On the ceiling, the darkness thickened. Kevin and Della left me writhing on the floor.

Blackness swirled about the room, thick as smoke. Stuck as I was, I had nothing better to do except attempt to control it. Breathing hurt my twisted ribcage, but I focused on slowing it to an even pace.

Who could really blame Kevin and Della for stealing a few moments of happiness? The black cloud dimmed and vanished as my sympathy for their plight kicked in. Left with nothing to do but tap the single finger I could move on the floorboards, I couldn't help but think of Carson, trapped in his own unforgiving body. Would I want to die, or would I want live like this?

After what seemed like an endless amount of time, creaky movement returned to my joints, like the Tin Man after a good oiling. I staggered robotically to my feet just as Vincent came barging through Xavier's door.

"Monica is heading to your room now. I'm not even going to ask what you're doing in here. Lucky thing I came to see you first and found you gone."

I stretched out my stiff joints, relishing the simple ability to move. "Kevin and Della have been using Xavier as a host for their parasitic love trysts!" I blurted.

"What on earth are you talking about?"

"Do you actually know what Della's Talent is?"

Vincent stepped closer to me. "Della is a genius musician. Her gifts for composing are legendary. Some of us are simply extraordinarily gifted in the arts."

"Della comes with a little something extra. She can shrug off her cerebral palsy, or whatever she's got, like a coat, and thrust it on someone else. This time she put it on me. From the number of times I've seen her waltzing out of here, I think she's been stealing Xavier's health and screwing Kevin the Scream Eater."

Vincent's aqua eyes ignited. "That's a very dangerous accusation."

"So you really didn't know, did you?"

Vincent frowned and rubbed his chin with an index finger. "Behavior like that is not sanctioned. The kind of abuse you're describing is certainly not tolerated here."

"Are you sure about that?"

Vincent glared at me. "Be careful what you say."

"What are you so afraid of?"

Vincent grabbed me by the wrist and pulled me into a not-very-gentle embrace, his heat roaring into my veins. "I'm not afraid for me."

"What about Xavier? Who's afraid for him?"

21

FTER I CHANGED INTO THE LOOSE–FITTING clothes Monica had left in the room for me, I raced to the library, where I found her already pacing. Clearly not happy about my lateness, she tried to cover up her annoyance with a tart smile. I thought about Xavier and my anger resurfaced, prickles of heat sliding up and down my spine. I'd have liked nothing more than to zap Monica with it, but that would only have landed me in way worse trouble than he was in.

I felt strangely naked without Vincent or Andre present, but Monica's pinched expression kept me from asking for them. We entered the grand space to find it empty. Dust motes swirled in the light that streamed through the tall windows that interspersed the book-lined walls. Along one of the inner walls, a shelf slid silently open. Monica led me through a dark entrance into a damp winding corridor.

We walked endlessly through the downward-sloping halls, the air getting damper and darker by the minute, and entered a dim windowless room lined entirely with red velvet curtains. At the room's center were an antique table, two wooden chairs, and three lit tapers flickering in a brass candelabra.

Monica nodded for me to sit and took the chair across from me. Without missing a beat, she leaned over the table and delivered a vicious ringing smack to my cheek. My head snapped back from the blow, and I gaped at her dumbfounded, rubbing at my stinging face. Already, a cloud of shadow hovered above us like a thunderhead. Monica looked up and smiled.

In a blink, I wasn't looking at Monica anymore. Instead, I gazed into the loving blue eyes of my mother.

The cloud vanished with a little poof and I was looking at Monica again. She reached across the table and touched my face with one manicured finger. The fiery ache was gone.

"We have a lot of work to do, Beth, and it's not without risk for either of us. But before we can even begin, we need to understand the lay of the land. No two Talents are the same. Each one has its own rules, its own trigger points and sources of origin."

I stared at Monica, my heart pounding, but said nothing. I was far too petrified to speak.

"I've read many books on the subject," she purred, "but there is still no substitute for trial and error. Our work is going to be slow, methodical, and tedious."

"How did you——?" I blurted finally.

"Change? The answer is simple. I didn't change. I didn't even slap you. My Talent is Sensory Illusion. I can make you see, feel, taste, and hear whatever I want."

"The time in the Evaluation when I couldn't move?"

Monica nodded. "Yes. It's quite a useful Talent. But like all Volatile Talents, it is strictly regulated, and is on the government's watch list. Like yours will be. If we are caught violating the rules of the Contract, our entire world will be put at risk. Our alliance with the Regular world is an uneasy one at best."

The words rushed out of my mouth before I knew what I was saying. "What about Xavier? Is his punishment all an illusion?"

Monica's face colored for a split second before returning to its usual creamy white, eyes sparkling like rare jewels in the candlelight's warm glow. "I don't know what you mean by punishment. Xavier's room detention is nearly over. Hopefully he has learned his lesson this time. The boy seems to have an allergic reaction to rules."

"But—"

Monica waved a hand dismissively. "I can assure you, this is all familiar territory for Xavier. If not for Gideon's generosity he would have been long gone, sent off to a more secure facility. Now, we need to focus on you."

"What about the mouse? At the Evaluation?"

"That," Monica said with a smile, "was totally real."

Then the room went utterly dark. I heard their chittering first, as what might have been an army of mice crawled up my pant legs in a mad rush to be the first up the mountain.

Real or imagined, I was going to scream, or burst into flames, I wasn't sure which.

"I know this is terrifying, Beth," Monica said from somewhere in the room, "and I'm sorry to put you through this, but it's necessary to locate the source of your power."

My breathing came in shivering gulps. The mice were scrambling up my T-shirt now. I shoved them off of me, but more kept coming. There was no way I could focus on anything but the fear.

"Focus, Beth. Do you feel it?"

All I could feel was my heart hacking its way out of my ribcage.

"You want them to die. Pinpoint the origin of your desire."

I scanned my panicked mind. Electric prickles writhed up my back, but without the ability to see, I had no idea where the shadow formation was, or if it was there at all. I was flying blind.

"I can't! If I can't see it, I don't know if it's there!" The mice were clawing at my collar. I felt their tiny paws grasping at my hair. I could barely draw in my next breath. "Please. No more. I can't do this," I pleaded. When this was over, I was going to kill Monica with my bare hands. If I survived.

"Search for it, Beth. The Death sense is like an underground spring. Find its source and it's yours to control."

The mice were climbing onto my head, their scratchy little claws digging into my scalp. More and more were on my legs and torso. I was bathed in sweat, nauseous, ready to faint. But beneath my crazily beating heart was a cold spot. Desperate, I centered my focus there. An electric vibration fanned out from the place under my heart, humming through my extremities. I sharpened my focus, imagining the heartbeat of each mouse shutting down.

There was a concussive blast that knocked me backward in my chair. My fingers and legs burned with the aftershock. Then I went numb.

Seconds later, I lay blinking on a floor strewn with the corpses of dead mice.

Monica extended a hand and pulled me to my feet. I looked around to find that there were only five mice, tops.

"Well done, Beth."

I grabbed for the back of the chair. I was so weak, I didn't think my legs would hold me upright. My recently mended leg screamed with pain. Monica's form wove in and out of focus.

"That is enough for today. We've accomplished a lot." She wrapped my arm around her shoulder to keep me from falling over. "Until you gain mastery over your Talent, using it will deplete your energy. You must build up a gradual tolerance."

We stumbled along, my feet dragging, her voice tinny in my ears. "And Beth," she continued, "it goes without saying that you must keep the nature of your Talent confidential. Only Vincent and Gideon know your secret. If word got out, there would be an uproar here at High Step. Many of the students are from old Talented families who wield a lot of influence in our world."

Somehow, Monica managed to guide me through the underground labyrinth and back to the library. Half-blind, my bones turned to sponge, I collapsed into the waiting arms of Andre, who carried me back to my room and tucked me into bed.

His touch soothed me into a fitful sleep and I was excused from classes for the rest of the day. When I woke, Dawn was sitting beside me, a worried Lila peering over her shoulder.

"They say you had a very bad reaction to your training," Lila said.

"We thought we could help ease your symptoms," Dawn added shyly.

Lila was staring shrewdly at me. "Thing is, no one really knows what your Talent is."

I rubbed my aching forehead. "It's the Chameleon effect. You know that," I lied weakly. After seeing a little of what Monica could do, there was no way I was taking her subtle threats lightly.

Lila slanted her head, lips pursed. Dawn ran her hands lightly over my torso.

"I understand," Lila said in a clipped tone. "We are taught that only the deadly Talents cause a strong reaction."

Dawn withdrew, leaving me feeling remarkably better. Lila was still staring at me, a mixture of disappointment and hurt stamped across her features. "I won't pry, Beth. I promise. But you need friends in this place. Real friends. Xavier's problem is that he never seemed to get that."

Dawn nodded from behind Lila.

"I just wanted to tell you that I found a pair of shoes for your Reveal. And that there's a dance party in the Rec Room after dinner tonight. It's not something you want to—or should—miss."

22

B Y DINNERTIME, I WAS FEELING MUCH BETTER. Vincent called for me and, without mentioning my afternoon training session, took me down to the dining hall. It was Wednesday night, two nights before my big Reveal, and the hall was buzzing with talk of the party later that evening. Bits and pieces of information spilled out until it became clear that this party was special, that it was basically a semi-annual pageant that High Step put on for its Benefactors. Though I asked repeatedly, no one, not even Lila, would explain exactly who these mysterious Benefactors were, only that they would be watching.

Monica entered the dining hall, breezily elegant in a gauzy silver gown that set off her gleaming eyes. Looking at her dazzling beauty, I was forced to wonder how much of it was real and how much was illusion. I caught Vincent staring at me, his mouth set firm, and looked away, thinking about how the shadows were filled with sharp things, ready to slice me to ribbons.

As I was thinking this, my gaze snapped across the room to where Della's wheelchair was being rolled in. Kevin, I noticed, was already seated on the other side of the hall. Poking dispiritedly at his food, he was clearly unaware of her entrance. Guiding the chair to their usual spot at the table was Xavier, looking as pale and cadaverous as a mushroom growing under a rock. His eyes darted nervously across the hall, landing on nothing in particular. He walked with a shuffling gait, one hand on the grips of the wheelchair, the other stuffed in a pocket.

I forced my attention back to the lively chatter. The dining hall bristled with a combination of anticipation and nervous energy.

"What are we supposed to wear to this thing?" I asked.

Lila's brows shot up. "It's come as you are. You'll see. It's crazy that they're having this two days before your Reveal, but there's never advance notice. They just thrust these pageants on us twice a year with no warning to keep us on our toes."

"Who are 'they?'"

Lila looked at me funny. "The Guild, of course. They run everything."

After dinner, we were each given a silk blindfold and instructed to lay a hand on the shoulder of the person in front of us. We were led on an endless trudge into the damp-smelling bowels of the compound; After what seemed like a long slog into hell, we were told to remove our blindfolds. Our eyes blinked open to a grand ballroom ablaze with the flickering light of countless tiny candles. Scores of giant flower-garlanded nests hovered three feet off the floor, while tiny, vividly colored winged creatures cavorted and swooped like hummingbirds.

Lila, inexplicably wreathed from head to toe in glorious sea-foam taffeta, her black hair crowned with diamond dust, cast me an amazed glance. Dazed, I scanned the room. All of us were clothed in silks and gowns befitting a Victorian dance. I was outfitted in an amethyst silk gown with a long flowing train studded with emeralds and sapphires.

"Monica's outdone herself this year," Lila proclaimed. "Too bad none of this is real."

I was too dazzled to comment, and my attention drifted. My breath caught. Vincent strode toward me across the ballroom. A black tuxedo set off the shimmering gold of his curls; his turquoise eyes were like slivers of tropical sea.

He looked me up and down. "You look——astounding."

"It isn't real," I said.

Vincent pulled me into his arms, his lips pressed against my ear. "Does it matter, *ma chérie*?"

Unearthly music floated on the air and I was dizzy with it, intoxicated by the flowers' heady perfume and Vincent's sweet breath. "I don't know."

Drawn into a whirling dance, our silk and taffeta gowns spun into a mass of wild color. Hooded figures lined the wall like sentinels, flanking the shadows, so still that I wondered if they were statues. I meant to ask, but was too swept up in the grandeur and the thump of Vincent's heart beating against my ribs.

The floor dropped away and we were lifted above the bowers, floating up to the rafters. Laughing, Vincent kissed me. We were lighter than air, all of us drunk on the opulent beauty of the Pageant.

Darkness blotted my thoughts for only a moment as I wondered how Kevin and Della experienced this dance, if the illusion was strong enough to include them. Then I spotted them whirling past like two happy clouds, Kevin with eyes the color of emeralds that were fixed on his elfin partner. I smiled ruefully as they passed, strangely glad to see them happy.

We settled to the ballroom floor like falling petals. The nests dropped with us, each one housing a table laden with overflowing platters of candy and fruit.

We took our seats and a hush fell over the room. The

candlelight dimmed. I caught Lila's gaze and she smiled back at me, cheeks flushed and eyes glittering.

Our tables were arranged like spokes on a wheel. At the center of the wheel, a raised circular stage lifted from the floor. Lit by a brilliant spotlight, a figure rose from within a haze of mist. It was only when the smoke cleared that I realized that the figure, who stood with arms extended, was Xavier. His eyes closed as if deep in concentration, he was dressed in a long-tailed white silk tuxedo, his shoulder-length hair a glossy raven black. His scarred skin was smooth and perfect, unblemished.

His singing started as a breathy whisper and gained volume until it shook the walls and vibrated inside of my bones. Candles surged brighter. Nobody breathed or shifted in their seats. Even Vincent, who squeezed my hand, was caught up in the magic.

Then the room went dark and silent. When the light returned, Xavier was gone, replaced by Monica and Gideon, who stood in his place accepting the thunderous applause that should have been his. Gideon was regal in a purple velvet robe, light sparking off his huge ruby ring and reflected in the russet tones of his hair. I still had no idea what Gideon's Talent was.

My throat was dry and parched. No amount of fluid would ever quench my thirst for Xavier's voice. Or for him. I glanced at Vincent, feeling guilty.

I wanted to ask what the purpose of all this fuss was, but his look told me not to question.

The party continued for what seemed an eternity. I danced and ate until I thought my stomach would burst and my feet might fall off. I'm not sure what was in the punch, but the room melted into a dizzy blur of color and laughter.

Eventually, the lights dimmed, the sounds quieted and our blindfolds were returned to us. We were led, disoriented and stuffed full of food, out of the ballroom through the endless twisting corridors. With each step the illusion faded; swishing taffeta, cool against my calves, giving way to jeans and sneakers. My giddy mood dissolved. My stomach growled with hunger pangs. It was as though the entire party had never happened.

As we trudged along, something hit me hard across the shins. I stumbled from the blow, falling to my knees on the cold stone floor. I was yanked away before the blind herd could trample me, taken by a captor with an iron grip and a slow shuffling gait, uneven breath scraping through their lungs. I struggled wildly to free myself as I became aware of the dark cloud that made its presence known in the space above us. Heart hammering, I called out, but my cries died on the damp air.

We stopped frequently for my captor to suck in tortured breaths punctuated by hacking coughs. When my blindfold was finally removed, I gasped. A shaft of moonlight cut across Xavier's gaunt face, the scarred half a pitted landscape of shadow and light. His black hair was plastered to his skull, his eyes feverish and bloodshot. The white tux was gone, replaced by a threadbare white T-shirt and torn jeans.

"Xavier! What the hell?"

Gesturing to his throat, Xavier shuddered, then coughed hard and long. Droplets of bright red blood trickled between his fingers and spattered the T-shirt. When the fit passed, he straightened. Looking at me sadly, he stroked my cheek with two fingers.

"You're sick. You need help."

Xavier shook his head. His jaw moved wordlessly until finally a sound rushed out, little more than a rasping breath. "Take this."

He pressed a scrap of paper into my hand.

I wanted to ask what I could do to help him but before I could, he was gone, disappearing into the dark damp corridors without a trace.

23

IT SEEMED AS IF XAVIER HAD WANTED TO TELL ME SO much more than he had, but couldn't. When I got back to my room, I was finally able to look at the note. I'd hoped it would shed some light on the mystery of what was going on with him, but it only added to it. All that was written on the crinkled scrap of paper was a crude doodle of a triangle punching through a circle. It meant absolutely nothing to me.

I tucked the paper scrap under my mattress with the Blast Mahoney button and tried to sleep, but a repeating loop of Xavier's terrible, bloody cough kept flickering across my closed eyelids. I tossed and turned, gnawing fear seeping through the cracks inside me that had never fully healed. The pinprick where Sam's Blast Mahoney button had pierced the skin of my palm throbbed and burned. I reached for the pin under my mattress and clutched it, but neither sleep nor any kind of peace would come.

The protective haze I'd been floating around in for the past few weeks was gone. Bitter memories came rushing back, razor sharp and crystal clear, and with them an avalanche of emotion no magic touch or meds could melt away.

I wanted to go home. I wanted my mother to hold me; I wanted to bury my nose in her soft hair and breathe her perfume. Even Carson's limp embrace seemed comforting compared to life in this place.

I glanced upward. A black film eddied across the ceiling like windblown smoke, its echo crackling through the nerve endings in my scalp. A sob welled in my throat, but I didn't dare let it out.

After a second sleepless hour I couldn't take it anymore. I threw back the covers, tugged on my robe, and crept through the halls to Vincent's room, something I'd never had the nerve to do before. I swallowed hard and knocked softly. It only took a few minutes for him to pad across his room and open the door, as if he'd been expecting me. I couldn't tell him about Xavier and hoped he wouldn't be able to decode the truth behind my emotional turmoil.

Blinking at me in his pajamas, his gold curls adorably disheveled, Vincent wordlessly folded me into his arms and guided me to his bed. He pulled back the covers and I slipped between them fully dressed; the sheets were still warm from him. He slid in next to me and I nuzzled against him. I slept cradled in his calming embrace and let my mind empty of troubles.

When I woke, the first light of dawn silvering the room, Vincent was already gone. I grabbed my robe and skulked out to the hall, palm burning, the troubles sifting back in like sand.

At breakfast, the dining hall buzzed with the excitement of last night's pageant and my approaching Reveal. Lila held court, dissecting how everyone had looked in their glamoured gowns. When she tired of that, and of batting her eyelashes at the oblivious Demetri, she switched to the level of artistry necessary to transform me into a zombie rock goddess and what on earth to do with my hair.

I poked at my eggs and watched Vincent from the corner of my eye. He was staring intently at me and placed his hand on my arm repeatedly. The tension ebbed at his touch, but returned with a vengeance when he removed his hand, anxiety twisting my insides in tighter and tighter knots.

Other than sorrowful glances from Zuber, no one seemed to care or notice that Xavier was not around. My anger burned slow and deep under the cold spot beneath my ribs. Only Vincent's touch kept it from boiling over.

Despite Vincent's efforts, the noise of the chatter echoing in my ears and the fury burning in my throat became too much. I fled the dining hall—headed where, I had no clue.

With Vincent unable to contain me, I was officially a human time bomb.

I stormed up the stairs to my room. I couldn't face class today.

I couldn't face life at all.

Monica was waiting outside of my room, arms crossed. "I thought you might be upset. You do fancy that boy, don't you?"

I heaved in a breath and tried to slow my heart. Faint ribbons of shadow scudded across the ceiling. "I don't know who you mean."

Monica glanced up, then locked her gaze to mine. "You have more important business to concern yourself with than Xavier and his mishaps." With iron fingers, she grabbed me by the wrist. "I don't think you understand the position you're in, Beth. I'm doing what I can for you."

"I don't want to be here. I never asked for this. I just want to go home."

Her fingers pressed into the flesh of my arm. "I'm afraid that's not possible. You're a danger to yourself and everyone you know. It's imperative that you master your Talent."

My gaze snapped to the ceiling again. The shadows were thickening, electricity pinging in my veins. Their presence made me braver. I could kill her if I wanted. I really could.

"What's happening to Xavier? Tell me."

Her eyebrows lowered. "As I said, he is not your concern. You need to dress for your training session."

"I'm not up to it at the moment."

Monica's fingers tightened on my wrist. "I'm not *asking* you, Beth. Perhaps you'll allow me to explain the need for urgency."

I hesitated, but short of striking her dead, I could see by the look in her eyes I was not going to win this one. "Well, okay."

The frost melted away into an even more chilling smile. Monica strode into my room ahead of me. "Allow me to clear things up a bit. I suppose we owe you that. We haven't been entirely open with you regarding the nature of your abilities. I've been protecting you from the Guild's wrath."

I blinked back tears. Somewhere inside, I must have known that no governing body would tolerate a deadly weapon with no safety lock.

Monica continued. "After your Evaluation, the Guild reclassified your Talent as a Level 10 Volatile, which means you were subject to a mandatory Recall. Gideon and I managed to buy some time, given our past successes with other, lower-level Volatiles. Unfortunately, this business with Xavier is putting a strain on our efforts." Monica stared at me, opal eyes burning fiercely.

"I don't understand. What does Xavier have to do with me?"

"Let me clarify. Recall is a euphemism for whatever the Guild deems necessary. We don't really know what happens to the Talented that are removed from our charge. And I'm not sure you want to find out."

"Xavier's been Recalled?" My mind raced over the

implications of the word. What did it imply? Brainwashing? Enslavement? Execution?

"If the Guild sends in the Knights of the Blood Rose, or KBR," she said, crossing her long legs, "anything is possible."

"What are you talking about?"

"There is much you need to learn about the world you're a part of, Beth." Monica paused, watching the emotions I couldn't hide flicker across my face. "The Knights," she continued, "are the Guild's judicial arm. Since the Middle Ages they've investigated, tried, and sentenced those deemed a threat to the well-being of the Guild. But mainly, they are assassins."

I shuddered. My face must have turned whiter than milk. Blood rushed to my head. "S-sounds archaic," I said, my lame response sounding forced and shaky to my own ears. "Like a cross between the Knights of the Round Table and the KGB."

Monica's gaze remained leveled at me, her voice calm and measured. "The KBR are no joke, Beth. They operate in secret. I have no idea if they've been dispatched or not. They do not consult me. I merely try to stay off of their radar."

Monica studied my reaction. If she was frightened, either by me or by an unwelcome visit from the KBR, she didn't show it. "On second thought, let's do this tomorrow. Perhaps you should practice on your own in the meanwhile. Until you have yourself under control, I suggest you remain in your room. Your classmates will be told that you are ill and encouraged to leave you to rest."

I couldn't breathe in the stale air of my room. Assassins could be lurking, ready to kill me. To kill Xavier. I wondered if they were like me, Talented who had managed to wrestle their murderous rage under control, or if they carried actual weapons.

Either way, I had to get out of this place. I wondered where Xavier could have gone in the terrible condition he was in, and prayed the KBR hadn't already gotten to him.

Outside my window, lightning streaked between the skeletal branches. The sky opened and unleashed its wrath. A shadowy figure slipped between the branches, with barely more substance than smoke. I heard the tinkle of piano notes in the wind.

I'd grown used to the shadow figure lurking in the woods of the compound and wondered if its presence was just another part of my weird Talent.

As much as I wanted to escape the compound and this crazy nightmare, I still couldn't risk leaving until I learned how to control my monstrous ability. There was no evidence that the KBR assassins had come. Maybe if I developed some restraint, they never would.

Like a distant beacon off the coast of a full-scale panic attack, my music called to me. I heaved the window open, let the squall flap the curtains, and blew a kiss to the wispy figure. Pinning the Blast Mahoney button to my shirt, I settled down to play.

On some deep level, I needed the music. The more certain I became that Sam was dead, the more I needed to hold onto his memory in any way I could. Music was my only solace from the darkness closing in on me, and my only link to him.

Closing my eyes, I began to strum slowly, my fingers tripping clumsily over the cold strings. Tears slid down my cheeks for all I that had lost. For all that I had yet to lose.

I saw Sam's face in my mind—the glossy brown waves, the black fringe of lashes that ringed those stormy grey eyes, his pale, almost porcelain complexion. I always thought Sam looked like winter. I swallowed hard, realizing just how much Vincent made me think of summer.

At first the flat chords twanged hideously. But I played

until the cold dead music began to heat, then flow freely. I belted out "Fragile Forever" at the top of my lungs. I played until the walls rattled and the song came roaring out of me like a gale-force wind. Until my fingers cracked, then bled.

Beneath the numbness was a boiling reservoir of rage, pain, and grief.

I played until I broke through.

Above me on the ceiling, sooty clouds gathered and swirled into a billowing vortex. I sang on, hoping that I could coax them toward me like a snake charmer. Tendrils of darkness dropped and twisted around my throat, the blood chilling in my veins. I kept singing, even as my air supply choked off. But I was fading.

I'd somehow managed to call down my own death.

A flutter of wings crashed through my open window. The shadowy tendrils loosened their grip on my throat and shot toward the intruder. A small object thudded to the floor as the dark clouds dissipated.

Shivering, I poked at the still-warm body of a crow on my carpet and let out a cry.

I'd killed Lila's pet bird, Pluto.

Hit by a sudden wave of exhaustion, I was too tired to contemplate what I'd just done. Instead, I curled up on my bed next to my guitar, clutching the Blast Mahoney button, listening to the faint tinkle of piano keys as I drifted off. Insistent pounding at my door woke me before I had the chance to actually fall asleep.

"Beth! Let me in!"

Groggy, I shuffled to the door in a trancelike fog. Vincent barged into my room, grabbed me by both shoulders, and pinned me to the wall, aqua eyes on fire. "What the hell did you think you were doing?"

"Taking a nap?"

Vincent's lower jaw trembled. "Do you think I'm stupid? Do you think I didn't feel that?"

"Oh. *That.*"

"*That*, as in, you almost killed yourself."

"It was an accident. I didn't know I could do that."

Vincent shook his head and raked a hand through his curls. "You have to get a grip on yourself."

"Why? Who would miss me? Maybe it's for the best."

Vincent slammed me against the wall and hissed through gritted teeth, "You don't get it, do you? Don't you want to know why I knew exactly what you did?"

"Shit," I said, finally understanding. "I almost killed you, too."

"They warned me the link was dangerous. If you kill yourself, Beth, you take me with you." Panting hard, Vincent stepped back as if surprised by his own anger. "Crap. I'm sorry. I just... It was the shock of it. I couldn't breathe. My heart was racing. Everything was going dark. I didn't... Listen. We're in trouble. If we can't get you under control, then—"

It was at that moment Vincent's gaze fell on the dead bird on my floor.

"That's Pluto."

I nodded. "If not for him, I would have killed both of us."

Vincent couldn't seem to tear his gaze from the tiny corpse. "Lila was worried about you. She sent him to check up on you."

"You're not going to tell her I killed her bird, are you?"

Vincent shook his head, gaze still glued to the bird.

"I'll bury him," I said. "I'm the one who killed him."

Vincent leaned over and kissed my cheek, his lips cool and feather-soft. His hand glanced off my shoulder as if my touch could burn. When he dared to look at me again, his features had rearranged themselves into their usual mask of calm. But I wasn't fooled. I'd caught a glimpse of the fear behind it. Vincent was plainly terrified of me. "I won't say anything about this. You have my word," he said, then left.

I crawled back into bed and dreamed about dead birds,

dead boyfriends, and bruised clouds with mouths full of razor-sharp teeth. No one came to disturb my sleep.

When I woke it was quiet and dark. I still wanted to turn my deadly powers on myself. But there was no way I could take beautiful summer-sweet Vincent with me.

I just had to go on living.

24

I WRAPPED THE SMALL BODY IN A SILK SCARF. EVEN though I was its murderer, I owed the bird a decent burial. How I would inter it in the frozen ground was another story.

Though a full moon flooded the woods in silver light, mist hugged the ground in ghostly drifts. The night air had bite. I trudged through the snow, Pluto's cold body like a stone in my pocket, the Blast Mahoney button clutched in my fist. Droplets of blood leaked from the tiny pin wound where the button had pricked my palm the first time. It burned and ached and I wondered if it was infected. In the whistle of the wind, I heard faint piano notes, but I marched stubbornly on in search of a proper burial site.

Disoriented from the hike through the cold persistent fog, I found myself standing at the tree where I'd first seen the crude message that had been carved into its trunk—"Fragile Forever," surrounded by the outline of a heart. I'd forgotten about it in the chaos of everything that had happened since then—but there it was, clear in the bright moonlight. I still had no idea what it implied or who had put it there.

At the base of the tree was a hollow place where less snow had accumulated. With a stick I was able to poke at the frozen dirt and chip out a shallow hole large enough for the dead bird. I placed it in its cold grave, said a brief prayer, and told it

I'd never meant to kill it, then covered it back over with dirt.

Maybe it would be better if I let the KBR take me away and lock me up somewhere before I did any further harm.

My gaze fell on something strange gouged into on the tree trunk right above the hole in the tree's base. Faintly carved into the bark and darkened with what looked like blood was an outlined circle with a solid triangular spike thrust vertically through it from the top. The symbol from Xavier's note.

I still had no idea what the symbol represented and wished I had paid better attention in class or knew more about the history of this bizarre world I was now a part of. But at least finding out would give me something to do besides dwell on my own troubles.

I reentered the building silently and crept up the stairs to my room. I'd gotten pretty good at prowling around the compound and couldn't resist taking a detour past Xavier's room.

No guard stood in the hall. I pressed my ear to the door, then knocked, but there was nothing but silence. Xavier was gone.

I slipped through the darkened halls, afraid of what I'd do if I were cornered like a rat. I was so deep in the swirling cauldron of my thoughts that I plowed right into the person who blocked my way. I looked up into Lila's tear-filled eyes. She'd been pacing the halls in her robe and pink Hello Kitty slipper boots.

"Have you seen Pluto? I-I sent him to check up on you. I was worried."

"N-no," I said. "I've been sleeping. It's the flu."

"Oh." Lila looked me up and down. "You do look awful. But what are you doing up at this hour?"

"I was homesick and bored," I said, truthfully. "I needed to get out of my room and stretch my legs."

Lila tucked a strand of hair behind my ear, her big eyes moist. "We all feel that way at first, Beth. It's not easy living like this. But you'll get used to it."

I wanted to hug her for her kindness, but I didn't deserve it. I'd killed the one thing she loved the most and when she found that out, she would hate me. But I couldn't come out with it and risk an involuntary backlash to her anger.

"Thanks, Lila. I'm beat now. Maybe I'll see you at breakfast tomorrow."

Lila smiled through her tears. The future loss of her friendship blew through me like a cold wind. "*Maybe*? If you're not better in the morning, I'll send Dawn in to work on you no matter what Monica says. Tomorrow night is the Reveal, or have you forgotten?"

My insides pulled into knots. In the swamp of my fears, I had completely forgotten. "No. Okay. But I'm already feeling better. I just need to rest."

Once under my covers I dropped into a dreamless sleep until someone shook me gently awake. Zuber's dark stare pierced through the gray half-light of my room. I wiped the sleep from my eyes and wondered if I was dreaming, because another pair of familiar blue eyes peered back at me. Xavier.

I threw off the covers and bolted upright in my bed. "What the hell?"

Zuber put his fingers to his lips. "Shhh."

It *was* Xavier. Dark hair fell over the scarred half of his face. He was even paler and thinner than before. The cocky half-smile was long gone, the vivid blue eye now clouded by a haunted look. He looked half-dead. But the KBR assassins hadn't gotten to him, at least.

"Where have you been? What's going on?"

Xavier pointed to his throat.

"He can't speak," Zuber said.

Xavier lowered his head and coughed into a tissue. Flecks of red peppered the white.

"Monica did this to him," Zuber said. "She's been exploiting Talent for years. If the Guild comes to investigate, it's because of *her*."

"Won't they help stop this?"

"He's an unregulated Volatile. First they'll use him to implicate Monica." Zuber glanced at Xavier. "Then they'll kill him. He's got to leave. There's no way he's getting out of this alive. But despite my protests, he insisted on seeing you one last time."

Xavier nodded and smiled grimly. I shivered as he leaned closer, his lips brushing my cheek and the edge of my mouth.

"Where will you go?" I blurted. "Let me come with you. I don't want to stay here."

Xavier's cobalt eye bore into mine. Wincing, as if it was a great effort, he lifted his black shirt above the waistband of his jeans. Carved into the taut muscles of his abdomen and still beaded with blood was the same symbol he'd scribbled for me on his crude note.

When he started to reach into the pocket of his pants, Zuber was on his feet, shouting. "What the hell are you doing? You'll kill yourself, idiot!"

I'd never heard Zuber raise his voice or move so quickly. He lunged to tackle Xavier, who sidestepped him neatly, and Zuber crashed headlong onto my bed. He rebounded and tried again, but he was no match for the speed and liquid grace Xavier still possessed despite his weakened condition.

The two of them wrestled, Zuber trying to grab whatever it was that Xavier had clenched in his fist, until finally a stinging back-handed smack across the mouth halted Zuber.

Zuber rubbed his swelling lip and watched sullenly as Xavier staggered backward to the wall, his back pressed against it before his legs gave way and he slid down to the floor.

"He never learns," said Zuber. Xavier sat dazed, gasping for breath, blood trickling from the corners of his mouth. "It looks bad, but it will pass," he said. "This time, at least."

"What's wrong with him?"

"Monica's got him under an illegal compulsion so he doesn't break under the Guild's interrogation. He's obviously got a lot of dirt on her. He's trying to fight the hold she has on him, but the effort is killing him. Every bit of truth he gives up, he pays for in blood and suffering. Even if he writes it down. Or carves it into his own skin."

"But what does that symbol mean?" I pressed.

Zuber shrugged. When Xavier's coughing fit had finally subsided, he motioned for me to come closer. Resting in his open palm was a small object, drenched with his blood. I peered closer at the triangular disc.

It was a guitar pick etched with the name of my old band, August Rebellion. Frozen with disbelief, I flipped the pick over. The words I'd inscribed on it the night I'd given it to Sam were still there. *Love you forever.*

And beneath that, scratched in a shaky hand were the words, *There's a way out.*

In an instant I was on my feet, my face inches away from Xavier, fury raging in my veins.

"Where did you get this? *How do you know Sam?*"

Zuber grabbed me by the collar and flung me across the room. "Leave him!" he shouted, crouching protectively near Xavier. "He's told you enough!"

"If you knew Sam, I have to know!" I roared, pulling myself up onto my hands and knees.

Above me the cloud, black on gray, had already begun to gather. My hair stood up by its roots.

"He's told you enough," Zuber said quietly.

The shadows dipped like low-hanging clouds. "I have to know," I sobbed. "Please."

Zuber glared at me. "You have no idea the strength it took for him to give that to you. You'll have to figure the rest out on your own."

Zuber dragged Xavier to his feet and threw one slack arm around his neck. "I sure hope you're worth it," he added, before the two of them walked straight through the exterior wall of my room and out of the compound.

25

TRIED TO CRY MYSELF TO SLEEP, BUT IT WAS NO use—I remained awake, questions rolling through my head like ocean breakers. How on earth could Xavier have the pick I had given to Sam over a year ago?

How could he know him?

Had Sam been *here*?

It made no sense and only fueled my fury.

I craved oblivion. Craved freedom from my surging rage. How easy it would be to let it sink into my skin and put an end to this nightmare.

But there was Vincent. I still couldn't justify sacrificing the life of someone so noble and beautiful—no matter how bad it got.

In the morning, Vincent came to tell me I was expected at breakfast as if nothing had happened at all. As if I hadn't been confined to my room. He was distant and courteous, the mask of placid serenity firmly in place. When he took me by the arm, I could feel our energies collide and war with each other.

He was scared to death of me, and it hurt. But I couldn't really blame him.

Finally, midway through our walk to the dining hall, I

couldn't take the silence. I jumped in front of him to block his way. "I can't stand this, Vincent. Why won't you talk to me? What's going on here?"

Vincent raised an eyebrow. His self-control was remarkable, but I could see the slight twitch in his jaw. "We're going to breakfast. After that, you have practice and I have class. Monica wants you to have some extra training sessions today."

"Cut me some slack, Vincent. You had to *feel* it. The Guild is coming, aren't they?"

Vincent stopped and sighed. "If you mean, *did I sense your inner turmoil last night,* yes, I did. But was I prepared to help you? I'm sorry, Beth, but I have to be careful about intervening when you go off the rails like that. Contrary to popular belief, I do not have a death wish."

"But you don't know why I was upset, do you? Or *do* you? Do you know where Xavier is?"

"No. I don't. And I can't say that I care." Vincent stared back at me, the twitch in his jaw more pronounced. "I truly thought I could help you gain control of yourself. But it may be safer for you to learn on your own. I care about you. But I—I underestimated your strength and I'm not sure I can— I wish it could have been different between us."

"What about our connection?"

Vincent stared at me for another beat, sorrow and regret forcing its way through the cracks in his mask. "Our connection," he said, "will take many months of separation to fade."

He looked away, then, rearranging his beautiful features, stalked ahead of me to the dining hall.

The chatter in the dining hall was like garbage can lids clanging in my ears, loud and unbearable. Zuber bent as if in prayer over his omelet, never once looking up. Demetri delivered lame jokes that fell like stones on his miserable and silent audience. Vincent's seat was empty. A blur of gold curls, he dashed around the hall like an industrious insect, avoiding me like I was a Venus flytrap. Lila pushed her food around, her eyes still puffy and moist. With false gaiety she tried to engage me about my shoes and dress for the Reveal. I wasn't having it and kept my mouth clamped shut as if my jaws had been sewn together. Across the room, Kevin struggled to feed Della in the seat Xavier used to occupy.

I couldn't choke my food down past the bile that rose in my throat. Above us, tendrils of shadow slithered between the chandeliers.

I somehow made it all the way through breakfast. Once it was over, I found Monica waiting for me in the hall, a smug smile pulling on her lips.

"Are you ready to get to work now?" She paused and arched an eyebrow. "Yes. I thought so."

Gideon shuffled toward us up the hall behind Monica. He was dragging one leg slightly as if he favored the other, and his usually glossy auburn waves hung lank and dingy. His shoulders were hunched, the normally vivid blue eyes filmy and dull. Even his oversized ring seemed to lack its usual luster. "May I see you for a moment, Monica?" Gideon asked, trying to draw himself up straighter.

Monica pivoted on her heel. His sickly demeanor must have set her off because she stalked angrily over to him. They argued in urgent whispers, apparently forgetting I was there.

A whiff of dampness, decay, and rot surrounded me. The smell of impending death.

Directly over Gideon's head, a vague whirlpool of shadow had begun to form. I turned abruptly and started to run.

Monica grabbed me by the shoulder and whirled me around to face her. "Not so fast. We have an engagement." Her eyes sparkled, the red lips pulled back in a brittle smile.

Gideon shuffled away down the hall, even more bent and hunched than before.

Whatever disturbing news he'd shared with Monica, she wasn't about to let me in on it. She hustled me roughly down the hall, heels clacking on the marble tiles of the main floor, toward the library wing.

In the dank tunnels of the compound, the acrid scent of death seeped from between the stones, carrying hints and warnings of past crimes. I shuddered and wondered if I could decode their messages, if my new sensitivity to smell was another aspect of my Talent.

After a long trudge through the bowels of the compound, we arrived at the training room. Just like before, a single candelabra glowed in the red-curtained room. Monica gestured for me to sit at the antique table at the room's center.

The sharp scent of violence and danger still clung to my nasal passages. I struggled to breathe evenly and rein in the murderous rage that thundered in my temples.

She'd hurt Xavier. How many countless others had she harmed?

If I killed her here and now, I would bring the Guild's punishment down on myself. And no one would ever know the truth about what she'd been up to.

And I'd become like her.

Monica smiled at me and tapped her red nails on the scarred and pitted table.

"Tell me where he is," she said, her smile turning suddenly venomous.

"What?"

"Don't play sweet and innocent with me, Collins. Xavier. He's gone and I want him back."

"Why's that?" I said, leaning toward her over the table, knowing it would make her flinch. She knew better than anyone just how fragile my control was.

"I may not have the ability to physically harm you, but I

can make you wish I did. We have need of his services here, and their loss could be devastating," she said coolly. But a slight quaver had crept into her voice. Even Monica the Great was frightened of me.

I straightened in my chair. "Even if I knew where he was, why would I tell you? So you can hurt him more than you already have?"

"Why, you ask?" Monica's voice lowered, her eyes flashing. "Because *your* very existence depends on it. Sometimes individuals must suffer for the good of the whole. I never meant Xavier any harm. He is the victim of his own stubbornness."

"You've been using him. How can that be helping him?"

"You would never understand the complicated machinations of our world. You are far too simple. And until you master yourself, the less you know the better. Now tell me," she said, rising to her feet. "*Where is he?*"

A column of flame enclosed me in a ring of fire, the searing heat melting my clothes to my skin. I howled as my flesh blistered until white bone shone under the charred skin.

It isn't real, I told myself between screams. From behind the curtain of flames I could see Monica smiling.

"Where is he?" Her cool voice boomed inside my head. "Everything you feel, dear sweet Vincent feels. Who means more to you—Vincent or Xavier? *Choose!*"

Not real. Not real. Not real.

"I swear! I don't know where he is!" Latching onto an icy reservoir in the pit of my chest, I reached down into it, beyond caring about anything except stopping the agony. Teeth gritted, I directed the cold shadow around me like a shield to block the flames. The illusion faded. I crumpled, completely unscathed, the deep pain sending aftershocks across my traumatized body. Shadows shimmered around me like a beaded curtain.

This time Monica didn't smile or clap. She gaped at me,

her face white, her lips parted in shock. "How did you do that?" she hissed.

I heaved in a breath and the curtain of shadow crystalized and sifted to the floor like sand. "I have no idea."

Monica sat erect and placed both her hands on the table. She spoke with a tremble in her voice. "Your Talent is more potent than I ever imagined. Why would you want to fall under the Guild's control, Beth, when they kill off or stifle every Volatile? With my help you can be invincible."

"I don't want to be invincible," I said. "I just want to be in control of my own mind."

"I can help you to do that," she said, a full smile blooming. "Just tell me where Xavier is."

"I don't know!" I jumped to my feet. Tendrils of darkness sprouted around me, forming a thicket of shivering vines. Monica backed away as the vines branched off and twisted toward her.

"You need me," she said softly. "But until you tell me where Xavier is, you are on your own. Remember, if the Guild marks your Volatile Talent, which I assure you they will, you'll get no protection from me."

She strode toward a thick wooden door, the room's only exit. "Let's see how well you do without me."

She slipped through the door and it slammed abruptly behind her, the sound of it echoing in the curtained chamber like the close of a coffin lid. I rushed for the door as it shimmered and vanished, leaving only a wall of seamless velvet curtain in its place.

26

PULLED BACK THE DRAPES WHERE THERE WAS ONCE a door to find nothing there but stone, as if I was at the bottom of a well. The tapers in the candelabra were burning low. Soon they'd gutter out, plunging me into complete darkness.

Monica had sealed me in my own tomb.

Fury and fear clouded my thinking, the cold reservoir of death sending icy spikes of rage through my veins. My deadly Talent would do me no good down here. I needed to think clearly. I pushed back on my terror, forcing down the lethal waves clamoring to escape from deep inside.

As the last of the candlelight sputtered out, the light resurged, then burst back into full flame, the tapers restored to their original length. Another of Monica's tricks, I figured. Which meant there had to be a door here somewhere.

I closed my eyes and fingered the stone behind the drapes, determined to feel my way past her illusion. When that proved to be of no use, I crawled across the floor in search of a trap door.

I searched until my fingers were numb, holding the line on my growing hysteria.

Then I heard it. A scratching, chittering onslaught— growing closer. An army of white rats burst from under the curtains, a seething squirming mass of teeth and claws. They swarmed around me, piling on, climbing under my shirt, scratching my skin, even plugging my mouth so I couldn't scream.

The rage welled up inside me until it burst like a geyser, filling the room with choking darkness. The army of rats vanished, but the death cloud covered the ceiling, a billowing menace.

The cloud descended, a thunderhead of death. It was getting hard to breathe. I thought of Vincent and wondered where he was as the life got squeezed out of him. And the more outraged I became, the more death oozed from me, killing us both.

No, I vowed. I couldn't let him die like this.

Vincent deserved to live.

And Xavier needed my help.

Monica wanted this. Monica wanted me to suffocate on my own poison.

And I wouldn't let that happen.

I focused hard on drawing the darkness back into myself, but it wasn't working. My limbs were going numb, ice freezing in my veins. My breathing was getting slower, like sucking air through a straw underwater. The closer I got to death, the more death flowed from me.

I lay sprawled on the floor, too numb and weak to care anymore, and whispered my apologies to Vincent, who was most likely dying wherever our still-linked connection had found him.

Through slitted eyes, I watched the blanket of oblivion drop from the ceiling. But instead of thickening, the darkness was somehow thinning, drifting toward the opposite wall.

The curtain parted. Darkness rushed toward the door-shaped cracks in the stone. Pressure built inside me, built inside the room, until finally, the force of the explosion blew a hole through the stone.

I lay, stunned and barely able to move, on the damp floor.

The candles had been snuffed out. Weak light filtered in through the opening from the tunnel beyond.

With barely any breath left in my lungs, I dragged myself toward the opening and out of my intended tomb. In the cool moist air of the tunnel, I could breathe a little easier, and I wondered if Vincent had survived this onslaught.

I was too weak to stand, so instead I crawled through the dark tunnels, finding my way more by touch than by sight.

So many times I wanted to stop and just go to sleep, let death finish the job it had started, but something kept me moving. Maybe it was the hope that if I survived, Vincent would make it through this, too.

Finally, I felt the ground slope upward and recognized the familiar ramp that led to the secret library entrance to the tunnels. I wondered what Monica would do with me once she realized I'd escaped.

I clawed my way up the last leg of the tunnel. At the library entrance, a woman's body sprawled across the dirt floor blocked my way. I rolled the body on its side.

The black hair was unmistakable. Monica.

At my touch, she coughed and looked up at me. In the dimness the rivulet of blood that trickled from her lips looked black. Her eyes were unfocused at first, then widened with shock. Then she began to laugh.

"Amazing," she cried between hacking coughs. "This is perfectly wonderful. I believe you now. My mistake."

Monica staggered to her feet and helped me to stand. She drew my arm around her shoulder to steady me. The two of us limped into the library where Monica eased me onto one of the soft couches, then flopped beside me, breathing hard from the exertion.

"This is so much more than I dared hope for. You are a miracle, Bethany Collins."

I tried to get to my feet to protest, but my arms and legs were made of lead. Instead I closed my eyes and said. "What are you talking about? You tried to kill me."

Monica laughed. "It was a test. And you passed. You passed with flying colors. Obviously you have no idea where Xavier is."

"Your test nearly did both of us in."

"It was worth the risk. And better than the alternative."

"You should have let me die."

"That would have been a complete waste of your Talent. And if I let you go on the way you have been, the Guild will be at our doorstep. They regulate all Talent, and they worry about such potent weapons falling into the wrong hands."

"What are you saying?" I muttered through gritted teeth.

"What I'm saying, Beth, is that, at least according to the Guild doctrines, *I* am the wrong hands. So what will it be? Take your chances that they'll try to train you to be one of their KBR assassins and eradicate you when they find they have no idea how to control you? Maybe they won't bother and will kill you on the spot. Or let me continue to train you how to channel and control your deadly Talent."

I opened my eyes to find Monica's face inches away from mine, lips parted to reveal white teeth filmed with blood. She laughed, tears streaming from her eyes. "The Guild doesn't want to hear about my experiments with Volatiles. Their answer has always been to Recall and Eliminate. Now they will be sorry."

"Why do you want Xavier so badly?" I muttered. I didn't want to stay and discuss politics with Monica. I just wanted to go and check in on Vincent to see if he'd survived my attack. But if I stood, I'd only fall over again, so there was no point in trying.

"I've been working on this project a very long time," Monica said gleefully. "Though you are another important part of my plan, Xavier is the key."

I would have pressed her about what her plan was and why

Xavier and I were such an important part of it, but at that moment Andre came barging through the library doors.

"Beth! There you are! Vincent is in the infirmary. He collapsed in the middle of English class. He's asking for you."

As much as I wanted to, I couldn't stand. I was still too weak.

"He's slipping, Beth," Andre urged. "The nurses don't know what to do for him. Even Dawn's tried to heal him, but it's not working."

I swallowed hard, my mouth dry. I closed my eyes, willing myself to get up. If Vincent died, it was because of me.

Monica stood, her strength apparently restored. "Thank you, Andre. I'm afraid Beth will require your able assistance herself. She's taken a fall during our training and is a bit woozy."

Andre helped me to my feet, his touch softening my worries over Vincent. But my legs buckled underneath me. Andre caught me before I went down, and heaved me over his shoulder like a sack of flour.

Monica strolled toward me and whispered in my ear. "Make sure you take care of our poor sainted Vincent. He's not nearly as strong as you. And do keep an eye out for Xavier. I'm sure he'll surface eventually."

Halfway to the infirmary I insisted on being set down. My legs were already stronger and, with Andre's support, we walked through the metal double doors into a bright fluorescent space where nurses in scrubs scurried back and forth.

We encountered Gideon on his way out, looking decidedly healthier than when I'd seen him last. Turning his oversized ring in an almost compulsive manner, he greeted us heartily. The shine was back in his hair and the spring back in his step, though his eyes still looked weary. The smear of shadow that had hovered above him before was gone.

"Ah, Beth. It's good you came quickly. He's been asking for you. But you shouldn't feel responsible. He volunteered for this. He's a natural-born risk taker."

A nurse led Andre and me into a room where the lights had been dimmed. There were rows of beds, but only one was occupied. My throat tightened. The last time I'd been in a hospital had been to see my newly disabled brother. That had been my fault.

And now I'd nearly killed Vincent.

I closed my eyes and let Andre lead me to the bedside, dreading what I might find there, dreading the sight of a death shadow hovering hungrily above him.

Vincent's gold curls fanned out on the pillow. Even in the dim light I could see that his tawny skin had gone ashen, his lips almost blue. His closed eyes were sunken, the dark lashes damp with the sweat that beaded his forehead. A nurse came by and wiped down his brow, then took his blood pressure.

Andre touched me softly on the arm. I found the strength to step closer to the bed to witness the damage I had wrought.

"Vincent," I whispered.

The dark lashes fluttered. His chest rose and fell in quick breaths. "Beth. You're okay. I thought maybe this time…"

I took his hand and squeezed. "I almost killed you and you're worried about me?"

Vincent smiled, his eyes still closed. "Monica warned me not to get involved with you. Not with my medical history."

"What medical history? What are you talking about?"

Vincent smiled. His eyes snapped open, still their same vivid electric aqua. "It's a congenital heart defect. Don't worry. There's this stuff they shoot me up with to get it beating like it should. They've sent someone to a local hospital to get an emergency dose. I'll be fine."

I lifted his hand to my lips. "Yeah. You'll be fine. As long as I don't kill you next time."

After I left Vincent, Andre escorted me back to my room, his touch working its magic. With each step I felt better and stronger and more resolved to master my Talent.

I had to, for Vincent's sake. No wonder I terrified him.

When I opened the door to my room, Andre at my elbow, I found Lila rooting around in my closet. "Oh thank heavens. How is he?"

I must have frowned at her, because Lila laughed, the delicious tinkling sound of it soothing my frayed nerves. "The Reveal is in three hours, or did you forget? Vincent will never forgive you if you miss this on account of him."

Andre shrugged and eased backward toward the door. "Girl stuff. That's when I take my leave."

"So, you're okay?" Lila asked, studying me carefully. I let her concern lap over me like warm waves. Maybe she'd never find out about the bird.

"What about you?" I asked.

She smiled sadly. "I miss Pluto. But he's a bird. The scare with Vincent put things in perspective. My friends are more important. And in our crazy world, they tend to drop like flies."

She pulled me into a hug, then held me at arm's length. "No more moping. No way I'm going to ruin the biggest night of your life. Now what on earth are we going to do with that hair?"

We laughed, the worry and strain peeling away. I wasn't

sure if I was still riding high on Andre's magic touch or not, but I was determined to cling to every delicious feel-good drop.

"It's time to turn you into a zombie rock goddess."

It took about an hour for Lila to transform both of us into rock and roll zombies—deadly pallor, torn clothes, and all. As we giggled and admired her artistry in the full-length mirror, we were interrupted by a jaunty knock on the door. It swung open, and Vincent, looking only a little pale beneath his golden mop, stood in the doorway applauding.

"Holy crap!" I ran into his arms. "That was one fast recovery."

"Miracle drugs and the remarkable Dawn saved the day and regulated my heartbeat. Unfortunately, she's a little under the weather and will be missing your Reveal. But she's not much for parties anyway. I, on the other hand, would not miss this for the world. And I already have the costume, since I've recently returned from the dead."

He smiled down at me, and I raked him with my gaze. There was no trace of a shadowy cloud anywhere. "Please don't joke about that, okay?"

"Amen to that, Saint Vincent! Glad to see you're still walking among us." Lila rushed up and gave him a quick kiss, then ducked into the bathroom, leaving us momentarily alone.

Vincent's smile faded rapidly, replaced by something far more intense. But there was no trace of fear. His velvet voice resonated in the hollow of my chest. "I am fine. I am used to these types of attacks. I have had them my whole life. But this one was worth it. I learned something about our connection today. Something I hope I never have to use."

"I don't understand."

Vincent lowered his head and drew closer. He kissed me tenderly on the lips, the energy fizzing into me through his touch, skittering under my skin and raising shivers up my neck. I gasped, the heat rushing to my cheeks.

"I was going about things totally the wrong way, *cherie*," he whispered. "I just needed to let go of my fear. To let you be you."

Lila emerged from the bathroom just as Vincent took a step back, the smile still flickering across his lips. Confusion and desire warred inside of me. I couldn't deny how much our link made me want him more than ever. But I feared for him. He looked to be the picture of health, but he was fragile. Breakable goods. And if anything happened to him, I couldn't live with myself.

Lila stalked up to Vincent and poked a finger at his chest. "You'd better let that ticker of yours get some rest before it cuts out on you for good. If you die, we'll kill you, ya hear?"

Vincent chuckled, but his glance seared into me as he backed toward the door. A small hope ignited within the cold place inside me. Maybe with his help, I could learn to master and control my dark Talent and still make a life for myself. And maybe there was a place for Vincent in that life.

"Later, ladies," he said with a wink. "You will knock them dead, zombie princess."

27

INALLY, MY COSTUME WAS READY. I GAZED AT myself in the mirror, astounded at the radical transformation. My skin was translucent and glowed a silvery blue; my hair was a shock of fluorescent turquoise with shimmering lapis streaks. The blood that dribbled from my zombie mouth was neon pink. Lila wore a slashed deep purple gown, orange "blood" soaking through. She sported five-inch silver fingernails that threw off trails of iridescent light.

"How the hell did you do this?"

Lila shrugged. "I'm just that good, I guess."

From under my bed, someone cleared their throat. "Okay," Lila said, "Caught in the act. C'mon out."

A willowy blonde with exotic eye makeup and half her face made up like a lizard stood in front of me, hands on bony hips. "Heya. I'm Pam, but call me Psyche. You can thank me for the finishing touches."

"It was my vision," Lila huffed.

"Of course." Psyche waved a hand and the lizard scales on her face became alarmingly real. A forked tongue flicked from her mouth as she turned and exited my room.

Lila shook her head. "Help these days. Wait until you see the decorations. Psyche's sister Violet is great with inanimate objects. And much less of a diva."

I rolled my eyes and laughed. "Takes one to know one."

When we were finally ready, we left my room arm in arm. Heading towards us from the opposite end of the hall was Vincent, dressed simply in a white collared shirt and jeans. The sickly pallor was gone. His skin glowed with radiant health, and his brilliant eyes lit up even brighter at the sight of us.

"Wow. Amazing. You've really outdone yourself, Lila. Now step aside, please. I'm the escort for the evening."

Vincent wedged himself between us and gave the royal nod to Lila.

She arched a brow, then stepped out of the way. "Pushy. So much for those courtly Euro-manners. What are you supposed to be, anyway?"

Vincent chuckled. "Her next victim."

Others had already started to gather in the main lobby. In their ripped clothing and garish make-up, only a few scattered partygoers really came close to Lila's and my level of outlandishness. Demetri Prishkin glided through the crowds to greet us. He was done up in jet-black armor, his white hair threaded with metallic copper. His eyes glowed ruby red. Psyche's mark was on him, clearly a favor from Lila. Demetri flashed a haughty smile, took Lila by the arm, and spirited her away. I smiled, happy for her that he'd finally taken notice, at least for this night, and vowed to break his fingers if he broke her heart.

Vincent nuzzled my cheek. "You smell good, too."

I stared into his eyes, unable to fathom how someone who had nearly died of heart failure in the afternoon could look so incredible that night.

At that moment, Monica waltzed up to us, a slightly

uneasy-looking Gideon on her arm. Her costume was subdued but magnificent. With pomegranate red lips and a demure bloodstain on her white satin gown, her black hair hanging loose and long, she was a study in red, white, and black. "Ah, young love. Isn't it wonderful? Lila did quite a job on your costume, Beth."

I forced a polite smile. "Thanks. You look great yourself."

She nodded her head regally as if that was a given and gestured toward the closed doors of the dining hall. "Wait until you see what we've done with the decorations. I wanted this night to be perfect, so I pitched in a little, didn't I, Vincent?" Monica stared pointedly at Vincent, who looked away.

Gideon cleared his throat and nervously twisted his gaudy ring. "You are a remarkable woman," he interjected with a quick smile.

Vincent squeezed my arm and warm reassurance coursed through me, emboldening me. "Well, thanks for helping out," I said breezily.

"I hope you appreciate the flawless quality of my work, Beth. I did it just for you."

I caught a glimpse of Vincent at the precise moment his gaze went fuzzy and distant. On his next step, he tripped and nearly fell.

"What did you do to him?"

"Please, Beth," Vincent said, holding on to my arm a bit too tightly. "No one did anything to me. I'm perfectly fine."

I caught Gideon's guarded expression. Monica's lips curled up in a cat smile, eyes glittering. "I'm very good at what I do. Very good. Now don't overdo it tonight, Vincent. Tomorrow you're back on bed rest."

Horrified, I glared at him. "Liar. You said you were fine."

Vincent shrugged. "I am at the moment. Monica's glamours go beyond skin deep."

I was about to chew him out for being a complete idiot for

playing fast and loose with his shaky health when Lila grabbed me and dragged me toward the double doors that had been flung open to admit the guests.

The dining hall was set up like an underground nightclub. Flashing colored lights strobed as zombie waiters wove around the room serving trays of snacks fashioned to look like body parts—sushi that looked like severed ears, finger cookies, cheese and olive eyeballs, cupcakes frosted to look like bloody brains. The walls shimmered with falling water backlit by blue, green, and pink lights that matched my costume.

At the far side of the room, a raised stage was set up with a full array of instruments. Andre had already taken his place behind the drums. A kid I didn't know practiced low booming scales on the bass guitar. My electric guitar gleamed on a stand beside my amp.

I sucked in a breath, pleased and relieved that there was no piano. I didn't need any reminders of Sam to pop my tiny little bubble of happiness.

Propped up next to a stool was a violin case. I whirled on Vincent. "You're kidding. Are you really up for playing in your condition?"

Vincent leaned in to tickle my ear with his nose. "Of course, yes. As I have said repeatedly, I am perfectly fine. You very much wanted to hear me play, *ma cherie*. This is my Reveal gift to you."

Vincent's lips pressed to my ear raised goose bumps on the back of my neck. From the corner of my eye, I spotted Monica motioning for me. I cringed, apologetically broke away from Vincent, and trudged over to her. This was not a good time to defy her.

"This is a Reveal, as you may recall. It's the night where you share your special Talent. And with my help, everyone here tonight will believe you to be a Chameleon, someone who can disappear into their surroundings."

"Got it." Suddenly exhausted, I was wilting in the heat of

her opal stare. My head pounded. Vincent had leapt onto the stage to tune his violin and I rushed over to join him.

The opportunity to perform with Vincent for this jazzed-up crowd of freaks was making me more insanely happy than I had any right to be. The acoustics in the dining hall were exceptional, thanks to its high ceilings. The audience fell silent as our first chords rang through the space.

We started off a little shaky. But Andre and I were a finely tuned machine, intuitively used to playing together. Vincent, with his supple bowing, was nimbly able to follow our lead. The bass player jumped right in. We launched into a few classics from Blast Mahoney, eventually meandering into some crazy improvisation.

Any worries I'd had about Vincent's well-being were obliterated by his virtuoso violin chops. Perspiration flew from him as he slashed maniacally away at the strings. His bow unleashed a torrent of furious notes that danced and leapt around the scream of my electric guitar. Andre's drumming boomed like rolling thunder, while the new player's bass line anchored us with its deep thrumming undercurrent.

Our impromptu band didn't have a name, but we were epic.

Wild energy sizzled between Vincent and me as we played. At times when he seemed to be fading, he rebounded, drawing strength from the music and the heat of the frenzied crowd.

We played for forty-five minutes straight, with the audience jumping and yelling the entire time. It was wilder than the wildest band slam I'd ever been at. Drunk on the excitement, I might have played all night had Monica not shut us down.

She strolled casually onto the stage and simply cut our amps. The crowd booed, but when she announced that it was time for my Reveal, they applauded and stomped the floor so hard the stage shook.

The lights dimmed. A single white spotlight trailed Monica as she exited the stage and cut through the crowd, which parted to let her pass. A circle opened for her in the center of the floor. Zombie waiters emerged from the perimeters to flank her in a protective ring. I tensed. If she'd gone to the trouble to costume her goons, Monica must have been expecting trouble.

Another spotlight swept down from the ceiling and caught me in its glare. Monica's voice drawled in my ears, weirdly projected as if she stood right beside me.

"Won't you come down and join me in the circle, Beth?"

I glanced at Vincent. He nodded and smiled, but something bittersweet in his expression made my breath catch. He didn't even reach out to touch me.

I stood as tall as I could manage and made my way off the stage. The crowd gave way for me. When I reached Monica, it was hard to see beyond the brilliant light that enclosed us. All I could see in the spotlight's glare was Monica, smiling back at me, cold and beautiful as a marble statue.

"I bring to you," she called out in her announcement voice, "Bethany and the Talent of..." Monica paused for effect, letting the rapt audience hang on her words. I marveled at what a natural showman she was. "Chameleon!"

The audience erupted in raucous applause, hoots, hollers, and whistles. I looked down at my hands, which now reflected my surroundings as if my skin was covered in tiny, mirrored scales. I'd gone invisible.

When the applause finally died down, the sound of one person clapping slowly lingered on. A man in white robes, his shaven head gleaming like polished stone, stood on the stage, bathed in white light.

"Bravo, Monica." The robed man stepped to the edge of the stage and spoke in a low voice. The sound carried across the hushed hall, every syllable clear and sharp. "You've done an admirable job of executing this spectacular fraud."

The zombie waiters tensed and edged closer. Monica replied in her steady alto. "How nice to see you, Inquisitor Ward. What brings you to our tiny compound in the hinterlands?"

"Allegations," the man said, leaping down from the stage. The crowd made way for the Inquisitor, who strode imperiously toward Monica. "Allegations that you have been dabbling in dark experiments and Volatile Talents. I came to see for myself. Do you deny it?"

"That's utter nonsense, Inquisitor," Monica said, raising her chin. "Surely you aren't falling for the gossip and hearsay that abound in our world. Rival compounds have always tried to make us look bad."

The man stopped a few yards from Monica, hands on hips. Monica's goons leaned in closer. Tension crackled through the hall as the crowd backed up, creating more space around us. "If you believe that the Guild operates on mere gossip and hearsay, you have seriously underestimated us. We have been conducting an investigation for quite some time. The evidence is rather damning."

"You're making a serious mistake, Inquisitor," Monica said calmly.

"Where is Xavier Smith?"

Smith? I hadn't recalled ever hearing Xavier's last name. I trembled in the fraught silence of the hall.

"I have no idea, Inquisitor. I thought perhaps he had finally got his due."

"Perhaps you tell the truth," said the Inquisitor. "But this is no Chameleon, Miss DeWitt, and the Guild knows it. You are under arrest, and this Volatile is coming with us."

In a blur of motion someone grabbed me from behind and forced me into a chokehold. Stars danced in front of my eyes. I couldn't breathe. Unholy rage, fueled by hissing fear, bubbled inside of me with no place to go.

I writhed wildly to get free from my captor. People were on the move, stampeding for the exits. But I was stuck.

Black-garbed assassins dropped from the ceiling on ropes. The mirror scales vanished, leaving me visible and exposed.

"Get her!" the bald man cried, pointing at Monica, who was furiously pushing her way through the crowd. Then, on cue, every person in the dining hall became a perfect replica of Monica.

Monica look-alikes shouted and shoved in a desperate panic to flee the hall. In the chaos, there was no way to know which Monica was the right one. I wasn't even sure if I looked like her or myself.

A billowing mass of black smoke cloaked the ceiling. If I didn't gain control, everyone in the room would die.

I struggled uselessly, still locked in the chokehold. An assassin dropped to the floor in front of me. He pointed a strange weapon at me, a short glass rod that glowed with crackling forks of blue-white light. Deep within the shadows of his hood, I could see him sneer. He extended the weapon and a jet of white-hot electricity shot out at me.

I closed my eyes, waiting for the blow.

It never came. Something barreled into me, knocking me to the floor. Above my head the streak of electricity jetted past and blasted into the assassin who had had me pinned. People behind him screamed and dove to the ground. The assassin crumpled to the floor, an empty heap of charred and smoking clothes.

"Let's get out of here." The Monica look-alike who'd tackled me helped me to my feet. The voice was unmistakable. Zuber.

The crowd of panicked Monicas pushed and jostled like spooked cattle, trampling anyone who'd fallen underfoot. I craned my neck for a glimpse of where I'd last seen Vincent, just as one of the Guild assassins swung onto the stage. He kicked at a body that was sprawled there. Though the body looked like Monica as well, I screamed. I began to push toward the stage, bitter rage howling inside me.

Zuber tugged me in the opposite direction, dragging my feet along the floor. We passed through the crush of bodies as if they had no more substance than mist. My surroundings had become a blur, the screams lowered to a muted warble.

"Vincent!" I continued to yell and fight until finally Zuber threw me over his shoulder.

I couldn't contain it any longer. The grief, fear, and outrage exploded from me in a concussive blast, blotting out all remaining sound and vision.

28

CAME TO MY SENSES, SHIVERING WILDLY. I LAY ON A bone-chilling surface in my torn costume. It was pitch-dark, and I was so numb with cold that I couldn't feel my fingers or feet. Someone had thrown a down coat over me, but it did little to keep out the frigid air. My head throbbed when I tried to sit. When my eyes adjusted, they were drawn to a dim sliver of light rippling on black water.

"Zuber? You there?" I called weakly.

Footsteps echoed in the dark space and grew closer. "Good morning."

"It's morning? Where the hell are we?"

"This is an underground cavern that I stumbled upon once, totally by accident. I know it's uncomfortable, but I had no choice."

When I tried to sit up, my head clanged with pain. "What about Vincent? I need to get back and make sure he's all right."

Zuber crouched beside me. A match flared, illuminating his face. Gray zombie makeup still clung to his dark skin, mingling with what looked to be actual blood. "You can't go back to the compound, Beth. Not ever. It was hard enough to

get

you

out. I brought you here to contain your—um—outburst."

I groaned and rolled over onto my side, facing away from him, the breath huffing out of me in clouds of mist. The frigid cold bit down to my bones. "Please tell me I didn't kill anyone."

Zuber lit another match, the brief glare illuminating the low-hanging ceiling of the small cavern. It would make a great tomb, I thought.

"I'm alive, aren't I?" Zuber asked, exasperation creeping into his voice. "I jumped through the floor when you started to go off and kept tunneling deeper. The rock must have absorbed the bulk of the explosion. I managed to get us here, to my handy little hideout."

"Thank you for saving me," I said, meaning it, though part of me wished he'd let that bolt of white light kill me.

"No problem." Zuber dropped a pile of clothes in front of me. I recognized my own boots and jeans, and someone's flannel shirt.

I rolled back over to face him. He'd made a little fire for us from some wood he must have gathered beforehand. "How did you get all this stuff?"

"I stole these for you from your room beforehand, since I figured you'd be in some skimpy Reveal get-up. I grabbed the wood and kindling from the lounge fireplace. I'd planned to spirit you out after the Reveal."

"You'd make a hell of a jewel thief."

Zuber poked at the little fire. "How do you think the Guild found me in the first place? Back in Baltimore, I used to help out my mama when we were low on cash. I'd walk into supermarkets after hours and help myself to some groceries. I guess word got back to them the third time I walked straight out of juvenile detention. Nothing could hold me. But I've gone clean. Now I steal only for the greater good."

"You're classified as a Volatile, aren't you?"

Zuber nodded. "Marginally. I'm only a Level 6. It's my association with Xavier that put me on their Most Wanted list. I wasn't even on the Guild's radar before that. Guess since my Talent is kind of rare, they hadn't considered how dangerous a guy who could walk through anything could be."

Zuber's profile was a dark silhouette against the flickering light. Suddenly, I felt claustrophobic. The thought that Zuber could entomb someone at a whim, miles beneath the earth, made me shudder. But what did the Guild fear about Xavier? How dangerous could a beautiful voice be?

My insides were hollowed out. I'd grown used to the compound and the friends I'd made there. If I were to be honest with myself, Vincent's weak heart could never have withstood my explosion. I'd killed him. If this cave became my tomb, I'd be just fine with that. A sob burst out of me. "It's not fair. Vincent was trying to help me. And look where it got him."

"No one could have stopped Vincent from helping you. It's the way he's made."

"What if he's alive? How can I just leave him?"

Zuber put a hand on my arm. "You have to, Beth. If he is, he'll understand. If not, it won't matter, will it?"

I brushed away tears with the back of my hand. "Everything and everyone I love dies, Zuber. How do I live with that?"

Zuber brought his face close to mine. "Would you rather Vincent's sacrifice be for nothing? Terrible things have been going on within the Guild, Beth. I don't know about Vincent, but Xavier has been trying to do something about it."

The shock of that name startled me out of my despondence. "What can he do?"

"You don't understand Xavier or his struggles. There's much more to this than you can imagine."

"So where the hell is he? How can he still be alive in the shape he was in?"

"He is. And he's waiting for you."

"Where?"

Zuber helped me to my feet. "It's a long story. It's time we get a move on."

After I changed behind a rise of jagged rock, Zuber took me by the arm. Our surroundings liquefied as we passed through rock and dirt, then surfaced. The moonlit woods surrounded us, cold and mist-shrouded. In the distance, the light of the compound glowed golden through the haze.

"We haven't gone very far."

"Bear with me. I'm looking for something."

We trudged through the freezing woods, the unrelenting fog clinging to our shins, obscuring the ground. It was like wading through liquid cotton.

"There," Zuber said, pointing to a low ridge that jutted from the mist. "That's the outer boundary of the compound. I've come in and out through here before."

I tried to peer over the wall, which was shorter than I was, but only caught a glimpse of gray nothingness.

Zuber felt carefully along the wall, then turned to me, his face grave. "The Guild has wards in place around all around the compounds. Kind of like a bubble of protection and camouflage from outsiders. They've neglected them for so long they've grown porous in places. Xavier and I used to slip in and out of this one and a few others. The bad news is that this one has been patched up. If all the other passages are closed like this one is, we're stuck."

"That's not cool." We'd spent a few minutes searching in vain when I remembered the carved tree and the scribbled symbol of a wedge through a circle that Xavier had given me at great cost to himself. I pulled it out and studied it. "This symbol. What does it mean? I found it carved into a tree."

Zuber sighed. "Maybe the tree is a marker. There was so much Xavier tried to tell me, but couldn't. I'm piecing things together just like you are."

Along with the note, I still had the Blast Mahoney button and the guitar pick in my coat pocket. I'd decided that keeping them there was the safest thing in case I'd ever had to make a quick getaway.

I clutched the cold disc of the button in my fist and the inflamed pinprick on my palm began to burn. "If we can find the tree with the carving, it might offer some clue I overlooked, since at the time I didn't know I'd be needing a clue."

"Maybe," Zuber said. "But we should check the rest of my usual spots first."

After we'd walked a good distance, checking on all of the exit points, Zuber was forced to conclude that, like the first one, they'd all been sealed up tight.

"They must have shored up all the holes right before the assault. If we try to slip through, they'll know exactly where we are," he said wearily.

"So we're trapped."

"We can hide out underground for a while. They can't occupy the compound forever. With luck, they'll conclude you died in the assault and leave."

"Wait. What if that carved tree points the way to another exit? Maybe Xavier wanted me to know that."

"Maybe," Zuber said, distracted. He sat on the stump of a tree and gazed into the distance, silent as an Easter Island statue head.

"Don't people come and go all the time?" I paced back and forth. "I know Monica and Vincent did. There's got to be a VIP gateway. Andre is always going home to deal with his sick father. Maybe the tree points to the official gateway into the compound. You don't think Monica climbs over walls, do you?"

"Even so," Zuber said sourly, "they'll have that entrance heavily guarded. It's probably the one they broke down to enter the compound."

I tapped my teeth with a finger. "I'm sure Andre can help us. We just have to let him know somehow."

"They'll be detaining everyone for questioning. They won't let him leave, no matter what. What good is he to us anyway?"

"You don't know Andre like I do. If there's a way, Andre will find it. He can say his dad is sick and he has to leave. He'll convince them with his touch. His Talent is much more Volatile than they realize. Then he can let us out."

Zuber clucked. "If you say so. Maybe Pretty Boy can make the Guild assassins feel so good they won't be in the mood to kill us."

"Never underestimate Andre. I'm sure he's looking for me right now... What was that good news you'd mentioned before?"

"Oh, good news. There's a little bit of that. For one thing, there's enough food stocked away in the cave to last a week, so if we do get stuck hiding out here, we won't starve as quickly."

I heaved in a sigh. "Not to be unappreciative of your heroics, Zuber, but this doesn't sound like you and Xavier had a very well thought-out escape plan."

Zuber shrugged. "Give me a little credit. I had to think fast with Xavier gone mute and deathly ill. He couldn't help me at all. I figured your Reveal would be the best time to bust you out. I didn't count on this full frontal Guild assault."

"Where exactly is Xavier, and how'd you get him out of here?"

"We travelled inside a cargo container by rail to his hometown. Xavier figured it would be the best place to wait for you."

I snorted. "Xavier's hometown. Where's that? Mars, or

Jupiter? And why would I want to go there?"

"It's about two hours south of here in Connecticut. Xavier thought you might want to join him there, since it's the same town you're from."

Zuber's words were like a hot poker stabbed straight into my gut. "Xavier's from Linford?"

Puzzle pieces were snapping into place. The strange connection to Sam, the intense interest in me from the start. Still, I didn't remember anyone named Xavier Smith and Xavier was not a person you could easily forget. Not all the puzzle pieces fit.

"It's been hard to get information out of him lately."

We walked through the misty woods, debating furiously. I wanted Zuber to take me back into the compound so I could check in on Vincent and tip off Andre. But he insisted it wasn't worth the risk. I seethed with anger, but somehow managed to keep my rage at bay. Maybe I'd depleted my stock of death rays. Either way, we were at an impasse. I couldn't sneak in without his help. And Zuber wasn't about to budge.

Abruptly, my palm started to burn more intensely. Before us, unmistakable in a swath of moonlight, was the carved tree, Pluto's final resting place.

I crouched to study the carving, placed strategically where the foggy ground cover ended. We peered at it in the scant moonlight.

"This one is different from Xavier's. Look." I pulled out the crinkled note. Xavier's hastily drawn sketch pointed straight downward. The one carved into the tree pointed slightly to the right.

Zuber and I exchanged glances before darting to an adjacent tree. After a bit of scrambling, we located another faint symbol carved into a trunk, tilted slightly higher. That symbol led to another, and another. Someone had been very busy carving these symbols. The more we located, the more the pinprick on my palm burned. I imagined I heard the tinkle of piano notes wrapped inside the wind. I thought of Sam and my throat tightened with a painful lump.

Could Sam really have *been here*? I'd never thought to ask Zuber directly. "Was Sam Bernstein ever a student at High Step? He was a piano player."

Zuber stopped in his tracks, gaped at me, and scratched his head. "You mean your old boyfriend? The kid that disappeared? Not that I know of."

"You looked at me funny for a minute, Zuber. You're not keeping anything from me, are you?"

Zuber squinted, his brow furrowed. "No, of course not! But it was weird. For a minute my brain kind of jittered, like someone shook it. Then, nothing. Just a blank."

"But you swear. You don't know anyone named Sam?"

Zuber slanted his head. "I can't swear I don't know *anyone* named Sam, but no piano-playing Sam Bernstein. I'm sure of that."

The lump in my throat hardened. I was certain Zuber wasn't lying, but I still couldn't shake the strong sense that Sam had been here. If only Xavier was able to spit out the truth locked inside him without it killing him.

After a series of ten trees carved with symbols, the woods seemed to end abruptly in a wall of fog.

"What the hell?"

"This way," Zuber said confidently, like a hound on the trail. I followed him into the mist…and came out on the other side. The mist evaporated to reveal a dirt road that led to a wrought-iron gate set in a high brick wall. Beyond the gate, a star-studded sky glowed a deep radiant indigo.

"That's it!" I rushed down the road toward the gate. "The entrance to the compound!"

"Don't, Beth!"

I stopped a few yards short, the pinprick on my palm blazing with so much pain, I almost keeled over. Zuber caught up to me, breathless. "It's booby-trapped. You didn't think they'd let us just walk out of here, did you?"

I glared at the gate that taunted me with its empty promise of freedom.

"We should go back to the cave," Zuber said. "It's only dumb luck some patrol hasn't caught up with us."

I hung my head and nodded, the thought of that cold dark hole filling me with dread. I shivered and turned to leave when a rumble, followed by the low beam of car headlights, approached from behind us on the dirt road.

"Shit," Zuber hissed and pulled me behind a broad tree trunk. We were about to burrow into the earth when a car door slammed and someone called out, "Wait!"

I twisted free of Zuber's hold and found myself buried up to my waist in the ground. Zuber blasted out of the earth like an angry geyser. "Why the hell did you do that? If I lose you underground, you'll suffocate before I can get back to you!"

He yanked me roughly out of the dirt and shoved us through the trunk of a massive tree. We stood listening on the other side of it, blocked from the view of the passing van. "Are you completely insane, Beth? Let's try that again. This time *hold on*."

I yanked my arm from his grip. "It wouldn't hurt to wait just another minute. It could be help."

Footsteps crunched back and forth. A figure, silhouetted by the headlight's bright beam, cast an elongated shadow on the dirt road. Zuber pulled me low to the ground.

"Beth? Is that you?" I let out my breath at the sound of that familiar voice.

"Andre!" Without hesitation I raced toward Andre and jumped into his muscular arms. "How did you know where to find us?"

Andre smiled and brushed the tangle of hair from my face. "They said you were dead. That you blew yourself up. I didn't want to believe it. With Zuber gone, too, I thought there was a slim chance he'd have slipped in and tried to whisk you out of the compound. But I knew it was blocked. I begged a guard into letting me go, claiming a medical emergency at home." Andre flashed me a lopsided smile. "It worked, as usual, and here I am. Your knight in shining armor."

He pulled me to his chest and I rested my head there, listening to the calming rhythm of his breathing. There was a tentative crunch of footsteps on cold dirt as another, slighter figure stepped from the glare of the headlights.

"I brought Dawn. Just in case anyone needs healing," Andre said.

Then he looked me straight in the eye and said, "I think it's about time I brought you home, Beth."

29

I HELD MY BREATH AS THE MASSIVE GATES SWUNG open, then closed behind us. The dirt road continued, then emptied onto a deserted country lane that wound through the night forest. There was no trace of the lingering mist that coated the compound's grounds, no evidence that the compound existed at all. There was just endless road and woods.

Illuminated by the headlight's beams, a sign indicated that we were 35 miles west of Springfield, and 120 miles to the west of Boston. This was news to me, since I had no recollection whatsoever of entering the compound in the first place.

Dawn and I huddled in the back seat. Dawn, never much company to begin with, fell promptly asleep. Zuber kept stonily silent in the front passenger seat, his puzzling contempt crackling like static electricity. Even Andre's calming effect could only partially defuse it. I didn't understand his mistrust of Andre. Though he could easily slip through the side of the van and onto the road, I doubted he would. He had no other choice than to trust Andre.

Despite my own frayed nerves, eventually the steady drone of the old van's chugging engine, the hum of tires on the road, and Andre's soothing vibe worked away my tension. I dozed off and woke as the first streak of vermillion stained the sky over Linford.

My stomach lurched at the sight of my hometown. The silhouettes of low buildings, blue-gray hulks against the backdrop of the lurid morning sky, reminded me that the girl I'd been here was lost forever. This was just to be a brief pit-stop to check in on Xavier before I went home to see my family.

"Did you know Xavier from home, Andre?" I blurted.

Eyes fixed on the road, Andre answered softly. "He's older than us. He came to the compound pretty young. We never met until I first went there."

We fell back into silence, the bare trees and frame houses drifting by in a pastel blur. People slept peacefully inside those homes, unaware of the terrors that lived outside their comfortable reality. Terrors like me.

"Do you think Xavier knew Sam from somewhere else? Some band thing? Because…" My voice choked off. Sam had been Linford's golden boy. Torn remnants of the missing posters that had cropped up all over town were still plastered to telephone poles. I swallowed hard and continued. "Because Xavier had something of his."

"Did he really?" Andre pulled the car into the empty parking lot of a familiar strip mall. Snippets of my former life bombarded me: Mom and me purchasing my sixth-grade graduation shoes at Adler's Shoe Emporium, stopping with my dad at the Linford Delicatessen. Zuber gazed silently out the car window, stiffly alert.

"I suppose it's possible they met through their music before Xavier went to the compound," Andre said.

"How old was Xavier when he left? Fourteen?"

"Sam was into music his whole life, Beth. It's possible they took a class as kids somewhere, right?"

"I guess. But that means they would have met when Sam was twelve." I slumped lower in the seat, the mystery of Sam's vanishing gnawing at me like a reopened wound. The view outside the car window mocked me, reminding me that I wouldn't find any comfort here in Linford. That I didn't belong here anymore. "It still doesn't make sense."

Andre turned to face me and touched a hand to my knee. "Life doesn't always make sense, Beth." The words were just that, words, but combined with the warmth of Andre's hand on my knee, they lowered the boil of questions in my mind to a gentle simmer.

"True," I said, slumping in the seat, exhaustion washing over me in a heavy wave.

"I can take it from here," Zuber said abruptly. "Take Beth to her mother's house in Finley Lake. Thanks for the ride."

Zuber had already emerged outside the car and began to stalk off. Andre jumped out and followed, his long strides quickly overtaking him, his voice muted through the car window. "This is ridiculous. I didn't take you all this way for you to storm off in a huff."

Zuber whirled on Andre, his normally stoic expression bristling with emotion. "I've got to keep him safe, no matter what. And if that means trusting no one, then that's the way it has to be."

I slipped quietly out of the rear door, straining to listen from a distance away while they argued. Andre's voice dropped low, his body language relaxed and non-threatening. "I brought Dawn to help Xavier. He's seriously ill. If you let him die, how will that be helping him?"

"I can't take the chance," whispered Zuber, the reasonable veneer stripped away to reveal someone who was nearly unhinged. "I don't know who to trust."

"I know you never liked me, Roddy," Andre soothed. "But I didn't come all this way to be your taxi driver. Xavier and I used to be good friends before you came to the compound. Right now he needs all the help he can get."

Zuber flashed me a desperate look. I walked closer, hands in my pockets. "Andre's had my back for as long as I can remember. He took a big risk getting us here."

Zuber turned to Andre. "I hope I don't regret this. If any harm comes to Xavier because of your actions, witting or unwitting, I'm going to make sure you regret it to your last dying breath."

I wasn't sure if Andre did, but I recognized the cold threat in Zuber's voice. I shivered, wondering how many of the people who had crossed him had been buried alive somewhere deep under the ground.

Andre placed a hand on Zuber's shoulder, but he shrugged it off. "I would never hurt Beth or anyone she cares about."

"Save your sweet talk for someone who buys your brand of shit, Serrano. Just get back in the car."

Zuber directed us past the McMansions that lined the coastal road, past the long-deserted factories and down a dead-end street. At the end of the street was the burned-out remnant of the old school building that had once been Linford High. After the modern new building had been completed ten years before, the building had briefly housed a private school before the fire had destroyed it for good.

Zuber got out of the car and cast a glance at Andre, bald contempt in his dark eyes. "He's in there," he said coldly.

Andre woke Dawn and helped her from the car. She stood blinking beside him, wide-eyed and pale, her hair a frizzled cloud of dull red.

I shuddered, unnerved, thinking of how frightening it must be to be holed up, sick and alone, in this charred husk of a building. What if Xavier had already died in there, thinking that no one was ever coming to save him? I closed my eyes and choked off the thoughts of Vincent, who I had probably killed, my sorrow for him mingling with my still-raw grief for

Sam.

I had to save Xavier. And hope that my terrible powers were good for more than just bringing death.

Zuber took me inside first. We walked directly through the sooty brick exterior wall into the rubble-strewn halls. Morning light filtered through the collapsed roof, lighting our way past piles of debris. Creeping down an unblocked staircase into the basement, we felt our way to a set of double doors that led to the old school's auditorium. Thin strips of dusty light cut across the rows of seats. On the dark stage, a single light glowed.

My breath caught. Surrounded by empty snack bags, cans, and water bottles was a battered couch, a theater prop from days gone by. A blanket-wrapped figure was curled into the fetal position on the couch. I cried out, raced down the aisle, and jumped onto the stage, Zuber at my heels.

Death hovered in the space above the still figure, waiting eagerly but still unsatisfied. I pulled back the blanket. Lips cracked and blue, stubble on the sharp planes of his jaw, Xavier was alive. But barely.

30

"**X**AVIER?"

Not even the flicker of an eyelid. Blood streamed from the corners of his mouth, staining the blanket and the couch. I found the pulse in his neck throbbing weakly.

"Get Dawn," I barked at Zuber. "Now!"

It wasn't long before Zuber, followed by Andre and Dawn, came hurtling down the aisle. Dawn crouched beside Xavier, her fingers pressed to his neck.

Andre looked sharply at Zuber, who remained focused on Xavier's still form.

I glanced upward. The billowing darkness had begun to drop. "Hurry. Please."

"I'll do what I can," Dawn whispered shakily.

A faint shadow hovered above Dawn. I bit down hard on my lower lip. Dawn would pay a steep price for healing someone so close to death. "I'm sorry," I said under my breath.

Zuber took me by the arm and pulled me into the shadows. Andre joined us as Dawn began to work on Xavier, her hands gracefully weaving in the air above him like a harpist.

At first Xavier was unresponsive. The dark cloud continued its descent. Finally, his eyelids began to flutter, followed by a slight twitching of his head. He kicked off the blankets and began thrashing his arms and legs violently. His back arched as his body went rigid with convulsive spasms.

I focused on the lowering cloud. It was heavy, like a blanket of lead descending. I pushed at it with all my strength until I thought my chest would explode from the strain. I wondered about Vincent, and if he was still clinging to life, if this would do him in. I wished I could sense him as clearly as he could sense me.

It was like trying to shove an elephant over a cliff, but little by little, the cloud eased higher toward the ceiling. Dawn whimpered as the shockwaves continued to shudder through Xavier.

When it was finally over, Dawn sprawled unconscious on the stage floor. Andre sat cradling her head in his lap, stroking her hair. Drained of strength myself, I crawled over to Xavier just as his eyes snapped open.

"Beth," he said. His eyes skittered unfocused, and his voice was little more than a gruff rasp. "Everything hurts."

Zuber came up beside me. "Take it easy, bro. You're going to be okay."

Xavier smiled and closed his eyes.

I marveled at the improvement. Color had returned to his sunken cheeks. He had his voice back. But Dawn wasn't doing so well. Andre stood and walked over to us.

"She just needs rest and she'll be fine. So do you and so does Xavier. Maybe this is a good time for me to take you to see your family, Beth. If you'd like, that is."

I glanced at Zuber. "Will you be okay alone with them?"

"We'll be fine. I couldn't live with myself if you missed the chance to see your family," Zuber said.

Andre nodded gravely. The implication was clear.

This might be the last time I'd see them.

Andre and I picked our way out of the ruins to his van. It was already noon. The midwinter sun bathed us in light and shadow. Walking to the car arm in arm, we could have been anything or anyone. No one would guess that we were refugees from a secret society of freaks.

The ride to Finley Lake went by too quickly. Now that I was to be reunited with my family, I wanted the drive to last. I wasn't sure what I would say when I barged in on them, or what condition I'd find my brother Carson in.

"You don't have to worry, Beth. Shelly goes to see them a lot. She helps your mom with the shopping and does a little cleaning for her."

"Great. I cut out on her and so she has to rent herself a replacement daughter."

Andre frowned. "She doesn't pay Shelly. Shelly's just good-natured that way."

My hands balled into fists. "Where do they think I've been? Don't they think it's odd I haven't been in contact?"

"Beth," Andre said cautiously. "High Step has its own unique way of dealing with things like this. It's called Plausibility. They plant an idea in the mind of the subject, and whenever a doubt or suspicion arises, it's overridden. I know it sounds awful, but considering the nature of our abilities, it always made sense to me."

"Nothing about High Step or the Talented world makes sense to me. If I could rip my Talent out of myself, I would, and I'd run as fast as I could."

"But you can't, Beth." The muscle in Andre's jaw twitched. There was nothing reassuring in his words. "It's in our DNA. It's who we are."

We pulled into the driveway of Gram's lake house. I hadn't been here since Gram died, but it was clear Andre had. It rankled me that he had been allowed to see my family more than I had. I sat in the car hyperventilating, trying to muster the nerve to go in. It turned out I didn't need to, because Shelly came running out of the house to greet us.

"Beth? Is that Beth? Oh my God!"

She pulled open the car door before I had a chance to react and was all over me, a tangle of hair, perfume, and jangly jewelry.

"Oh my," she said, cocking her head. "You've gone *au naturel*." We'd stopped at a gas station to get me cleaned up, but I knew I was a sight.

"You don't have to say it. I'm a mess. Rough trip."

I noticed Andre touch a hand to her arm and her expression softened, her eyes gone moist. She smiled and leaned in to kiss him, then turned to me. "Your mom and Carson are going to be thrilled. I wish someone would have told us you were coming. I'd have made breakfast!"

Andre hugged Shelly closer and smiled at me, too. And then, for a split second, Andre's beautiful mask of serenity slipped. His eyes went hard, the warmth gone. He reached over to touch me and the chill that had shot up my back departed.

I was home. I might not have remembered being here, but I was going to see my family. That was going to have to be enough for now.

"How is Carson?"

Shelly's smile widened. "He's in great spirits. His crew comes to visit at least once a week and takes him out. He's always got a joke. And, it's amazing, but he's been accepted to Duke for the fall semester."

"Wow," I said. "That *is* amazing." I couldn't imagine how my athletic brother had adjusted so quickly to his new life in a wheelchair.

"It's because of your mom," Andre said. "She wouldn't let him give up. She's relentless."

It wasn't my triumph. In fact, it may have been my absence that allowed Mom to focus without distraction on Carson's rehabilitation.I looked at the ground. I hadn't been there to help. I wondered now just how long I had been gone. On my timeline it seemed like only weeks. I shuddered.

"C'mon! Let's go in!"

I glanced at the elaborate ramp Mom had had constructed and marveled at the speed in which she'd gotten it done. Mom was unstoppable when she put her mind to things, but this was really mind-boggling.

Shelly skipped up the ramp, opened the door, and called inside. In moments, the oval of Mom's face appeared at the door and the emotions I'd been trying to keep down came gushing to the surface.

I raced up the ramp and flung myself into her arms, my face in her hair. I inhaled her perfume, wishing its scent could seep permanently into my skin.

"Oh, Beth," she said. "We've missed you here so much." She pulled back to look at me and stroked my hair. Andre touched her arm and the worry lines softened. "I see you've let all the blue grow out. I like the new look."

I wasn't really sure what the new look was, considering I'd given zero thought to my appearance other than for the Reveal. It was then I realized that in the fuzz and confusion of my time at High Step, I hadn't noticed how long my hair had grown, and that the bright ultramarine tips had faded to a pale powder blue.

"What's today's date?" I blurted.

"March 10th, silly," Shelly laughed.

I swallowed down panic. The last date I remembered was late October. Apparently, I'd been gone for five months. I couldn't make sense of how this was possible. How chunks of time could be totally missing from my memory.

"It's so good to see you," Mom said, ushering me inside. "Carson! You'll never guess who's come to see us!" she called.

I cringed. To them, my absence was normal and unquestioned. When I disappeared forever, would they even notice? I glanced again at Andre, who seemed deep in concentration.

There was a soft whir as Carson rolled into the foyer. His face and hair were the same as ever; glossy sandy-gold hair flopped across a handsome face. Strapped into his chair, Carson's entire body was slack and immobile with the exception of the few fingers he used to control the wheelchair.

"Beth! Excuse me if I don't get up."

The smile was the same, broad and without irony. His eyes twinkled with life. Carson was making the best of things.

Andre touched my arm and the warm feelings coursed through me. Whatever hurt I felt was totally selfish. My mother and brother were doing fine without me. I'd just be in the way.

I leaned in to kiss my brother, felt his warm stubbly cheek scrape against my own. I hugged him hard, though I wasn't sure he felt it.

"I missed you, Carson."

He stared into my eyes with a depth I'd never seen from him. "I know." The intensity disappeared in a glowing smile. "The game's on, guys. Mind if I go back to it? Maybe it's sick, but I still get a thrill out of watching seven-foot dudes run around and try to toss a ball into a hoop." He winked. "Besides, I've got some bets lined up with the guys. Feel free to join me."

Mom shrugged and smiled, her cheeks blooming apple pink. "Carson does watch a lot of TV. But he reads a lot, too. More than he ever did before. I got him an e-book reader. That's how he finished his GED in record time..."

She ushered us into the expansive living room, where her

tasteful design sense was evident in the polished wood floors, cathedral ceiling, and wall of windows overlooking the sunlit lake. I wondered where she'd found the funds for it when she'd claimed we were going broke only months before. In minutes, with Shelly's help, a spread of cheese, crackers, and sparkling cider had been laid out on the coffee table. Mom followed with a piping hot casserole of macaroni and cheese and set it down on a trivet.

The normalcy only added to the anxiety that flamed my insides. Had they been paid off for their compliance? Mom would not knowingly consent to that. This, I concluded, was for me. To allow me to let go so I'd know they were fine.

I shivered. Someone feared my wrath enough to eliminate the possibility of my going postal.

I glanced at Andre, who beamed back at me, and squelched the urge to shudder. As much as I wanted to, I couldn't stay here. I didn't belong anymore.

"I hope the food is decent at school, honey. Bet you miss my famous macaroni and cheese."

"Um, yeah, Mom. It's good," I said, choking down a mouthful. It was as I remembered it, but I seemed to have lost my sense of taste. "And I did."

"The chef at High Step is five star," added Andre with a smile. "No one starves there."

Mom beamed. "That's what I want to hear!"

After a round of meaningless chatter wherein I couldn't really answer Mom's questions with anything approaching truth, I decided to check in on my brother.

In the den, which Mom had managed to transform into a modern track-lighted entertainment center, Carson's wheelchair faced the giant flatscreen TV. He pivoted his chair toward me when I entered.

"Hey, sis. How is school treating you?"

I plopped down on the leather couch and sighed. "Fine. It's all fine."

Carson stared at me a beat. "You may be fooling Mom and Shelly, but you're not fooling me."

A chill tiptoed up my back. "About what?"

"C'mon, Beth. Remember the time in the hospital room? How you fought so hard to keep me alive?" Carson jerked his head to flick the hair from his eyes.

"N–no. I don't know what you mean."

He maneuvered his chair closer. Any trace of a smile was gone. "It's not easy living like this, Beth. At first I did want to die. But I'm only alive because of you."

I wiped away hot tears with the back of my hand. This is what I'd dreaded. What I couldn't face. "I-I'm sorry. This is all my fault. I should have warned you something terrible was about to happen."

He cut me off. "That's a load of bullcrap. Get the remote and hit the mute button, will you? Can't even do that myself, damn it."

I did what he asked and returned to my perch on the couch opposite him, my heart ticking like an old clock in the silence of his penetrating gaze.

"When will you believe me that it's not your fault I'm stuck in this chair?" he asked. "They wanted me dead. You kept me alive."

I struggled to clear my throat. The floor felt insubstantial, like it might give way. "Who wanted you dead?"

"People," Carson said, his gaze still fixed on me. "People like *us*."

He looked up. I followed his gaze to the trace of dark vapor that scuttled across the ceiling. "I learned how to beat it back," he said quietly. "But I'm not as strong as you."

I tried to slow the pounding of my heart. "What the hell are you saying, Carson?"

"Quit playing dumb. You and I are the same kind of freaks. I've known it for quite a while. Ever since I killed Dad."

The floor buckled beneath me. I clutched the arm of the

couch, certain the couch and I were going to fall through. "D-Dad died of a heart attack."

"It seemed like that, didn't it?"

I closed my eyes, breathing in and out slowly. Maybe I would wake from the nightmare to find that my brother was just an unfortunate kid in a wheelchair and not some broken and discarded freak.

"It's true, Beth. I figured out that I could do this at fifteen. I was getting pretty good at it. Maybe too good. And the sick thing is, I kind of liked it."

I said nothing, just continued to breathe in an attempt to control my mounting panic.

Carson continued. "I was so caught up in my own little drama that I failed to do the one thing Sam asked me to do. Protect you."

My eyes snapped open. "What did you say?"

Carson quirked an eyebrow. "Sam used to tell me that he had this theory that our kind were drawn to this area because of some weird type of magnetic resonance. But I don't think that's it. I think our families were all lured here somehow."

I kneeled beside my brother's wheelchair, took one of his limp hands in mine, and squeezed it almost hard enough to break a bone.

"I can't feel that, you know," he said, looking at his hand. "I have the tiniest bit of sensation in the fingertips of my left hand. And just enough movement to control this chair."

"What happened to Sam?" I whispered through gritted teeth.

Carson's eyes grew watery. His voice caught. "I wish I knew, Beth. But I tried to distract you. To keep you from thinking about him. It's what he wanted."

I sank to the floor and tucked my head between my knees, wishing Zuber had left me in that cold dark hole in the ground.

Carson continued, his voice gruff. "I'm sorry. I wish things were different. I wish *we* were different."

I couldn't look at my brother, couldn't stifle the sob that forced its way out of my lungs. Finally, I swallowed it down and, my eyes clenched tight, managed to speak the truth that had been staring me in the face all along. "Sam was like us."

"He was."

"What kind?" I pressed my knuckles to my lips, still unable to look at Carson.

"I don't know, Beth. Probably something dangerous. Something that needed to be taken down. Linford is a nest of people like us. There are predators. And there are prey. You figure out who's who."

I pried my eyes open to look up at my brother. "Are you saying the Guild tried to kill you and Sam?"

"If that's what you call them," Carson said quietly. "It's been going on since forever. Think of all the missing kids around here. I'm betting there are more. Kids who died in freak accidents. Kids who moved away suddenly."

"Xavier," I whispered, my insides churning. "Did you ever know a kid named Xavier?"

Carson pulled in a long breath and took a sip from a tube attached to a canteen of water strapped to the back of his chair. Mom's ingenuity again. "The only Xavier I knew was the Smith kid who died in that boat explosion five or so years ago. But I think that was his middle name."

"How could you remember that?"

"I always had a mind for details."

I chewed on a nail. It would explain the horrible scars. "Are you sure?"

"It was on the news nonstop. William Xavier Smith, the son of that annoying preacher, Barclay Smith. The one that showed up in my hospital room right after the accident. His dead kid is the reason that guy is on his missing kid crusade."

My hand flew to my mouth. "Xavier is *that man's* son?"

"The guy you know can't be the same person. That kid

died."

"What if he didn't? You didn't."

Carson took another sip from his water tube. "I'm really glad you came, Beth. Really glad we had a chance to have this talk. Up to this point, I've been able to keep it from Mom and I'm proud of that. But I don't have long and I worry about her."

"You don't know that, Carson. You can't just give up."

"I'm fighting like crazy, Beth. My lungs are shot. I hate the thought that Mom's going to be alone."

Tears flooded my eyes. I pushed back on the dark cloud that had massed on the ceiling, biding its time for the right moment. Deep in my gut, I knew my brother was right. He would lose his battle soon and I wouldn't be there to help him. I squeezed his useless hand harder. I wondered if Dawn could be of some help, but thought better of getting his hopes up.

"Andre and Shelly will take care of you and Mom."

"You think so?" Carson swiveled away from me, pulling his hand free. "Ask your good friend Andre why I sometimes catch him watching me like a cat looks at a fish in a tank. His magic touch doesn't work on me because I can't feel it. I can see right through him."

I tried to slow my breathing. To steady my voice. "Andre cares about us. He's been trying to help as best he can."

"Andre's out for himself. Even Sam could have told you that."

I followed Carson's gaze to the door. Andre stood in the threshold. He wasn't smiling. "We should get going, Beth."

31

I PRESSED MY CHEEK TO CARSON'S, THE SOFT STUBBLE on his jaw scratching my skin.

"Don't give up fighting, Beth," he whispered.

I pulled away and caught Mom watching us, her eyes damp. Andre touched her arm and a warm smile shone through her tears. "It was so lovely to see you, honey! You've done wonders for Carson's state of mind."

Shelly watched us, frozen like a deer in headlights. Her expression seemed to shift like sunlight on a mountainside until Andre pulled her into a quick hug. After they separated she smiled, too, her jewelry jangling like wind chimes. "Go out and knock 'em dead, kiddo!"

I almost gagged, then forced a smile. Andre cringed visibly at her word choice, but kept his smile in place. "Ready?" He held out my coat and I snatched it from his hands.

"Yes," I snapped.

He tried to take my arm as we trudged to the car and I reeled away. "Don't touch me, okay?"

"What's wrong, Beth? It's *me*."

The setting sun turned the woods crimson and gold. I could run. But with no money or safe haven, where would I go? Zuber was the only person I could really trust. And Xavier. I had to no choice but to cling to the hope that Andre meant me no harm, that he just had his own agenda. If he wanted to hurt me, he'd had so many chances.

I slouched low in the front seat. Andre got in and started the car. He reached out to touch my shoulder and I pressed against the door.

"What is it? Are you afraid of me?"

His hand grazed my cheek, the backs of his fingers pressed lightly against my skin.

"Of course not," I lied. "It's just hard saying goodbye to them, not knowing when and if I'll see them again."

Andre continued to stroke my cheek and despite myself, I felt the hard kernel of my anger soften.

"I understand," he said.

I cleared my throat. "Carson said some nasty things about you."

"Did he?" The warmth of Andre's touch seeped through my skin and into my veins, smoothing out my emotions. I pushed my fingernail into the infected wound where Sam's button had pierced my skin hard enough to make it bleed. The pain helped me untangle my thoughts from Andre's sway.

"It's sad to see him so bitter and angry when he should really be trying to move on," Andre added.

"He's trying very hard to adjust to his new life."

Andre kept his reasonable tone, but his gaze grew sharp. He backed out of the driveway and the old van chugged noisily down the quiet country road. "I don't know what Carson said, but if you ask me, he's just looking for someone else to blame for what he did to himself. He couldn't handle his Talent, so he drank. He caused his own accident, Beth. He could have had a place at the compound along with you and he regrets his own stupidity."

The narrative sounded plausible. I stared at the passing trees, their indigo shadows weaving an intricate pattern on the road's surface. Andre's touch was in my blood, headed straight for my brain. Plausibility, I repeated in my mind.

"What about Sam, Andre? What do you have to say about him?"

Andre kept his gaze fixed on the road, his expression unreadable. "I tried to warn him to keep his nose out of places it didn't belong. I think Carson might have tipped him off, but he got curious about the disappearances. He started poking around. Maybe he poked in the wrong place."

I closed my eyes. Again, an acceptable answer. One I could live with. But something nagged at me. "Carson said he was one of us."

"Carson is delusional. Sam was just an ordinary guy."

We drove on in silence and I grew sleepy. What Andre said made sense. Plausible. And I couldn't deal with the alternative—that Carson was right about Andre.

And that Sam was a freak like the rest of us.

We pulled up to the ruins of the old school building well after nightfall. All was silent except the waves of the Long Island Sound on the beachfront a few hundred yards away. The night air was chill and fraught with silent dread. A shadowy stain lingered, dark against the night sky.

"Something's wrong," I whispered.

Andre placed a hand on the small of my back and I let his touch smooth my taut nerves so I could think. In the cone of Andre's flashlight beam, we picked our way through the piles of debris to the basement auditorium. It was completely dark, no trace of Zuber's lantern.

No trace of anything except a faint whiff of lingering death.

"This is not good," I said. We walked hesitantly down the aisle to the dark stage.

"Xavier?" I called. "Zuber? What do you think happened to them, Andre?"

"I don't know," he said quietly.

I picked my way across the stage. I found Zuber's lantern and flicked it on. Glistening in the pale light were bloody footsteps. *Recent* bloody footsteps. I followed them to the wings of the stage, where they ended at a pile of tattered costumes stained with drops of blood. I shoved the clothes aside and peered closer. Beside a bloodstained box cutter were words carved into the stage floor.

FIND THE RESISTANCE THEN YOU'LL FIND SAM

Gouged roughly under the words, blood pooling in the crevices, was the circle and the wedge symbol.

"Andre! You've got to see this." I whirled around to face him. No one was there. "Andre?"

And then I smelled it. Sharp and acrid, voracious and relentless, the shadow cloud dropped from the ceiling... enveloping me, warning me that I had to run.

Except someone had me by the neck, with the barrel of a gun pressed to the back of my skull. There was nothing warm, kind, or soothing about it.

32

"I'M SORRY," ANDRE SAID, HIS VOICE AS measured as ever. "But I'm just doing my job. Walk. One foot in front of the other. Do as I say or I'll blast off the back of your head."

"Why are you doing this? What did you do with the others?"

I tried to kick at him. To focus on the cloud that billowed around us.

"Come with me peacefully and you'll find out."

Since I had no idea how to turn the deadly cloud on him before he pumped a bullet through my skull, I did what Andre said.

I'd believed him. Trusted him. And now we were all screwed because of it.

Outside the ruined school, on the sandy strip of beach in the cold moonlight, a circle of figures surrounded a body lying on black sand. Blood-soaked sand.

Xavier.

I froze and stifled a scream. Andre pressed the gun harder into the base of my skull and shoved me along.

"The cerebellum is the true source of Talent, Beth. This is a valuable piece of knowledge that has eluded the Guild, which is why they have failed so miserably," he said in his smooth tone. "I've been studying the way our minds work. A bullet in your brain will cut off your power before you can do any harm." Andre's voice turned sharp. "And don't think I won't. You're a danger to all of us and so is your precious Xavier. Talent like yours needs to be controlled. Or eliminated."

No warmth flowed into my veins. Only deadly calm and cold conviction.

A figure in a dark coat with platinum hair that glowed white like a second moon knelt beside Xavier on the sand.

It was Demetri Prishkin, his eyes closed in concentration. My gaze travelled the circle of people huddled around Xavier's body. They were chanting, their voices joined together in an ominous thrum that made the pulse in my neck beat wildly.

Above them, death swam and swirled like a funnel cloud, the composite of my anger and fear, mixed with Xavier's impending demise. I knew that if I didn't keep that cloud in check, Andre would pump a bullet into my head.

My eyes fell on another familiar face. A portly older man glared at me, his eyes brimming with pure hate. It was the guy from the hospital room. The missing kid guy. Reverend Barclay Smith. Xavier's father.

Then I spotted Zuber. His wrists were cuffed in thick steel manacles linked together by heavy chains. He'd been beaten, his face swollen and darkened by bruises. Another length of chain fastened to the manacles connected him to a hooded figure in a long dark coat. The figure threw back its hood and my legs nearly buckled.

His curls shone gold in the silver light. Vincent stared straight at me, then looked away.

"*Et tu, Brute*?" I whispered under my breath.

The fix was in. And it hurt worse than a bullet in the brain.

Demetri lifted his face skyward, his hands resting lightly on Xavier's chest. I had no idea what he was doing to Xavier and I didn't dare ask Andre.

Xavier's back arched. His face turned crimson. He seemed to be screaming, but no sound came out of his mouth.

"In the end, my research paid off," Andre said in my ear. "I'm the one who finally figured out how to break Mr. William Xavier Smith."

I didn't have the luxury of asking why it was so important to break Xavier. What he had that everyone seemed to want.

Above me the darkness thickened, obscuring the moon. Sweat broke out on my forehead. I couldn't contain this rage much longer.

"Andre, please," I moaned. "I can't hold on."

Andre cocked the trigger. "Try harder."

Apparently my life was not worth as much as Xavier's.

I had maybe seconds to live.

Then all hell broke loose. Zuber plunged straight into the ground, yanking the chain and slamming Vincent flat onto the sand in a belly-flop.

Andre yanked the gun from the back of my head to shoot wildly at Zuber. I took my cue and kicked him in the groin with the back of my heel, knocking him off-balance. He dropped the gun. I scrambled over sand to the street as fast as my legs could carry me. Downtown Linford was only a mile away. If I could make it there, maybe I'd be safe.

Andre had staggered to his feet, apparently grabbed the gun, and now pounded after me. Bullets sang past my ears, death following me like a swarm of bees.

I ran as hard as I could along the coastal road, my lungs screaming for oxygen. Andre was gaining ground. Then something clutched at my ankles, and I was whisked through the layer of pitted asphalt and pulled clear through the cement to a cold dark space.

Zuber and I landed in a breathless tangle in the sewer

tunnel that drained Linford's rainwater to the sound.

"What the—"

"When I said no jail could hold me, I wasn't exaggerating."

In the dimness, Zuber flashed me a jaunty half-smile. I just stared back at him, too stunned to respond. "Please explain to me what the hell is going on here."

"Where should I start? As soon as you left, they came. I'm pretty sure Dawn wasn't in on the plan. And I won't tell you I told you so about Serrano. Suffice it to say I always thought he was a pompous kiss-ass."

"What the hell was Demetri Prishkin doing to Xavier?"

Zuber shook his head. "All this time, I thought I could trust that bastard. That he was my best friend. I never suspected Prishkin's Talent for convincing people to do what he wanted was Compulsion. That's a Level 10 Volatile. Monica's been using him to force Xavier into submission."

"So Demetri put a Compulsion on Xavier?"

"He tried. Thing is, the Compulsion never fully worked on Xavier. Never worked on me either."

"Why?"

Zuber rolled up the leg of his jeans. A dense network of horizontal scabs striped his shin. "I cut myself. Pain keeps it in check. It's why none of their brainwashing efforts worked much on Xavier. Because of his old injuries, he's in constant pain anyway."

I closed my eyes. Only in our twisted world would pain be our best defense. I showed Zuber the infected pinprick on my palm. "Could this have helped keep my mind clear?"

"Most likely," Zuber said. He seemed to be breathing heavily, gulping in air in quick swallows.

"Do you think this is the Guild's doing?"

Zuber shook his head. "They'd never use so many Volatiles. They don't trust them. I think these goons are working for Monica. I think she's been planning something crazy all along."

The image of Vincent and his expression churned my stomach. "So Vincent and Andre are working for Monica. And that makes them traitors to the Guild. But they're all after us."

"The Guild or Monica," Zuber said, wheezing. He seemed unable to catch his breath. "Pick your poison." Above us, darkness pooled and my scalp tightened. I wondered if I was sensing Xavier's death.

"Zuber, when I was alone with Andre I found a message from Xavier. It said that if I found the Resistance, I'd find Sam. Does that mean anything to you?"

"The Resistance? Its existence has always been a rumor. If this is the secret Xavier's been sitting on, it's huge."

"The resistance to what?"

"To the Guild and the corrupt monsters who exploit Talent. Like Monica."

"Where are they?"

"The old sixty-million dollar question. I have no clue." Zuber laughed, but it ended in a gurgling cough. My gaze snapped to the dark stain blooming on his T-shirt where he clutched his side. "And I'm afraid I won't be going with you."

The air above Zuber darkened and descended over him like a shroud of smoke. Andre's aim was better than I thought. He'd hit his mark.

Talented were dangerous.

But they were still no match for guns.

Zuber smiled, his eyes losing focus. "I'm sorry, Beth. I'd go with you. But it hurts when I move."

I helped Zuber to lie down on the wet tiles and watched the shadow drop.

"I'd give anything to go with you," he whispered. Then his eyes slipped closed.

The darkness rested softly on his chest. He shuddered, then sank through the floor tiles and deep into the earth as the cloud rose and drifted away.

33

LEFT THE BLAST MAHONEY BUTTON ON THE SPOT where Zuber had died and disappeared into the earth.

I'd come to the end of the line. Two people I cared about and trusted had tricked and betrayed me. And now, because of them, my friend Zuber was dead, my friend Xavier was a captive, and I was a fugitive.

I wanted to turn that dark cloud on myself, and this time, I wouldn't hesitate to take Vincent and his glass heart right along with me.

But I couldn't rest until I knew what had happened to Sam. I thought back to the times I'd seen a shade roaming the woods, watching me. Was that his ghost trying to reach me?

I clung to the conviction that if Sam was dead, I'd know.

But I felt nothing.

I had to find the Resistance and learn the truth.

Then I'd return for Xavier. And use my lethal Talent to kill every last one of my enemies.

And I'd enjoy it.

Tears streamed down my face as I walked the network of tunnels under my hometown. Life went on for the people who slept above me, blissfully ignorant of the nightmare world right outside their windows. I slogged through the watery sewer tunnel, a nuclear explosion in a holding pattern. My anger could have obliterated the entire town.

I needed to find a place where it was safe to let it go.

Even if I did manage to escape Linford, I had no idea where to find the Resistance. I had no money. I was hungry. But my mind was clear and my thoughts were finally my own.

I didn't have much, but at least I had my thirst for revenge.

I waded through the filthy water. Slivers of moonlight streamed through the drainage grates to light a path for me.

The sound of sloshing footsteps sounded behind me. Voices bounced off the tunnel tiles.

I splashed blindly ahead to where the tunnel split into a fork. More voices wafted toward me from one of the forks, so I raced down the other, running mindlessly.

"Beth!" hissed a voice from the street above. "I know you're down there."

The voice reverberated inside my bones.

It was Vincent, come to reel me in like the catch of the day.

I gritted my teeth and rushed on without comment.

His voice poured down from another grate. "I know where you are at all times, Beth. If I wanted to turn you in, I could have them here in minutes."

My lungs were on fire, but I kept running. I hated the fact that despite everything he'd done to me, I wanted nothing more than to be cradled in his arms like when we'd once fallen asleep together.

Like it or not, we were bound. Not even my outrage over his betrayal could break that connection until it faded on its own.

Then he was standing in front of me, thigh-deep in the filthy water, wet curls plastered to his head.

"You can't run forever, Beth. Monica's people might not have the resources, but the Guild will never tolerate a Level

10 Volatile going rogue."

I spat at him, turned, and ran off in the other direction. He took a gamble. He knew I wouldn't kill him. Couldn't kill him.

"Please. You have to trust me." His voice shivered in my ears, a siren song to my battered emotions. Then my elbow was wrenched behind my back in a painful hold.

"Please hear me out," Vincent pleaded. "Why would I take this kind of risk alone if I wanted to turn you in?"

"Because in your conceited head, you believe I won't kill you." I struggled crazily to break free. "Maybe you're wrong. You and that bastard Andre sold us out. Zuber's dead. Are you happy now?"

Vincent held tight. I wasn't fooling him. He could read my feelings and intentions like a road map. He spoke, his voice thick with emotion. Gone was the measured, careful tone. "I'm so sorry. I wanted to prove myself loyal to the Guild. I thought I was doing the right thing."

I stopped struggling. The heat of his face pressed against my neck worked its way into my bloodstream, uncoiling my tight muscles. "Fucking Saint Vincent. What would you possibly need to prove?"

"I was—my father was a traitor to the Guild. A Tribunal gave me a chance to redeem myself, since I was so young when they arrested him."

I paused, weighing his words, pushing back on the sway of his real grief and pain. I couldn't let him persuade me. "How was he a traitor?"

"My parents raised us far away in a remote part of Northern France. My mom and sister were Regulars. Papa was arrested when I was thirteen for training me outside of the Guild's auspices. They brought charges against him. I was sent overseas. I never saw my parents or my sister again."

"How do I know you're telling the truth? You and Andre

are world-class liars."

"I can't speak for Andre. I can only speak for myself."

It all sounded very reasonable, but I wasn't buying it. Vincent had already proven himself to be an accomplished actor. I pushed back hard and he stumbled, falling onto his ass into the putrid water.

I didn't waste any time laughing at him. I just ran like hell.

But Vincent's legs were much longer than mine. He overtook me easily and pinned my wrists roughly to the slime-coated tunnel wall. "You shouldn't make me run like this, Beth. You know how easily my heart can just give out. And you need me."

"I don't need you!" I thrashed about, but it was pointless. The only way to get free was to kill him.

He smiled, painfully beautiful even drenched in slime water. "You're a liability to the Guild, Beth. Monica was going to unload you and turn you over to that Holy Roller guy, Reverend Barclay Smith. He takes care of surplus Talent."

I tried to wrench my hands free of his grip, but he only leaned in closer, his lips inches from mine. The breath heaved in and out of my lungs.

I could fight a lot of things.

Vincent at close range was not one of them.

"That asshole is Xavier's father. What do you mean by *he takes care of surplus Talent*?"

"Just what it sounds like. He takes the unruly ones off Monica's hands if things get too hot. He calls Talented the devil's children. He's a homicidal lunatic on a sacred mission to wipe us all off the planet. He considers it God's work. Monica feeds him crumbs to keep him interested."

I finally stopped flailing and sagged against the wall. "Don't you think it's a strange coincidence that his own son was supposed to have died in an explosion, only to turn up alive a few years later?"

Vincent's aqua eyes were iridescent in a slice of moonlight. "That's how it all started. His own son, William Xavier Smith, had a strangely hypnotic voice. Barclay thought he was possessed and tried to exorcise the evil from him, as he called it. Xavier was horribly injured, but survived because a Guild member rescued him and spirited him away to the compound."

Vincent's lips were now millimeters from mine.

"I still don't know if I believe you," I murmured. His face was close enough to mine for me to taste his breath. "Or trust you."

"Promise you won't run and I'll show you something."

"Promise." I was disgusted with myself. I was so losing this battle.

Vincent lowered his hands. He unbuttoned his coat and lifted his flannel shirt, revealing the lean muscle of his abdomen. Carved into the tender flesh just above the waistline of his jeans was a raised white scar—the circle and a wedge, the same symbol Xavier had shown to me numerous times.

"What the hell?"

"Just before my parents were taken away, I howled while my father held me down and burned this into my skin with the heated end of a spoon. He placed an undetectable glamour on it, which was his Talent, and told me that if I ever needed him, he'd manage to find me."

We found a dry ledge and climbed up, huddling together for warmth.

"They tried to reprogram me, as they call it. There are Talented who can wipe your mind of your true memories and intentions and replace them with false ones. This is what Gideon does so masterfully. But it never worked on me or Xavier because of our damaged bodies. My heart murmur and his painful scars rendered us immune, which got us instantly classified as Volatiles. I tried to play their game. Xavier never did."

"What exactly is Xavier's Talent? Why is there such a big fuss over him?"

"Xavier's voice is like steroids for Talented. It amplifies the abilities of others, and re-energizes the ill and weak. To be honest, his voice is what kept me alive."

"I thought you hated him."

"I was protecting him from himself. Xavier never had a lick of sense. Instead of running from trouble, he ran toward it."

"Holy crap," I said.

"It is also what's kept Gideon alive," Vincent continued. "He should have died from his cancer years ago. So now do you understand why Monica wants him so much? Xavier's voice grants godlike powers to those who can harness it."

"But they couldn't make him cave to their wishes."

"Actually, he was fine for a while. As fine as someone could be after surviving a murder attempt by his own father. That is, he was," Vincent said, "until Sam Bernstein came to the compound."

It was as if someone had dropkicked me in the gut. I couldn't breathe.

Vincent continued. "Not only was Sam resistant to reprogramming, but he could reverse it in others. He could nullify the effects of any Talent by just pointing a finger. His control was masterful. Try to imagine the uproar his presence created. He and Xavier wreaked havoc on the compound. It was pure mayhem. The Guild was on its way when Sam somehow escaped and disappeared into the night. Xavier was taken away for detention. They tried to make us all forget everything. But I never did. Then Xavier returned, bitter and changed."

I shivered in the icy water, tears burning my eyes. It must have been Zuber who had helped Sam to escape. I wondered if he'd lied about knowing Sam, or if he had been made to forget.

I couldn't ask him now.

"If you knew all along, why didn't you tell me?"

"If Monica found out that you knew, they would figure out that reprogramming didn't work on me. Which would lead to instant Elimination. I'm not as valuable as Xavier. So I hid what I knew, and lived in fear they'd find me out."

Vincent gazed into my eyes, the warm aqua haunted and fearful. "Do you believe me now? I'm walking away from them because I believe in you."

I swallowed hard and nodded. We held onto each other, shivering together on that cold ledge, until we finally fell asleep. We woke as the morning light sifted down the gutter grates and spilled across the filth-strewn floor.

"They're gone," Vincent said.

"How do you know?"

"I'm a Tracker. It's a side benefit of my Weaving Talent. Once I've touched someone, I can track their unique pattern from any distance. It's most likely why they never considered Eliminating me. Cooperating like I did, I was far too useful to the Guild. If I've marked someone once after Weaving, I can sense them when they're near. Andre and I worked as a team. He scouted new Talent. I marked them. I never really trusted Andre, so I marked him, too."

I chewed a broken nail. "So Andre was the scout that brought us all in to the compound. What did he get, a cash reward or something?"

"Probably. But I don't think money was is his main motivation. Andre has other issues. But never mind him. I marked all new Talent. You know what that means, don't you?"

I shook my head. My thoughts were murky. I wanted to sleep, preferably wrapped in Vincent's arms.

"It means that if Sam is alive, I can find him because I'd marked him. And if I can find Sam, we'll find the Resistance."

Vincent smiled, triumphant, apparently missing the elephant in the room. My stomach lurched.

"What if he's dead? I've felt this shade watching me for a while now. What if that's his ghost?"

"Did you feel his death? Wouldn't you? What about Zuber?"

"That's different. I saw him die."

"You saw him sink into the ground. What if he's just healing there?"

I closed my eyes and shook my head. "No. He's dead. I'm certain."

"But you're not certain about Sam."

Vincent leaned in to kiss me gently on the forehead, then pressed my head against his chest. I listened to the thump of his faulty heart and willed it to keep its steady rhythm. "So there is still hope."

Who would I choose if Sam was alive? Had I ever loved Sam as deeply as I needed Vincent?

"The first thing we need to do after we get out of this rank pit," Vincent murmured, his hand stroking my hair, "is to get you a new guitar."

I chuckled softly. "You've got to be kidding. What about clothes that don't stink like a cesspool? And with what money?"

"My family has millions. Another thing Dad had glamoured onto me was the access code to our fortune."

"So I hit the lottery, huh? Why is my guitar so important? You want me to serenade you to sleep in our slime-coated home?"

Vincent tipped my chin up toward his face and pushed the hair away from my eyes. Then we kissed, long and sweet, our thoughts and emotions woven together like a tapestry.

There was no getting him out of my system now.

"Because I'm going to hone your skills," Vincent said, a little breathless, "and your music is the key. There's a battle coming, and we're going to win."

Then he leaned in to kiss me again. It was a long time before we came up for air.

TO BE CONTINUED...

ACKNOWLEDGMENTS

First, I want to say a huge thank you and wish a fond farewell to the incomparable Kate Kaynak, fellow Squirrel on Crack, and founder of Spencer Hill Press, who has stepped down as the Grand Poobah to be replaced by the equally awesome Jessica Porteous. Without the belief that you've both shown in me these past nearly four years, and all you've put up with, I'm not sure where I'd be as a writer.

That brings me to my editorial A-team of editors at SHP—Vikki Ciaffone, Laura Ownbey, and Eagle Eye himself, aka The Closer, Rich Storrs. Along with my copy editors, Shira Lipkin and Hannah Ringler, they have scraped and polished this manuscript until it gleamed. To my publicist, the unstoppable Brooke DelVecchio, who also serves as my muse and Head Cheerleader (and occasionally therapist) and has worked tirelessly to make sure this book got into your hands. To Meredith and Kelly, and all the other members of the publicity crew who work to get the word out there. To my fellow designer, Errick Nunnally, who does most of the layout now.

And certainly, not lastly, a very critical member of my "team." To my brilliant agent, Shannon Hassan, and the entire amazing agency, Marsal Lyon Literary—you all rock. I can't even begin to explain how comforting it is to belong to the best agency in all of children's publishing.

There are many others I wish to thank, but first, I'd like to recount the tale of exactly how this book, the third I've published with Spencer Hill Press, came to be.

You might be surprised to know that I had written this book before *Breaking Glass* or *Vision*, then stuck it in a drawer to gather dust, abandoned while I knocked out *Breaking Glass* and subsequently sold it, and then *Vision*, to SHP. Back in 2010, it had won runner-up for second place in a Writer's Digest contest, got me my second agent, garnered interest from a bunch of others, and then never sold. Back then I'd called it *Life And Beth*. So I apologized to it, and set it lovingly away.

But something about this book would not let me go. I'm not sure if it was Beth herself or just the cool title, but the summer before *Breaking Glass* came out, I decided it had to be revisited. I tore it apart and inserted my favorite character orphan from one of my other, less beloved unpublished books (that you will never read). His name is Xavier. Once Xavier found his way into *Until Beth*, I knew I had found the spark to finally bringing this book back from the dead. So thank you to Xavier, my favorite fictional character ever. Your book may be gone, but you get to live again in the pages of a totally different story.

This brings me to the saga behind the cover of *Until Beth*. Some of you may know that not only do I design many of SHP's covers, but am also allowed the great privilege (and burden) of designing my own. I don't think I've ever had a worse client, thankfully. The story of the cover of *Until Beth* is as twisted as the story of how the book came to be written and rewritten.

In the summer of 2014, I'd created a cover that everyone loved and signed off on. Except one little graphic design sophomore with very definite opinions. My daughter, Becca, did not approve of my original cover, claiming it was pedestrian, boring, and took no chances. It would not, she insisted, sell my book.

At first, I balked and brushed her off. After all, I'm the design professor and she's just a student. But she called me from a design event and adamantly repeated the advice of a world-famous cover designer she'd met, with whom she'd discussed my cover. Finally, I got tired of arguing and listened to her. In a day, the idea for the guitar-shaped grave popped into my head. I sketched it and got instant approval from SHP and Shannon. And thus, I created what I believe may be my favorite cover I've ever designed.

So I am indebted to the "monster" I have created—the talented, outspoken little genius that is my daughter.

That brings me to the many other people who support, tolerate, and stand behind me. My family—husband Rick, son Ben, the photographer (who currently resides on the opposite side of the planet). My parents, Gene and Sherry, who never once discouraged my unruly creativity. Also to my Aunt Arlene, Uncle Roy and cousins, Sue, Nancy (and Dan) and Judy who and act as a kind of family publicity mafia. Love you all.

And the friends, who are really not that different from family—to Joanne, my first reader. To Jill, and her son David, who listened to me read this book to them when it was only a few creepy chapters and insisted I keep writing. To Debbie, Andy and Josh—who have always been huge supporters. To Dhonielle Clayton, who started out as my "Baby Cuda," but is now my Guru for all things writing. And to all the Cudas—Cyndy, Kate, Trish, Cathy, Linda, Lindsay, Christine, Pippa, Heidi, and of course, Dhonielle, who kept me afloat during the writing droughts, and edited this thing to death. To Christian, my first fan, who not only works for me, but follows me around to all my book signings. To Kristin, and all the other new pals who support and read my writing. To all my writer friends, all over the Internet for being there when needed. To the Binders, a massive group of YA writers I am fortunate enough to belong to.

And lastly to Bronx Community College—my day job— the place I get so much of my inspiration and support. Thank you to the young people who inspire me every day, and to the faculty who validate the fact that I write. And gratitude to an administration that actually helps promote my book.

In short—thank you, world. I'm grateful to be a part of you.

Lisa Amowitz was born in Queens and raised in the wilds of Long Island, New York where she climbed trees, thought small creatures lived under rocks and studied ant hills. And drew. A lot. She is a professor of Graphic Design at her beloved Bronx Community College where she has been tormenting and cajoling students for nearly twenty years. She started writing originally because she wanted something to illustrate, but somehow, instead ended up writing YA. Probably because her mind is too dark and twisted for small children. Lisa is represented by Shannon Hassan of Marsal-Lyon Literary Agency. shannon@marsallyonliteraryagency.com

Breaking Glass, released in July, 2013 from Spencer Hill Press, is her first published work. *Vision*, the first of the Finder series was released September, 2014. *Fractured*, a novella combining the worlds of *Breaking Glass* and *Vision* released as an ebook only, June 7, 2015. Amowitz is currently working on the unnamed sequel to *Breaking Glass*.

Website:

http://lisa-amowitzya.blogspot.com
http://www.lisaamowitz.com

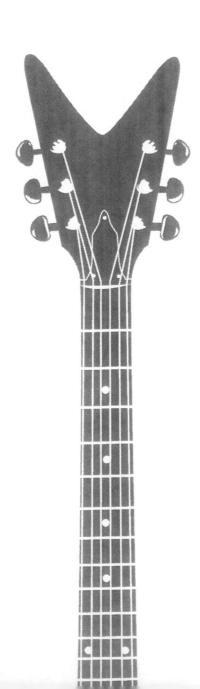

CPSIA information can be obtained at www.ICGtesting.com
Printed in the USA
LVOW06s0331260815

451445LV00002B/2/P

9 781633 920330